D0952560

RIPTIDE SUMMER

LISA FREEMAN

Sky Pony Press
New York

Sky Pony Press books may be purchased in bulk at special discounts for sales promotion, corporate gifts, fund-raising, or educational purposes. Special editions can also be created to specifications. For details, contact the Special Sales Department, Sky Pony Press, 307 West 36th Street, 11th Floor, New York, NY 10018 or info@skyhorsepublishing.com.

Sky Pony® is a registered trademark of Skyhorse Publishing, Inc.®, a Delaware corporation.

Visit our website at www.skyponypress.com.

10 9 8 7 6 5 4 3 2 1

Library of Congress Cataloging-in-Publication Data is available on file.

Cover design by Sammy Yuen

Photo credit: iStockphoto

Print ISBN: 978-1-5107-1167-9
E-book ISBN: 978-1-5107-1168-6

Printed in the United States of America

RIPTIDE SUMMER

PEARL HARBOR

HONOLULU

KAIMUKI

PARADISE

POPULARS
POPS

CANOES

WAIKIKI

QUEENS

GRAVEYARDS

KAHALA

PUBLICS

CASTLES

OLD MANS

DIAMOND HEAD

RICE BOWLS

TONGGS   ZEROS

Southside Surf on OAHU

This book is for Lucie and Bea.

TABLE OF CONTENTS

I

June 10–July 7, 1973

Strawberry Moon

BEGIN AGAIN.

CHAPTER ONE

The Keeper of Secrets

I hurried into Roy's, twisting the tips of my hair to one side so I wouldn't sit on them. At the familiar booth in the back, Rox and Claire sat, head to head, plotting.

Rox and I had a special something going, but I never forgot she was the most dangerous sign in the zodiac: a Scorpio. She had a famous wink and a killer body, but when she saw me, her eyebrows furrowed into a tight little V. She dropped her shades down her nose and said, "What, Nani?"

I had to tell her the message from our boyfriends: they had bailed and gone surfing in Porto.

When I did, Claire laughed. "BFD." She stood up, adjusted her hip-hugger bell-bottoms, and flipped her blond hair to one side so I could easily gaze into her dreamy turquoise eyes. She whispered in my ear, "Rox has news," then strolled out. Guys hooted and whistled at her, but of course she didn't acknowledge them. That was against the rule:

Younger guys don't matter.

Summer had officially started, and the local surf grotto was jammed.

The best part was that Rox and I were going to Fiji tonight. Not the one near New Zealand. We go to Fiji in my room. It's our code word for getting naked and warm.

When I slid into the booth, the seat was hot where Claire had been sitting. Rox bumped her knee into mine and put her sandy foot next to my thigh. I beamed at her.

Meeting Rox last summer was like finding treasure without a map. Her perfectly streaked brown hair hung down to her elbows, and she fidgeted, tapping the side of her coffee cup. I knew better than to ask what was going on. She'd explain when she was good and ready.

"We have to postpone our trip to Fiji," she said, after a long pause.

I swallowed, even though there was nothing in my mouth. *Now I'll be alone all night. That blows.* We'd been planning this sleepover for weeks. It was going to be special. A real party to celebrate her graduation, for just the two of us. I even cleaned my room and changed my sheets, especially for her. And I made sure my mother would be working the graveyard shift at St. John's.

Rox tossed a few ice cubes from her water glass into a milky cup of coffee, then sipped slowly. I took hold of her hand under the table like, *Ain't no big thing. I'm cool.* Inside though, I was crumpling like burning paper. But before I could say anything, Rox told me, "*Tubed* magazine is coming to State." That was the biggest surf rag in town. "If I have my way, I'll be in the September issue."

"Surfing?" I asked.

"Don't be stupid. Just standing there. Looking hot. In this."
She pulled a bikini out of her pocket. It was so small, I almost
thought it was a headband. Then she hesitated. "There's something else, but I'll tell you later. Did you lock your bike?" she
asked.

I shook my head.

"Then there's no time to waste," Rox told me. "It could be
gone in seconds." She slipped her feet into her wedges. The
heels made clacking sounds as we charged through the crowd
of our admirers. Rox pushed me forward as the boys ogled
her low-cut top and tight jean shorts. *Good luck with that*, I
thought. *She's mine.*

Once we got outside, I noticed the sign: PATRICK'S. It was
taped in the takeout window. Underneath, it said, ROY SPLIT.
"What does that mean?" I asked Rox.

"The food's gonna get better." She lit up a smoke and let
me take a drag, never taking her eyes off mine. Marlboro Reds
tasted like sawdust, but I pretended to enjoy it, making the
moment last as long as possible. Since I could see my bike
right where I left it, I linked my arm with Rox's and cautiously
escorted her around several dogs sleeping on the sidewalk. The
locals' mutts are mellow, but Rox hates it when they sniff her.
When I pushed up the kickstand on my bike, Rox grabbed the
handlebars so it was hard to move. There was a twinkle in her
eye as she brushed against me one more time. It was her way
of showing me I was special.

I sailed home on Dad's four-speed, past the neighborhood
gay bars, where Mom hung out and drank in peace, knowing
none of the guys were interested in picking her up. The wind

lifted the hem of my hot pants, and my poncho clung to my arms.

I loved living by the beach, but I hated our house. When I saw the dome-shaped mailbox covered with marbles, I knew that, unfortunately, I was home. I'd decorated it to look like a candy jar and covered the wood post in pear-shaped shells and soda caps spelling out 33 Sage, my address.

There was a large package leaning against it. The brown paper wrapper was smashed and torn on either side. It looked like it had been to Vietnam and back. I didn't have to wonder what Jean, my wino mom, bought during one of her drunken stupors; I could see it without opening the box. There were reusable bowl covers, because Tupperware was too expensive, and a hand-held magnifier, because eyeglasses cost too much. There was even another girdle to hold in her thunder thighs. You know, the important stuff we couldn't afford and she couldn't live without. Seeing that package wouldn't have bothered me so much if I were still going to go to Fiji with Rox. But no Fiji meant no vacation from my sucky life.

CHAPTER TWO

Take Cover

I prepared for the worst as I opened the back door. My home was past the point of no return. I swear, this house was a bummer magnet.

I wanted to set Jean's package on the kitchen table, but her mess from breakfast was still there. She'd left the newspaper open, a few headlines circled in red for me to read. I tried not to look at the news anymore. Nixon swore he was innocent, but investigators found out that he talked about the cover-up more than thirty times with his lawyer. What a dweeb. He was such a liar. Jean still thought he was a good man. I thought she was living on Mars.

The dishes in the sink didn't matter since Fiji was cancelled, but I washed them anyway. I took a plate from my secret stash and some food from the cabinet. Jean didn't get to the grocery store much these days, so I always kept my favorite dinner hidden: rice, Spam, and canned pineapple.

What I hated most about being alone was the silence. It was scary. Once I was sure 33 Sage was more secure than the Pentagon—windows closed and locked, closets inspected, and doors double bolted—I took Jean's package into her room and placed it beside her bed. Right next to the urn of sand, which she still thought was filled with Dad. Sometimes I felt kind of bad about stealing his ashes, but I was glad he wasn't still stuck in that bottle, like some genie waiting centuries to be freed.

I tiptoed down the dark hallway to my room and stood in the doorway for a minute, assessing everything like a soldier. I have a photographic memory. It's like I'm a camera. I remember everything that I see, so I place things in certain spots so I'll always know no one has entered but me. That way I can work up the courage to go into my room, knowing it's safe.

"You are sixteen. Get over it," I reminded myself again. "The windows are locked. The doors are closed. You're okay."

Still, my skin prickled. I made a barricade out of the small display case I got for my toys at a garage sale. It was easy to pull across the doorway. I placed my black-and-white TV on top. TV was my best friend—when I wasn't with the lineup. Lisa Y. and Lisa H. were going to be the rulers this summer. They'd been at each other's throats all year, vying for the top spot, and Jenni was still so shy she barely said a word.

I wished Rox were here. She'd keep me company and trim my Bowie bangs for me. They looked dorky when they got too long. I listened to the silverware wind chime clanging outside, and another surge of loneliness welled up inside me. I wrapped my arms around myself and squeezed as tightly as I could. What a pathetic hug. If I could have unzipped my skin and stepped out of this feeling, I would have. But I was stuck with myself.

I looked at the bed. When I was small, I was afraid of things hiding under there, but now that's where I kept my biggest secret safe. The one that no one, not even Rox, knew about. It was shipped here in my mom's station wagon—sent by boat to the mainland. I still missed Hawaii, my real home, but having this present from my dad helped me live without it.

Dad was going to give this to me for my sixteenth birthday, but he died seven months before that happened. I found this beauty in the back seat wrapped in towels, with a birthday card taped to it. It read: *Hau'oli lā hānau*, which meant happy birthday. Then he wrote:

> For my darling daughter, Haunani. I hope you enjoy this Tom Parrish Lightning Bolt board. Can't wait for some waves.
>
> Love,
> Dad

I got on my knees next to my bed. Touching the board sometimes made me feel better. It was the most beautiful stick in the world, and the only solid thing in my life. It had never seen the ocean, and it most likely never would. But dreaming about surfing tonight was almost as good as going to Fiji.

It was so quiet that when the phone rang, I must have jumped a mile. I tried to ignore it, but it kept ringing. If it was Jean and I didn't answer, it would be my fault when she freaked out, got drunk, and wound up fired. Then we'd really be broke. But if it was a bill collector, I'd have to pretend I didn't speak English again. Or I could pick up the receiver and just wait—that's what I did.

"Are you still in the mood to travel?" Rox sounded like she had her hand cupped around her mouth.

"Yes," was all I managed to say before she hung up.

I squealed. A high-pitched girl sound jetted out of my mouth as I clenched my fists and jumped up and down, like a contestant on *Let's Make a Deal* who just chose door number three and won the big prize. I was stoked, hopping down the hall, forgetting my stinky thoughts with just enough time to gobble up dinner and zip into the shower.

CHAPTER THREE

The Pact

Rox slinked toward me until we stood, face to face, on either side of my bed. I tracked every move she made: the bend in her wrist as she lifted her hand and curled her finger, gesturing for me to come closer; the touch of her cool palm on my cheek; and the black licorice taste of Sen-Sen breath freshener when our tongues slowly touched.

There's a powerful center in the heart of Fiji, where volcanoes explode and cool into the sea. The first step to seeing the truth of who we really were was turning out the lights. We responded to each other's every need without words. I knew what to do without thinking. Like magic, we left one world and entered another.

I loved everything about Rox—the fuller curve of her hips and how her pointy edges had softened recently. Even her face had a glow to it—not from the candle, but from within. How did she keep getting more beautiful? I took a picture of her with my mind. Then she put her hand on my chest, feeling its rise and fall. I could smell my scent on her fingers.

I lit a Lark 100 and offered it to her.

"I quit," she told me.

"When?" I asked, stunned.

"Just now." She smiled, slipped out of bed, and squeezed into one of my nightgowns. I was amazed. How did her boobs get bigger and better?

"Do you have any peanut butter left?" she asked.

"Probably." We stayed close as we moved from room to room, like one person instead of two. I scraped what was left of the peanut butter out of the jar and put it on toast, on celery, and finally on a banana before she was full. Rox only chows down when she breaks up with her boyfriend—the incredible, edible, dark fish, Jerry Richmond, who surfs so much he's rarely dry.

"Did you and Jerry have a fight?" I asked, carefully. That would make our summer perfect. Maybe beyond perfect. Especially since Nigel, my demigod, born-again boyfriend was going to India with his twin to convert Calcutta to Christianity. With both of them out of the way, we could practically move to Fiji permanently.

But Rox was laughing at me. I hated when she did that.

"Quite the opposite," she said. "Jerry and I are getting married."

My heart plummeted like an elevator when its overhead cables have been cut. I imagined myself smashing into thousands of pieces as I hit the cement.

Bam. Inside I was blown to smithereens, but I tried to keep an even keel. "When did he pop the question?" My voice sounded thin and strained.

"He hasn't. But he will."

"Why?"

"Can you keep a secret?"

Hello? I travel to Fiji, I'm in the Sisters of Sand, and I know every single thing about you, I thought. But I just nodded to appease her.

"Promise?"

Oh, please get a grip, I wanted to tell her. *Spit it out. Why, at just eighteen, would the hottest girl, fresh out of high school, want to get married? And right after an amazing trip to Fiji?*

"I'm pregnant." She put her hands on her hips and did a little twist, shaking her ass.

I couldn't move.

Rox thought I didn't understand, so she continued, "There's a bun in the oven." She waited for my reaction, then laughed at me again. "There's a pea in the pod!"

My body stiffened as Rox kept talking. "I have a plan, and it will be *better* than okay." She paused dramatically and announced, "I'm going to marry Jerry and have kids, and you are going to marry Nigel."

Was she kidding? I am a *Funny Kine.* If I ever get married, it will be to a girl. As if.

"Let's make a pact. What do you think?"

Last year we became blood sisters. Now what did she want? Rox was so happy, I couldn't bring myself to break her good mood. Even though a part of me wanted to slap her.

But marriage and babies? That was going too far. With women's liberation, we didn't have to do that anymore—at least, not right out of high school. A pact is more binding than a promise. It's like an oath. Rox had created a prison with no escape, and I was just waltzing right into it.

When I still didn't answer, Rox stood up and pulled me in front of her, looking into my eyes. She said, "I promise to take you as my Fiji-loving mate." It sounded like *we* were getting married. That almost made me forgive her.

"Now you say it," she said.

"I promise to take you as my Fiji-loving mate, too." The smell of sulfur filled the air when Rox lit a match, inhaled quickly, and then took a long drag to hotbox her smoke. So much for quitting. The end of her Marlboro sizzled and sparked a bit before she jabbed it into the inside of my left arm. She didn't push hard, but the burning made me gasp. I liked how much it hurt. It put all my other pain somewhere else.

But it was weird, doing the same to her. I didn't like scarring her.

Still, now the pact was sealed. We'd be together forever. One way or another.

CHAPTER FOUR

(

Joyce

Rox woke with a start. "What's that?"

"Just my mom," I told her. I listened as Jean's keys dropped to the floor. Then I waited for the familiar sound of a beer being popped open.

Rox didn't notice. She whined into the pillow. "When I wake up I always feel like I'm going to barf."

Jean knocked on my door, and I jumped since Rox and I had been sleeping naked. I yelled, "Wait!" Rox jumped into her clothes as I lifted my arms and pulled my nightgown over my head.

Jean kept pounding. "Do you *mind*?" I yelled. It was so embarrassing. Then it got worse. Jean flung the door open and tripped over some books, landing on her hands and knees. Her beer spilled all over the rug.

"I want to talk to you."

"No!" I hollered.

She smelled like the hospital and the medical lowlifes she hung out with. I felt my face turn red as the heat of shame rose up in me.

I don't think she even noticed I had company until Rox said, "Morning, Mrs. Nuuhiwa."

I pulled the covers over my head. How embarrassing. My mother sucked the oxygen out of every room she went into.

"If it's okay with you," Rox said, putting her hands up as if to stop the fight before it started, "I'm going to leave before the shit show."

What was I going to say? *No, please stay. I want you to see how loaded my mother gets.* Rox stepped over Jean and was gone in an instant. I'd never live this down. And if the Sisters of Sand or the McBrides ever heard about it, I wouldn't be able to show my face at State again.

I didn't want to hear another word out of Jean, so I ran into the bathroom and locked the door.

I stared blankly into the mirror. I looked like a sad sack, so I gave myself a mini beauty treatment: smearing my face with Noxzema until it stung, then rinsing it off with cold water. I dabbed on lip gloss, pinched my cheeks for extra color, and rubbed primrose behind my ears. Nigel and Shawn were picking me up soon, and I wanted to make sure I didn't smell like Fiji. Then I combed my hair from the part to the tips.

That's when I saw the burn on my arm. I thought, *This will last forever. Just like me and Rox.*

I looked downright sweet in my coral necklace and bikini. This summer my colors were going to be Cyprus and yellow. They would bring out the green in my eyes. What used to be the worst thing about how I looked would become the best, I decided right then and there. The buttercup-yellow flowers embroidered around my top and the soft, bamboo-green bottoms with thin satin ties would help me maintain my local superstar status. Even though I wasn't born here, Santa Monica was my home now—and I *had* to keep it that way.

I snuck out of the bathroom and listened for my mom. The coast was clear. The smell of coffee wafted down the hall. That was weird. I'd assumed Jean would be passed out by now, like she usually was after working the night shift.

I could hear the coffee percolating as I cautiously slipped into the kitchen. Sitting with Jean was a well-dressed woman. Her purse matched her shoes and belt, her makeup was meticulous, and I could tell her gold jewelry was real. She stopped talking when I walked in.

A chill spread down my spine.

"Who died?" I asked. Who was left in my family? A *tutu*—my dad's mom, who I'd never met—in Hawaii, my dad's best friend, Uncle Mike, and my mother's brother, who sent Christmas cards occasionally. When nobody answered, I tried asking again, with manners this time. "Would you please tell me what's going on?" And then I asked, "Did you get fired?"

The lady gently patted my mother on the back and Jean whimpered, looking down at the floor. "This lady is going to help me stop drinking," she said. "I've been trying to do it on my own, but I fell off the wagon again."

I could hardly believe my ears.

Jean grabbed me around the waist. She was shaking so hard I had to cradle her in my arms for fear she'd slip to the floor. I held her tight as she kept saying, "I'm sorry."

"What do I do?" I asked the lady.

"Just hold her," she said. "And by the way, my name is Joyce."

I'd never talked to an adult without calling them Mr. or Mrs. It was strange. And when she stood up, I could see that

Joyce was a big gal—wide and tall. She had salt-and-pepper hair pulled up in a French twist, and there were no chips in her firecracker red nails. Everything about her was calm and centered.

She told me, "Your mom is sick," and pulled up a chair for me. "Jean here has been trying to stop drinking for a while."

"Really?" I asked.

Joyce said, "It's going to be okay," as she gently touched my hand and nodded sympathetically. "I was once like your mom."

That was hard to believe. Jean had buried her face in my lap, and I could see an inch of dark roots in her blond hair. "How can that be?" I asked. This Joyce was like nobody I'd ever seen. I couldn't imagine her having a hard day in her life.

"Once, I did a face-plant right in a bowl of risotto," she said. "My husband and kids were so disgusted, they left me there and went to bed." Joyce started laughing. *Was that funny?* "That was eight years ago," she said. Then she asked, "Are you hungry, Nani?"

You're not going to believe this, but Joyce made me French toast and scrambled eggs. I peeked at Jean through my hair. She was trying to be wide-eyed and alert, but her face looked sort of like a mug shot. Then we drank coffee together while Joyce told us more stories. "When my son was about your age, I drove the car into a brick wall and tried to blame it on him. I had blacked out, and I didn't even remember it until my husband told me the next morning." She was laughing again, so I laughed, and Jean laughed too, sitting up straight for the first time in months.

I said, "Good thing you don't drink anymore, Joyce."

She held up her coffee cup and said, "Cheers."

Most grown-ups ask dumb questions and talk at the wrong time, but Joyce was okay. And thank God she wasn't from a church. What a relief. It seemed she belonged to some secret society that doesn't accept money, and basically talks to anyone who drinks too much.

The doorbell rang, and Jean bolted to her room, gasping, "I can't see anybody." She hid herself halfway behind the door as Joyce reassured her, "Why don't you take a shower? I'll be here when you come out."

Let me tell you something. That Joyce is a sharp one. She saw the way my eyes zeroed in on her before I opened the door. "Okay if I hang out with your mom for a while?" she asked.

I crossed my arms and turned to her. "Why are you doing this, really?"

"Because somebody did it for me." She pulled a smoke out of her giant purse. She was a beauty shop type, but there was nothing sugarcoated about her. I decided, right then and there, to trust her. To hand over my broken-down mom.

When I took one last look at her, Joyce was dabbing her eyes with a crisp, white handkerchief, then patting her forehead like a gospel singer. I opened the door just a crack and slid out to meet Nigel and Shawn.

CHAPTER FIVE

☾

Déjà Vu

When we got to State, Shawn and Nigel zipped out of the van to inspect the waves. Both of them were wearing red trunks, and their hair was the exact same length, just below their shoulders. Of course, my nemesis, Jerry Richmond, was waiting for them.

He was a real piece of work these days, with his foxy-boy body. That was something I couldn't compete with. But what irked me the most was, he was a great surfer. No—he was beyond great. He was righteous in the water. Sometimes when I watched him, I secretly dreamed I was in his body, clipping and cutting back into each wave. How incredible would it be to surf again, breaking through the endless rhythms of the sea, rearranging reality so it fit my needs?

After an executive meeting with the guys, Nigel gave me a big, salty kiss. "You don't mind if we split, do you? Zuma is going off." I tugged at his pretty, long, blond hair and put a smile on my face. It didn't matter how close we were; surfers didn't like girls who tagged along. I knew the rule:

Waves before girlfriends.

Besides, soon Nigel would be on his way to the slums of Calcutta. Until then, every wave counted. Looking at him, I felt like a chunk of my heart was vanishing right before my very eyes. The combo of Rox and Nigel was the perfect balance of yin and yang. My life worked this way, and I never wanted it to change. But I knew better than to make a fuss, so I just gave Nigel a flirty tap on the butt as he walked away.

The extra bummer was, now I was stuck with Lord Ricky and his raunchy sidekicks, Brad and Stu.

"Did you hear? *Tuuuubed* is doing an article on me. Hey, Glenn!" Lord Ricky pointed at a man with a long, gray ponytail and a camera swinging around his neck. He was barefoot and wearing rolled-up white linen pants and a matching shirt that looked like he'd slept in it. "He's the man who's going to put me on the cover."

Dream on, you dweeb, I thought. I hated the way Lord Ricky elongated every vowel, making each word an event I wanted to forget. He moved in closer. "Where's my kiss?" Lord Ricky loved to do this whenever Nigel wasn't around.

I shrugged my shoulders like a dumb girl, which I am not. He tried to stretch out his arm to beckon me closer, but he was wearing his uniform: an old lady's yellow bathrobe that fit so tight that if he moved too quickly it would tear right off him. He had a hickey on his neck and was sitting on his throne: an upside down trash can. Lord Ricky was insatiable—and disgusting—when it came to young girls.

I was never so happy to see the Lisas and Jenni in the parking lot.

"You're not bugging Nani, are you, Lord Ricky?" Lisa H. had an overbite and big smile like Joni Mitchell's.

He gave her a stern look, which made it possible for me to sneak around him, and Lisa Y. skipped over to me. Some of her wavy, gold hair got in my mouth as she stumbled. She has bad vision. Story goes: she blew up firecrackers in her face. She refused to wear glasses. But none of the guys knew about her eyesight because she always kept one of us by her side.

The four of us inspected State. Everybody was in their assigned place: the old guys were in the volleyball courts with a few Lakers celebs—the only non-white people on the beach besides me; the gay guys were partying on the left side by the green wall; and the locals were sitting all around us, but nobody dared park their butts in front of the Sisters of Sand. They had to look at our backs while we watched the takeoff zone and everything that goes with it: surfing and surfers. Nobody with a brain got too close to us.

Nobody, except Melanie Clearwater. Since she had taken over the Topangas with her sister, Nicole, they had started inching closer to our spot. The Topangas were a bunch of retro-hippies who lived in the infamous canyon just before Malibu, hung out at the Elysium nudist resort, and grew their own pot.

The Lisas hated Melanie—especially since she had moved the group into their Earth Mother phase, drinking vanilla extract for breakfast and wearing see-through tops with petticoats. Today they were testing their chakras by touching pressure points on each other's bodies.

Melanie's saccharin voice chimed out, "Hi, girls."

"Hey, Mel," Lisa Y. said unceremoniously, watching the Topangas tap each other. "That should keep them busy for hours," she whispered.

Lisa H. covered her mouth with her hand and said, "Lesbos."

"Disgusting," Jenni chimed in.

I twisted the tips of my hair. "Yeah, for sure." What a phony baloney I was.

I looked closer at the Topangas, crammed together on one big blanket, as we passed them. *Thank you, Pele,* I thought. If Rox and Claire hadn't called dibs on me last summer, I'd be stuck with the Topangas, suffocating on the cherry incense they were burning.

It was Claire's last day at State, and we wanted to get everything just right before she got there. We made sure her towel faced the sun and that her and Rox's ice-cold Tabs were in the right place. When horns started honking down the Pacific Coast Highway, I knew they were arriving. I had a sudden thought: this is what it would sound like when Rox and Jerry tied the knot. They'd probably have a Just Married sign in the rear window and go to Catalina for their honeymoon. It made me cringe.

I took Rox and Claire's graduation gifts out of my Levi's pocket purse and placed them in the center of the towels. The SOS had gotten them dolphin necklaces: one turquoise, the other ruby red. The dolphin was Pali High's mascot, and my family's 'aumakua. They were my protectors.

"Hey!" Lisa Y. pulled at Lisa H.'s top to show her how sunburned she'd gotten: more burnt than the little girl in the Coppertone billboard over State Liquor.

"Stop being the boss of me," Lisa H. snapped.

"You're fried," said the other Lisa, pointing a tube of sunscreen at her.

This is going to be a fun summer, I thought, walking to the water and thinking about Jean. I was worried about her, but I reminded myself that Joyce was a Sturdy Gertie. I couldn't let my mom distract me. Not today.

I had just gotten knee-high in the water when I heard, "Hey, love," from behind me. I turned. Glenn snapped a shot of me pushing the bangs off my face. They were bugging me so much, I think I was frowning.

"Is that going to be in *Tubed*?" I asked, concerned that it wasn't a very good shot.

"Sorry, love. We have a No Girls policy. Just wanted to make sure my camera was in focus." *Typical,* I thought to myself.

Then, looking beyond me, he asked, "Are the waves always this good?"

"Yep." At State, the Pacific is a silver indigo. It's restless and rough. Nothing like Waikiki.

Bob, the lifeguard whose tower stands to the left of the SOS, hoisted the yellow caution flag over his station, carefully watching another numb-nut kid struggling to catch a wave. Bob shook his head, then yelled to me, "Watch the rip." I wanted to ignore him, but instead I smiled and waved.

Only surfers were allowed out right now—no civilians, and *no* girls—but that couldn't stop me from getting wet before paying homage to the outgoing rulers. I watched the water—unlike that wannabe surfer boy who'd just lost his board. He had no idea what he was doing. But I could see the riptide from where I was wading out.

In some places, the rip was smooth and calm. The tourists always swam directly into it, not knowing it was dangerous. State Beach had a fixed rip. It was almost always in the same spot, smack dab between where the lineup sat and Bob's perch. It looked like a river within the ocean, white water rapids, muddy and dark. Anything in its path was sucked out to sea. You have to know where the danger is in order to avoid it.

In a way, life is like a riptide.

"Yo!" Bob yelled again.

If only that knucklehead had swum parallel to shore, he'd have stayed out of the narrow current that snagged him. But he was panicking, trying to go against the tide. He'd gotten himself into the worst part of it, between the breakers and the whitewash. He was like a hamster stuck in a wheel: not going anywhere. He didn't realize he would be okay if he just stepped out or treaded water. It was too late; he struggled to keep his chin up, then waved his arm, signaling desperately for help.

"Look out," Bob called as he ran past me, throwing a red buoy over his shoulder as he rushed into the water. Even just standing there, I could feel the current yanking at my legs. I didn't fight it. I just moved one way and then the other downstream. I zigzagged serpentine lines without losing my cool, and voilà—I was back on dry sand.

I assumed the lineup was watching the rescue, but when I turned around, I saw them all staring at Rox and Claire, who were both smoking. I knew Rox couldn't quit. They strolled arm in arm down the beach, just like I remembered seeing them strut when I first met them. Except, now they were older and more amazing. The sight of them stopped all the volleyball games. Men were transfixed by their strange, magnetic force.

CHAPTER SIX

☾

Total Perfection

Rox sat absolutely still, cross-legged on the striped beach towel.

I lifted her hair. "This one's for you." I hooked the necklace and watched her gently place it in the center of her chest. It was a sparkling speck of red to honor Pele and give Rox protection. Better late than never.

"It's beautiful," she said, clasping the tiny dolphin between her fingertips. She looked at me and said to the group, "I'll never take it off."

"Me neither," Claire chimed in. "Thank you, everyone," she said, hugging each of us.

It was turning into a great day. At least, until the Lisas started bickering about *Tubed* magazine again. Lisa H. looked at me. "Nani. Have you ever seen a girl in *Tubed* magazine?"

Rox took over. "No, but I'm going to be the first. You watch. Usually, in surf magazines, all you see are girls' butts. Who they are doesn't matter."

"She's going to change all that this summer," Claire said.

Lisa H. stood up, gyrating her hips. "Not if I get a picture first."

She trotted down to the water.

"She's becoming a problem," Rox said, under her breath, to me and Claire.

I nodded. The new seating arrangement was making her overly confident. Lisa H. was a Sagittarius, and too eager. Her desire for power was making her annoyingly stupid.

"Do you want the good news, or the bad?" I asked.

Rox said, "Good."

"Lisa isn't going to be in *Tubed*."

"What's the bad?" Claire asked.

"None of us are. There seems to be some kind of gentlemen's agreement: no girls allowed."

"There's a word for that," Claire said. "It's on the tip of my tongue . . ."

"Sexism?" I said.

"No Fair-ism. BS-ism," Rox replied. "Well, that changes everything, doesn't it?"

"Hey, girl," Melanie said as she walked toward the water.

Rox was just about to flip her off when one of those dark, excited expressions came over her face. "Hey!" she said, all friendly, which tipped Claire and me off immediately. "See that guy over there? His name is Glenn, and he told us how he chooses girls for *Tubed*."

Melanie looked at Rox. "And you're going to tell *me*?"

"Sure, why not? Claire and I are leaving soon. So, he said you have to keep your chest up and back arched a little. Shake your butt side to side when you walk. That catches his eye." Rox raised her Tab in a toast. "May the best butt shaker win."

Melanie thrust her shoulders back and said, "Neato. Bosso. Keeno," and gave us a peace sign. *Ick.*

When she was out of earshot, Rox said, "I hate her."

The sunnier it got at State, the gloomier Rox looked. She didn't talk again until a shadow fell over us.

There was only one person who would dare stand in Rox's sun. "Look what I found," Jerry said in a singsong voice. He playfully dropped some seaweed on Rox's butt, then sat on it, getting her all wet and sandy.

"Are you done?" Rox asked. I wasn't sure if she meant surfing or sitting on top of her, but either way, she was smiling again.

"Negative," Jerry said. "No waves at Porto down south, so we're going to spend the rest of the afternoon here." He gave her a quick kiss, jumped up, put his board on his head, and said, "Later, 'gator."

Nigel yelled, "Wait up, Richmond," and charged after him.

I loved Nigel's soft, Jesus-like vibe. In the year we'd been together, he'd gotten even sweeter—if that was possible. He'd also maxed out yet another wet suit with new muscles.

The Topangas nearly gave themselves whiplash watching the McBride twins walk by. I thought, *What a bunch of amateurs. Wait till they see me celebrate my one-year anniversary with that hunk when he gets back from saving souls in India.*

I was distracted by a van pulling in to the parking lot. It wasn't a cool van; it was a Ford with no windows on either side. It looked like an impenetrable cube of metal and sat there like a dare.

"Oh, no," Lisa H. said.

I lit Rox's cigarette as she said, very matter-of-factly, "Looks like the VPMs got a pass from Lord Ricky." No one drove into State's parking lot without permission.

Lisa H. groaned, too loudly, "Not those uncivilized sex fiends."

Claire shushed her. "The Van Patrol Members are not normal," she confirmed, "but they can surf."

What is *normal in this Haolewood?* I asked myself, lighting my Lark 100 off Rox's. I recognized these nutty white boys (a.k.a.: *haoles*) from school. Everybody knew this pack of nomads went from beach to beach. They were notorious ladies' men.

"Do you hear? They're blasting it," Lisa H. announced.

"Shut. UP," Rox said.

"What?" Lisa H. asked.

I tried to be a peacekeeper. "You know they always play that song by Iron Butterfly before they surf," I said.

"Is it true that Iron Butterfly was so stoned, they couldn't pronounce 'In the Garden of Eden'?" Jenni asked.

"Yes," Lisa H. said, with great authority. "'In-A-Gadda-Da-Vida.' Seventeen minutes and five seconds of it, to be exact."

"No one asked," Rox said.

The Lisas bickered for the entire seventeen minutes. When the van door finally slid open, pot smoke billowed out and several versions of the same blond surfer descended.

"They remind me of the Rolling Stones getting off their jet," I said.

Everyone could see that they were more than just a clump of guys who moved in a pack. Their hair was wild and uncombed, and they swaggered like no high schoolers I had ever seen.

These newbies weren't pretty like the McBrides. They were scruffier and more dangerous, with cracked teeth and black eyes. It made for a seismic shift in the ethos of State.

The Lisas and Jenni perked up and started going off on Johnny Brewster, the driver of the VPMs, and how cute he'd gotten.

The more they yakked, the lower Rox sank. I could tell their constant chatter was really irking her. They didn't know she was pregnant and feeling icky. If they'd done one more hair flip, I think Rox would have lost it.

But when I saw Coco Sinclair bringing up the rear of this motley crew, I got what all the excitement was about. He was a total surf maverick, and he and Johnny were ranked in the Competitive Under-Eighteen category. I had no doubt they were here for the *Tubed* article. It was going to be a summer of "see and be seen."

Lisa H. should have kept her mouth shut, but she couldn't stop herself. "You know, maybe I'll go for that Coco."

"Spare me," Rox said.

So much for flow in the lineup.

"Time to recruit," Claire said, clapping her hands all enthusiastically, like Mary Poppins. "Jenni, why don't you and the Lisas check out the public side of Bel Air. There might be some potentials hanging out."

"But the VPMs just got here," Lisa H. pouted.

"Go get some recruits," Rox ordered. "Do you want the Topangas to take over? Look at those space cadets. They're going to outnumber us if you don't get going."

Over in the Topangas' spot, Melanie laid out eucalyptus leaves, making pillows for each of her girls. Then she stood so Glenn could see her. She twitched then jiggled like something had just crawled up her butt—looking at Glenn all the while. Then her sister Nicole did it, too.

Glenn didn't know what had hit him. He kept adjusting his tripod and pretended not to see them, which made us snicker ourselves sick.

When Claire was done laughing, she said, "Come on, you guys. We need serious backup."

"But we wanted to hang out with you on your last day," Jenni said, cuddling into Claire's side. Jenni's blond hair was almost as long as mine, making her even more luscious in her violet bikini. She was so cute, guys called her by her last name: Fox. She was the protective Libra who watched over the Lisas.

Claire reassured her, "I'm only in Europe for a little while. I'll be back before the end of the summer."

"But then you're going straight to UCSB. When are we going to see you?" Lisa H. whimpered.

Rox pretended to play a little violin. "Do you think Claire and I busted our butts making this lineup, so you could let it evaporate? Get going." As they strutted away, she started talking about them behind their backs. "You better not let those dorks eff up. Or else, Nani." She held her finger cocked to my head like a gun, then said, "Pow."

Rox was looking right through me, acting like I was just another member of the lineup. She rested her head on Claire's shoulder.

Claire didn't even know Fiji existed. Their affection was girly and sweet. It didn't bother me. In fact, I liked it.

Seeing them made me smile to myself and lick my lips. I knew Rox was just acting tough, and deep down she couldn't resist me. At least, I hoped not.

CHAPTER SEVEN

☾

Lovebirds

Claire tested her tan by pushing two fingers into her forearm. If the spot went white, she would know she was burning. "I don't want to fry. Did you see how pink Lisa H. was?" She chewed her pinky nail off and nonchalantly spit it into the sand. "I need a swim," she moaned.

Claire walked toward the tower, and the whole beach stopped to watch. Glenn did, too—but I didn't hear a single click of his camera. Claire flowed into the breeze like some kind of deity and flirted with Bob the lifeguard until he brought the no swim flag down.

"I've got a question." Rox held up her left hand and admired her fingers. "What do you think? Diamonds with a white gold band, or regular gold?" she asked me.

"What's the difference?"

"White gold looks like silver. Regular gold looks like gold."

"Why don't you just get a silver band?"

"Well . . ." Rox paused and thought. "Gold is forever."

"What does Claire think?"

"Claire thinks . . . expensive. Like a typical Palisadian rich girl." She scooched closer. Her words tickled my ear as she said apologetically, "Claire is going to be the godmother; you're going to be the aunt, okay? You understand, don't you?" I nodded, surprised I could lie to Rox.

Jerry got out of the water, his board resting on his head, and began to walk up the beach.

"Well, it's now or never." Rox stood, pushed her boobs up, and spanked the sand off her ass as she walked up the beach to talk to Jerry.

Claire gave her a thumbs-up as she sat back down with me. Then she whispered, "Chain smoking can't be good for the baby."

What did it matter, anyway? That baby was half Rox and half Jerry, which added up to total perfection.

We turned onto our stomachs and positioned ourselves elbow to elbow, wiggling down as low as we could. This way, we'd be able to watch Rox's every move. Claire tossed her hair to the left, and I tossed mine to the right, so when we put our heads together it was like we were in a tunnel. It was great. And yet it wasn't. I was stuck in the front row watching my future being determined for me.

"Do you think he'll get down on one knee? Or maybe he'll break into tears of joy." Claire giggled, barely containing herself, as Rox took Jerry's free hand and held it close to her heart. We watched her put her other hand on Jerry's board. It was like some kind of surf sacrament. A triangle, a blessing. Yin, yang, and baby.

I almost got caught up in the moment and didn't think about what was really happening. I was losing my true love to some guy. If I married Nigel and Rox married Jerry, we'd be breaking the ultimate rule:

Never marry a surfer.

That was my mentor, Annie Iopa's, most important rule.
Annie used to work at my dad's bar. She was like my big sister
and taught me everything I know. "Surfers are no good as husbands," she had warned me. Why didn't I warn Rox? And why
didn't I stop this pact she'd dragged me into? I peeled back the
Band-Aid and looked at the perfectly round, red blister on the
inside of my arm. Love makes you do weird things.

"I think she just told him." Claire poked me in the ribs.
Jerry stepped forward, staring at Rox. Their hands were still
tightly laced together. His mouth dropped open, and his eyes
went wide. "I think it's going to be tears," Claire said.

"This is like watching a silent movie," I told her. "Even
though we can't hear anything, we can totally tell what's
happening."

"It's so romantic."

That made my flesh crawl. Claire squeezed my hand. Jerry
turned and gently positioned his surfboard against the metal trash
can behind him. He said something to Rox and looked away.

"Nope, looks like he's going to get on one knee!" Claire
squealed.

Then, like a rocket, with one convulsive kick, Jerry slammed
his heel in the center of his board, breaking it in two. The snap
was so loud it echoed down the beach.

I gasped. It was awful and violent, like watching a car crash.
Everybody turned to see what all the commotion was about—
including Glenn. Claire covered her face.

For the second time today, everybody's eyes were on Rox.
Except now she wasn't the little princess making an entrance.

She was the girl getting yelled at by the hottest surfer on the beach. Everyone could hear Jerry's incomplete sentences.

"What the . . . you said you couldn't!"

He picked up what was left of his board and hurled it, one piece at a time, into the empty trash can behind them, making the most brutal noise I'd ever heard.

He paced back and forth, slamming his fist into his hand.

"What's he going to do? Hit her?" I said. "He better not."

"This is *definitely* not good," Claire said, still covering her face.

I was not going to let Mr. Mellow lose it on Rox. I prayed to Pele, *Please make Jerry Richmond go away forever*, and stood up, not sure what to do next.

Jerry was just about to kick over the trash can when Nigel and Shawn intervened from across the beach. Nigel whistled through his teeth, and Shawn yelled, "Hey, lovebirds!" Before Jerry could make one more threatening move, they had him in the parking lot. And that was that.

When Rox trudged back to us, Claire and I scooched to either side so she could lie between us. I didn't know what to say, and neither did Claire. What would help at a time like this? What could we *possibly* say? I looked down at my hands, cautiously glancing sideways at Rox. "Sorry" seemed so pedestrian.

It was as if someone had switched off the light in Rox's eyes. Her neck and chest were covered in red blotches. She lit another cigarette and told us, "I've got to get this taken care of."

That's when my supernova Virgo side kicked in. At least abortion was legal now, so Rox wouldn't have to have some guy do it in a garage with a rusty hanger. Annie had told me about girls who tried to miscarry back home before it was legal in Hawaii. They'd eat baby goat livers and drink carrot juice. But Rox didn't need to know all that right now.

She didn't move. Everything went very still in our area, but the rest of State flowed with its normal rhythm: volleyball games, gay guys splashing in the water, Glenn with his tripod set up just to our right, and Bob on riptide watch as waves crashed into swimmers.

When Claire finally spoke, she tried to sound lighthearted. "We're going to need a code word for this operation," she joked. "No pun intended."

I knew Claire didn't mean to be a smartass, but she couldn't have said anything worse. Rox shuddered and narrowed her eyes. "Wake up," she said, snapping her fingers in Claire's face. "This isn't some game. This is my life."

For a moment, Claire was speechless. *That's a first,* I thought.

"I know," she said sharply. "But shouldn't we have a discussion, at least, about adoption?"

"I'm not getting stretch marks for nothing."

"No, of course you're not. I should have known better."

"You don't know anything." Rox pounced. "You just have your perfect little life and your perfect little parents who are going to take you and your brother on your perfect little European vacation. And then you're going to go to your perfect college that's perfectly paid for. The only thing that *isn't* perfect is your two-timing boyfriend, who hasn't gotten *you* pregnant yet."

"Shut up!"

"YOU shut up."

Claire stood and grabbed her stuff. "You know, Rox, why don't you just take care of this yourself."

"I will."

"Fine," said Claire.

"Fine," said Rox.

"I'm going to hang out with the recruiters," Claire said. "Have a great summer."

Rox pulled the towel over her face so tightly, I thought she was going to suffocate. As Claire turned to go, she held up her middle finger at Rox, mouthing the words that went with it. Then she looked at me. "I'll see you when I get back from France, Nani. Sorry, but you're going to have to take care of Her Heiny." She headed up the beach to Bel Air without another word.

After a few seconds, Rox yanked the towel off her face and fixed her gaze firmly on me. "Promise you won't leave?"

"We made a pact. Remember? I'm not going anywhere." I forced a smile.

CHAPTER EIGHT

Secrets and Cover-Ups

June fifteenth was going to be a historic day. Everybody was planning to get to State at the crack of dawn. There was a total solar eclipse, and it wouldn't be visible from California again until the year 2150. Nobody was supposed to go out when it was happening, but State was going to be a full-on party. The SOS had been planning it for weeks.

I had made viewing boxes out of cardboard. Each one had a wide piece of aluminum foil and a space for your head to go through, and when you stood with your back to the sun, the eclipse would be reflected on a white sheet of paper.

I was in a hurry to meet Rox. When I ran past my mom's room, I could see she was still in bed. "Get up!" I thought she'd be better when she stopped drinking, but she was worse than ever. The alarm clock was blaring when I turned it off. How could anybody sleep through that?

I rushed to the kitchen to heat up some old coffee, but when I took it to her, the bed was empty. Then I heard it: gagging. I ran to the bathroom. Jean was lying on the tiles under the toilet.

"Help," she whimpered.

I didn't know what to do, so I called Joyce. When she picked up, I didn't even say hello; I said, "Mom's sick. She's throwing up, and the sheets are soaking wet."

"Get her a beer," Joyce said calmly.

"No!"

"Nani, she needs alcohol or—"

"I threw it out."

"Get some chocolate, then, and put it under her tongue. I'm on my way."

"Chocolate?" But she had hung up.

I tore the kitchen apart looking for something like chocolate. I went crazy, pulling open all the cabinets. I called Joyce right back. "There isn't any chocolate. Nothing's here."

"Okay. Just stay with your mom. If she convulses, call an ambulance."

"What?"

"It's going to be okay. I'm on my way."

I hung up the phone, but as soon as the handle hit the receiver, it rang again. I lifted it without a second thought and said, "Yeah?"

"Is Jean Nuuhiwa there?" the voice asked, confused. When I didn't answer, it said, louder, "Hello?" Then, even louder, "Is Jean Nuuhiwa there? This is Sister Mary Helen from St. John's."

Holy Mary, Mother of God, I thought.

"Hello?" The voice was curt.

"Oh, hello, Sister. My mom—" I wasn't sure what to say. In the last three weeks, I had told Sister Mary Helen every lie in the book—from Jean getting a flat tire to the flu. We'd even had a couple "deaths" in the family when she was too hung-over to go to work.

"She's not here," I finally said. "Um." I yanked at my hair, trying to think of something. "I have a fever. And she went to the pharmacy to get some medicine, so I'll finally stop throwing up." There was silence on the end of the phone. "Is it okay if my mom stays home today? I don't want to be alone." I looked up and asked Jesus for help—knowing he spoke the language of nuns. "Would you hold on, please?"

Then I held the phone so she could hear Jean making heaving noises from the bathroom. I shuffled my feet and held the phone close to them, then slurped to make it sound like I was wiping my mouth.

"Sorry about that. But like I was saying, I'm sick. Okay if she stays here today?"

Sister Mary Helen didn't sound too happy about it, but what was she going to say? "Yes, dear. Of course."

And then, just to nail the deal shut, I said, "Will you pray for me, Sister?" I didn't expect her to start praying right then and there. She sounded like she was having one of those seizures, so I just let the phone hang and went back to mom's side, while the old bird kept praying.

The next day, when I showed up at State, Rox wasn't talking to me. I used all the change in my bag to get her Red Vines and a Tab, so she wouldn't be mad.

"You promised you wouldn't leave me," she said. "Where were you yesterday? I had to endure the Lisas alone."

"My mom was sick."

"Ha. Drunk, more like it."

I straightened my towel and turned away. I was desperate to hide—like I was the last one to notice that my insides were leaking into a puddle all around me. There seemed to be a stain everywhere I went, thanks to Jean.

Rox flicked a new matchbook from Patrick's at me. "You forgot I had my Chart House interview, didn't you?"

"No . . . yes. I'm sorry. Did you get the hostess job?"

Rox took a little bow. "You bet I did. I start after this is over," she said, pointing to her stomach.

Thank God Rox would have something to look forward to after this whole mess was done. I had heard that the Chart House was very romantic, with the sound of the waves and private booths. The ultimate date spot. All the waiters were surfers. Everybody wanted a job there, but only the chosen few got one. As the restaurant's new hostess, Rox would be the first thing each guest saw as they entered, the sunset reflecting in the floor-to-ceiling windows behind her.

Jenni interrupted us by cautiously tapping Rox. I swear she barely touched her. "Look," Jenni said. Lisa Y. was wearing a new pair of wire-rim shades with green-tinted lenses. And she was walking alone!

"Wow," Jenni said, "you look hot."

"I have the story of the century," Lisa Y. announced. But before she told us what happened, she held up her prescription glasses and declared, "I can see!"

"You're late," Rox barked. "When do you plan on recruiting?"

"Where's Lisa H.?" Jenni asked.

I had never seen one Lisa without the other. It was bizarre.

Lisa started talking so urgently that her words spilled out all jumbled together. "Remember the other day I was telling Lisa H. she was getting sunburned? Well . . ." Lisa Y. looked around to make sure the Topangas couldn't hear her. "I swore that I'd never tell Lisa H.'s secret, but . . . here it goes: Lisa is a hardcore Mormon. Like, her family wears that ginormous underwear. No cigarettes, no soda, no alcohol. They have, like, twenty children, and—if you're a girl—you have to wear a one-piece bathing suit."

I couldn't believe Lisa Y. was saying such disgraceful things. Back home, my Mormon friends up in Laie were really sensitive about what they called their "garments." They wore them as a sign of respect to God. It was this sacred covenant, like when Jewish people wear yarmulkes. But Lisa Y. couldn't have cared less. And I didn't say anything.

Rox put both hands on her hips. "That's not true," she said. "Lisa H. always wears a bikini."

"Exactly!" Lisa said excitedly. "We used to sneak into the gas station before coming to State so she could change."

I couldn't believe how easily Lisa Y. ratted out the other Lisa. Luckily for me, my secrets were safe. Rox was one hundred percent true blue, our friendship sealed with a Fiji pact.

"Yesterday," Lisa continued, "Lisa H.'s mom walked in when she was taking a shower, and Lisa got totally busted, thanks to those teeny-tiny lines on that pink skin. Well . . . her mom went bananas—and when she saw the smokes and empty Coke can in her purse? She went even more bonkers. Long story short, Lisa Haskell got shipped off to Utah first thing this morning."

"What?" Jenni said.

"She has to babysit her twelve cousins for the entire summer, then write an essay for her bishop, before she can come home."

"Oh, great," Rox said. "That means when I start working, there will only be three girls in the lineup!"

When I heard that dark tone in Rox's voice, I moved into my peacekeeper role. "So how did you get all this info?" I asked Lisa.

"She called me, crying hysterically, while her father was packing a suitcase for her."

Rox hardballed it in one sentence: "Good riddance to bad rubbish." Everyone froze as she slammed her cigarette into the sand like a period at the end of a sentence, lay down, and rolled over.

If Rox had been a sympathetic kind of girl, she'd have been concerned about how the lineup had shriveled, but instead she smirked. No Claire. No Lisa. No McBrides—they were getting ready to leave—and no Jerry. He had made himself scarce. Rox was in total control. And I knew it was important to her that it keep looking that way. This is when The Rules were obvious and important—even if I made them up as I went.

It's better to say nothing
than something you regret.

The lineup went into a bake session. No one talked. Like a clock ticking, the sun moved to another part of the sky. It had to be almost noon.

"The VPMs are here," Jenni said, all cheery. Even when there weren't waves, the Van Patrol Members showed up every day no matter what. They surfed in swarms of jellyfish, blown-out two-footers, and tsunamis. It didn't matter. They were always in the water.

"Lord Ricky gave them citizenship status," Jenni continued. "It looks like they'll hit State every day for the rest of their lives."

The VPMs were natural locals. Unfortunately, they hassled the gay guys and didn't think twice before slashing tires and breaking the windows of cars that didn't belong at State. I saw three of them on the bluffs standing watch with a walkie-talkie. They were guarding the beach for Lord Ricky, making sure that since a *Tubed* reporter had arrived, the incredible waves that broke here were for locals only. This beach may have been public, but it was private now.

"I've made a decision," Rox said, sitting back up. "Lisa, you'll be Number One. Jenni, you'll be Number Two. Here's the catch: when you graduate, Nani will be Number One, and she gets to choose her Number Two. Do you both agree?"

Jenni and Lisa looked at each other, smiled, clapped, and hugged. And then it didn't even take them a second to chill out and calmly nod.

"That sounds great, Rox," Lisa said. Clearly she had forgotten all about her ex-best-friend-for-life. *Poof.* Gone.

Quietly, I asked Rox, "What happens when Lisa H. comes back?"

She gave me that diabolical look that could freeze you to the bone and make you want to run home with your tail between your legs. "Lisa H. is *never* coming back to State."

"Why not?" I asked.

"I've taken her membership away. She's out." I froze, stunned. Rox's meanness was more hypnotic than a pendulum swaying back and forth. I had to force myself to look away before she started laughing.

Two VPMs startled her, tossing their boards a little too close to us while they were waxing up. "Oops, sorry, Rox." That gave Coco the opportunity to get a better look at Jenni. He stared so intently, Rox's frown dissolved. It was important to her that the VPMs and the lineup were on the same team. And if they were dating, better yet.

The chemistry between Jenni and Coco was unreal. Rox looked pleased when Jenni blushed and turned onto her side, so all Coco could do was gape at her round, little ass. Lisa noticed Coco's flirting, too. A move like that never got past the lineup.

Up close, I could see Coco's eyes were a shade of crystal blue. There was no escaping them. And on top of that, his hair was bleached white from the sun and hung in a V down to the middle of his tan back. It was easy to spot him on State, now that the McBrides were gone. Coco guzzled Hawaiian Punch from a can, then tossed it gracefully into the trash. He gripped his board tightly under his arm and walked calmly across the hot sand. As he pushed off into the water, Jenni looked at Lisa and said, "Let's get wet."

Rox grinned smugly as Jenni took Lisa by the hand and seductively walked her past the rest of the VPMs, not glancing back.

"And they lived happily ever after," Rox said. She locked pinkies with me, started to laugh, and then stopped. "I'm going to get it done on Thursday."

"Where?"

"In a doctor's office."

I thought, *Lucky for you Roe v. Wade got passed six months ago.* Nobody on the mainland seemed to know that, in Hawaii, abortion had been legal since 1970. Of course it was passed in the smartest state first.

Johnny Brewster stood above us with his board under his arm. He had to be least six feet tall with wavy, sandy-blond hair and a cute little face with thin lips. He was a typical crazy boy. But, most importantly, he ran the VPM empire.

I wondered what sign he was. I thought he was probably a Gemini, because he was smart. He paid homage to Rox by looking at her and saying, "Hey."

That daily acknowledgement to the lineup's leader is what gave him permission to move forward. This is a little known fact, but it's the girls at a great surf spot who permit new locals to enter the water. Without us, there would be no protocol. That's why we had to build the lineup fast—or else the Topangas really would take over. They were spreading like a virus.

Half wet and half dry in the water, Lisa looked different with her shades on and without the other Lisa hovering next to her. She seemed more alluring and sexy. Lisa and Jenni made a good set.

I thought the big excitement would come when Coco charged past them on his first wave. Maybe he'd splash Jenni to get her attention. But it wasn't Coco who made the first move. It was Johnny. He walked a little too close to Lisa, surprising her and making her turn. Then he actually touched her arm.

"Contact!" Rox told me, as if announcing a lunar landing. "This is going to work out fine. I'm such a genius," she said. Like I didn't already know. "You realize recruiting is up to you now," she continued. "Those two lovesick puppies are going to be useless."

Me? Recruit? That was ridiculous. It was the high-pressure responsibility of the new rulers. Not me. In an instant, my summer dissolved right before my eyes. I hardly had a minute to get a grip and conjure up a half-hearted, "No problem."

CHAPTER NINE

(

Our Father

After an exhaustingly flirtatious day, the SOS packed up. Lisa and Jenni couldn't stop talking about Coco and Johnny. They had sun-tight faces and greasy smudges all over from their favorite suntan oil, Bain de Soleil. They didn't even care that Rox had announced that it was her last day at State for a while. She made up a story about going to Esalen in Big Sur with her sister, but really she just wanted to sound cool, so no one would ever guess she was getting a you-know-what. This way, her squeaky clean reputation would stay intact.

It's so screwed up that when a girl graduates high school she has to look like she's getting serious about life. Guys can be goofballs for another four years, but girls have to grow up instantly. I've seen lots of them cut their hair and start wearing pantyhose. And when it comes to beachcraft, well, girls aren't supposed to go to State every day. Unless, of course, they have kids. Then it's okay for them to live full-time on the sand. But for ex-rulers like Rox and Claire, visitation rights have to be used sparingly. It's how they keep their fame intact.

I think Rox was relieved to be taking a few days off since Jerry wasn't showing up. It kind of made her look bad.

When I saw Nigel's baby-blue VW van parked on the bluffs, I grabbed my stuff with a sigh of relief. I told Rox I'd see her later, since she was treating me to the new James Bond movie in Westwood tonight. I waited my turn while one of the VPMs hosed off. Then I dipped in and quickly scrubbed the sand away so my skin would be shiny and smooth, the way Nigel loved it.

Just as I was about to step into his van, I stopped dead in my tracks. There was a strange guy in the driver's seat. I backed away. Two of the VPMs guarding State went on alert.

"Nani! Nani, it's me."

"Nigel?" I tried not to look like I was seeing a horror movie.

"No, Shawn. Sorry to freak you out."

I wanted to scream, but that would have set the VPMs off more. I don't think they believed Shawn was a local. He sure didn't look like one. His long hair had been shaved into a crew cut. I couldn't stomach that I was looking at a McBride. His neck was skinny, and his Adam's apple poked out. He didn't look anything like himself. Where hair once folded over his shoulders, I could now see pimples and moles. He looked like the plucked chicken I once saw on Kauai that had hideous bumps on its white, greasy skin.

"What happened to you?" I asked.

Shawn put the van into reverse and said, "I'll tell you on the way. You've got to help Nigel."

"What's wrong?"

"He won't come out of the fort, and we're leaving first thing tomorrow."

"Only if you promise no hanky-panky," I said. There was no way I'd get in a car alone with Shawn McBride under regular circumstances. I knew he would try to hit on me, so I waited until he crossed his heart, held up two fingers, and swore to God before I hopped in.

As we drove, Shawn told me about the Father's Day Massacre. It seems Mr. McBride insisted that the "boys" give him something he really wanted. And what he wanted was to have his barber come over during the family brunch, sit Nigel and Shawn down, and shave off their hair. They couldn't go to India, he insisted, looking like girls.

It sounded humiliating and awful. Poor Nigel. Shawn was better at shrugging things off, but Nigel was sensitive. Hair is a sacred thing. It holds what my dad called mana, which means energy. And cutting somebody's hair is sacrilegious.

Though I never wanted to go back to the McBride's Malibu home, I had to. Nigel needed me.

"How long has he been in there?" I asked.

"Since last night—but I brought him a pizza."

I thought about how my mom had avoided Father's Day altogether. The night before, she had taken a bottle of vodka into her room and closed the door. I had watched TV.

When the security gates bearing the gold initials MB opened, I saw the pink hacienda mansion with the red-tiled roof. I hadn't been here since that party when I got dosed last summer. That was when the bad blood started between me and Mary Jo. The SOS banished her and Suzie after they spiked my beer with acid. I did a rock-and-roll hula that sort of made me famous with the locals.

I was not happy about being back.

There were waiters everywhere, in black pants and white shirts, folding up chairs and putting plush cushions into bags. Others were taking down the huge tent, shaking out the white tablecloths and lugging outdoor heaters into a truck. Shawn explained that, the night before, his mother had hosted her annual fundraiser for The Blind Children of India. He parked the van and scurried into the mansion.

I knew my way around. I walked past the pool, through the rose gardens, to the far end of the estate, to where I'd find the notorious fort—the World War II bomb shelter where Nigel had been hiding. I opened the door to the Love Shack with its familiar smell of cedar, pot, and mold, and I made my way down the stairs in total darkness.

"Nigel, it's me. Are you there?"

I flipped on the switch, lighting up the rows of green and red Christmas lights around the brick walls. Then I saw him, crunched in a corner, hiding under the giant Santa and the rest of his mom's Christmas decorations. He pulled a blanket over his head, making a human teepee, and he wouldn't come out.

"I've already seen Shawn, so I know what you look like." It was painful to watch him timidly emerge, pouting like a little boy who had peed his pants in kindergarten.

"Pretty bad, isn't it?"

I went into girlfriend mode and said, in my most soothing voice, "To a degree—but not really," even though I was thinking: *FRANKENSTEIN!*

It took a while, but eventually I coaxed Nigel out to take a shower, eat a sandwich, and save India.

The McBrides' gourmet kitchen was bigger than my house, and it contained a feast of leftovers from the party. I made a killer turkey sandwich for Nigel and polished off the leftover lobster salad, eating it with my fingers. I put the sandwich on a fancy plate and garnished it with homemade potato chips.

Just as I turned to set it on the counter, I smelled the stench of vodka and Tabasco. Mrs. McBride wobbled in wearing furry slippers and a chenille robe over her formal attire from the party. It looked like she just woke up. Did she sleep in her clothes? Her hair looked like a termite mound, and she was crunching loudly on some celery from her Bloody Mary. Diamonds the size of grapes hung from her earlobes.

Unlike the rest of the SOS, I try to avoid sweeping judgments, but when I saw Mrs. McBride maneuvering so excruciatingly slowly, there was only one word that came to mind: drunk. We watched each other in silence. Then she removed a crushed corsage from her dress and let it drop onto the marble island between us. She looked at my sandwich and daintily handed me her glass.

"This looks lovely. Thank you, dear." She took the sandwich I had just made for Nigel and pulled some money from her bra. "This is for working overtime."

I had never seen a fifty-dollar bill before. It reeked of strong perfume and was so crisp I had to be careful not to get a paper cut. I was just about to slip it into my pocket purse when Nigel zoomed into the kitchen, snatched it out of my hand, and slammed it back into his mother's.

He put his arm around me as Mrs. McBride took a giant bite out of the sandwich. "This is my girlfriend, Mom." He was so tall and defiant. *But what I would have done with fifty dollars!* Mrs. McBride looked away as Nigel escorted me around the counter. Luckily I had untied my white lace blouse and tucked it into my jean shorts, so my midriff was covered. I guess when she saw my flip-flops she realized I wasn't the maid.

Mr. McBride entered the kitchen, filling the room with the kinetic force of a nuclear flash. I had never seen someone so famous before. He was, after all, the most prominent business tycoon in Nixon's inner circle, and he had a daunting presence. I tried not to gawk or stare. He was wearing a floor-length velvet bathrobe, his belly protruding and his thick, ash-white hair combed to one side over his head.

It was creepy the way he looked me up and down. "Well, well, who do we have here?" he asked with a Texan accent as he put his hand on my hip and pulled me in too close, slipping it down my waistband, almost to my ass. His voice plowed right through me. He looked at Mrs. McBride and asked, all friendly, "Is this Rosita's daughter? My, Anna, how you've grown!" He grabbed my waist tighter and felt me up.

I couldn't believe Nigel was just standing there watching. Where was the radical Jesus warrior I knew and loved? What, he could let his mom have it, but not his dad?

Then Mr. McBride went fierce and military. "Fix me some lobster salad, and next time, wear your uniform. I don't care whose kid you are; I'll fire you." I had to squirm my way out of his grip. Nigel wouldn't look at me.

Enough is enough, I thought. This was bogus. If I were blond, no one would be confusing me with the help, who they treated like trash. And that pissed me off even more than Nigel just standing there. Once and for all, I got it: because I was *hapa*, half white, in the eyes of people like the McBrides, I would never be more than half okay.

I turned to the son of a bitch and told him in my warrior voice, "You can't fire me because I don't work for you."

"What did you say?"

"Listen here, you *haole* bonehead—"

That was all I got out before he took a swing at me.

Mrs. McBride tripped over herself, pushing me out of the way. "Hurry," she said.

I swear, if it wasn't for Shawn running into the kitchen and taunting Mr. McBride by yelling, "Don't be a dick, Dad," he would have taken me out. But instead he chased Shawn upstairs, shouting, "You bastard! Get back here."

Nigel just stood there like a deer in headlights.

Until his mom shouted in his face, "Get her out of here."

There was no way I was going to marry into that snake pit—pact or no pact. The scale had tipped too far. Nigel and I moved sideways like a couple of crabs in a fast-moving tide. When we were outside, he had the nerve to toss me the keys. I'd never driven the van before, but I wanted to get home as much as he wanted to get out of there, and Nigel was shaking so badly, I knew he wouldn't be able to get it into gear.

"Want to listen to 'Locomotive Breath'?" Jethro Tull always made Nigel feel better because he was a Christian, too. I watched out of the corner of my eye as he shoved an entire pack of Juicy Fruit in his mouth one stick at a time and started chomping really hard.

He put on a faded Dodgers baseball cap, dark glasses, and a scarf to disguise himself. "I'm incognito," he said.

Then he launched into Father Nigel mode, like nothing had happened. He rambled on about how we were the last kingdom, and no one knew when everything would go kablooey, but most likely it would be soon.

"Uh, Nigel," I said, "I think things already went kablooey." When he ignored what I said, it made me wonder what else Mr. McBride had gotten his claws into. Until then, I'd had no idea that Nigel McBride just might have more secrets than I did.

I felt like I had been swallowed whole. I'd never realized how little Nigel's head was; without hair, he looked like a jabbering skull, clicking away, telling me which scriptures to study while he was gone. He even got his highlighted Bible out of the glove compartment and gave it to me, reminding me to fear God.

Fear God? I thought. "Fear your Father," I said. "Call the police on him. Do something." Mr. McBride had been milliseconds from belting me one. And the worst thing about it was: if he had actually hit me, there wasn't one cop in the world who would have believed me over him. I gave Nigel the silent treatment the whole way home.

When we pulled up to my house, he said, "You're a lot braver than I am . . . I'm sorry."

But you know, sorry didn't really cut it.

He slipped out of the van and came around to the driver's side. "Can I have one last kiss?" he asked. Then he pulled me closer and dipped his tongue into my mouth. Even though he was almost bald, he was still a gifted kisser.

I grabbed the hat off his head, popped him one, and put it on backwards. I was pissed, but I also felt sorry for him— especially when he quickly covered himself with the raggedy old scarf, arranging it to make sure both sides of his head were covered. Maybe absence would make my heart grow fonder.

When he got back into the van, he lit up a roach from the ashtray and took a hit as he handed me a pillowcase stuffed with a wet suit and old clothes. He laughed nervously. "Can you drop this off at the Salvation Army for me?"

"No!"

Then he smiled that McBride smile that I loved so much. "It's for the poor."

I grabbed it out of his hand, knowing this was the end and the beginning. I had seen the dark corner of his world. The surf god Nigel McBride had fallen from grace.

"Don't let your dad get the best of you," I told him.

I was never meant to see the chink in his armor. I wanted to yank his Saint Christopher off his neck, but there was too much sadness in his eyes. His strangled pride made him look even smaller as he pulled down his shades.

"Aloha," he said.

CHAPTER TEN

☾

Changes

Nigel had never said the word *aloha* before. It means hello and goodbye, and the way he said it, it sounded so final.

It made me angrier as I entered 33 Sage. The house was a mess. I just hoped Jean was still on the wagon. It had been seventy-two hours. But who was counting? She'd been seeing Joyce every day, but I still kept my eye on her. People who drink like Jean does can't be trusted.

"Mom, I'm home." She strolled out of the kitchen wearing an apron.

"Are you hungry?" she asked. With her hair up she looked like she was doing a Betty Crocker commercial.

"No, I had lobster salad at the McBrides'." I was trying to impress her. And I did. She perked up and said, "Really? How nice!" Then suddenly she added, "I don't like you up there unchaperoned."

"Mr. and Mrs. McBride were home."

"Oh?" She held up the *LA Times* and pointed to an article with her magnifying glass. "I was just reading about their charity. Apparently, they just had a fundraiser that brought in fifty thousand dollars in one night!"

If only she knew, I thought to myself.

"How are they?"

"Fine." Then I added, just to make it sound right, "Tired."

She waited for a moment. "What's *he* like?"

I wanted to say, *He's an ogre, a child molester, and a bigot.* "Nice," I told her.

My mom was shaking a little and sweating, proof that she was still sick. Her face was puffy and jowly, but I think she was getting better. As long as we didn't get talking about the Java Jones or Uncle Mike, who stole it from us, we could sit peacefully in her garden and do a crossword puzzle. I watched the moon rise higher in the sky as my mom ripped through the across words. Watching her figure things out, I remembered that once upon a time, she was smart.

When she finished whooping my ass at the crossword, Jean jumped up, looking at her watch. "I'm missing *Bonanza.* I've got to see Michael Landon." He was the cutest actor on the show. I charged after her into her room. She adjusted the antennas on top of her TV and turned up the volume before hopping into bed and stretching out.

"He's my new boyfriend. I love going to bed with Little Joe." She laughed.

Ick.

I sat down next to her, and she nestled her head into my shoulder. Neither of us moved, even during commercials. After Little Joe got the girl and rode off into the sunset, I finally stretched and cracked my toes. Rox would be coming by to pick me up soon, but for the moment, I realized, this was actually nice. I loved hearing my mom laugh, and I lit a cigarette for her without her even asking. During the break, I wondered aloud, "Would you ever do that?"

"What?"

"Get a boyfriend," I said.

"No. Your dad was it for me."

I hugged her. "I love you," I said, and I meant it.

A horn honked outside. It was hard to let go now that Jean was back. I kissed her on the forehead, tucked her into bed, and said, "Sweet dreams. I'll be home early."

CHAPTER ELEVEN

☾

Opposites

State looked different without the old members of the lineup at the center of it. Lisa was not easy to forget. I couldn't just erase her from my life. But then again . . .

I took a few steps forward and stopped. Sitting smack dab in the middle of the SOS was Mary Jo. Her freaky, white hair curled loosely down her back, making her stand out like a sore thumb. To stop myself from saying anything, I had to squeeze my butt cheeks and bite my tongue. I was afraid I'd collapse, so I kept tightening every muscle in my body. Then I took refuge behind my hair. I couldn't let my mind go into orbit.

Mary Jo was one of my least favorite people. But somehow she had become the star of the JV volleyball team. She'd gotten longer and leaner, strong as hell, and I had to admit, she looked good with her plum bikini, freckles, wild corkscrew hair, a ring on every finger, and that unstoppable, kinetic Leo energy. She was laughing.

I knew I had to do the exact opposite of everything I wanted to do. I pressed my fingertips into my temples and rubbed back and forth. I had to act indifferent, so as I began my walk—no, my stroll—no, my casual, leisurely stride—to the lineup, I reminded myself: when you want to kick sand in her face, say something sweet. When you want to flip her off, wave. When you want to shout, talk softly. Do the opposite of mean.

Mary Jo said hi, and I gave a little, low-to-the-hip wave. The smart thing for me to do was keep moving as we glared at each other.

I looked at Jenni and told her, "Come on, let's go for a swim." Non-confrontational and happy, like always. When Jenni and I were waist-high in the water, past the break, facing the horizon, I let it rip. "What the eff is going on?"

"It's just a day pass," she said. "We didn't want her, but the Topangas can't have her, either. We need to build our numbers, Nani. And besides, Lord Ricky insisted she get local status again. After all, Mary Jo's brother *was* his best friend."

Lisa splashed in on the conversation like she owned it. "Jenni and I can't go against him on our maiden voyage." We all three dove under a wave and popped up on the other side.

"It's our first day," Jenni continued.

"You know this is best for the SOS."

What was I going to say? *Judas, traitors?* I could get a lot more dramatic, but instead I went along with the morning routine. We took off our tops at the fifty-foot buoy, and I dog paddled and talked like nothing was wrong.

Later that morning, we had our first drop-ins: a couple gingers with pearly white skin, plaid shirts, and suspenders. Lisa whispered, "They're Eagles groupies."

No recruit in her right mind would show up in suspenders. I was impressed by how Lisa surveyed them with an unstoppable stare. They weren't the smartest tacks in the pack. They didn't even realize what was happening as Lisa walked behind them and made a thumbs-down motion. They just complained about what a drag it was to babysit their tag-along next-door neighbor, Tina, all day. I mean, they talked and talked until finally, Lisa said, "Don't you two have somewhere you have to be?"

Mary Jo added, "Like—now?"

I looked up at the sky, pretending to study the clouds.

"Okay, fine." They pulled up their suspenders as they charged off, yelling back, "You can take care of Tina then. We don't want her."

Lisa said, "I don't want her."

Jenni said, "I don't want her."

Mary Jo said, "I don't want her."

And then—what a surprise—everyone looked at me.

Lisa plastered a smile across her face and said, "Nani, she's all yours."

I held my chin tight and squeezed out, "Sure."

My eyes almost burst out of my head when I saw Tina fluttering out of the bathroom. I expected some annoying, knock-kneed little kid, but she looked like a bucket of stardust. I could see the future in the blond tips waving down her back. She was tiny and airy, wearing a creamy tangerine bikini. As she got closer, I could see her moss-green eyes were lighter than mine. They looked almost gray. I thought, *This girl would not wither in the heat.* It was like she had been anointed.

Tina stopped for a minute between us and the Topangas. I saw Melanie stand up, about to pounce on her, but before she could say a word, I called out, "Hey! Over here!"

She looked confused and asked, "Where are my friends?"

"First of all, they're not your friends." I said. "They ditched you. Second of all, how old are you exactly?"

"I'll be fourteen on August fourteenth." She had a sweet, little voice, but she was a Leo. I knew that meant staying power. I liked the way her low-slung Mexican purse hung on her hips as she waited.

"She's only thirteen," Jenni whispered, but Lisa and I were looking at each other, smiling.

"Who cares? She doesn't look it," I said.

"But she's a baby!" Mary Jo complained.

"Let's nickname her Baby," I said jokingly. Lisa perked up. And that, as they say, was that. I'd have to be more careful of what came out of my mouth in the future, because now Tina was Baby. Our fledgling and first recruit of the new lineup.

CHAPTER TWELVE

Baby

Rox and Jerry still weren't talking. I knew that because they called me behind each other's back. Like, the morning before her "procedure," Rox made sure I knew every detail so I could tell Jerry what time he had to pick her up. Then Jerry called me that afternoon because he'd forgotten the time. It had been going on like that for days.

Between that, taking care of my mom, and the nonstop recruiting, I was feeling pounded. Dozens of girls came out of the woodwork, but none were good enough, and it quickly became clear that Mary Jo's day pass was never going to expire. Lord Ricky made sure of that.

Baby's spot was next to mine. I didn't realize I had been craving a new friend until she was put in my care. I liked the way it felt to talk with her about things like pet rocks and her favorite Cher song, "Half Breed." I'm not sure she ever paid attention to the words—either that, or she had no clue I was *hapa*. Regardless, Baby made me concentrate. Taking care of her helped me forget the fact that no one was taking care of me.

In the ocean, I liked Baby even more. She had a strong underwater kick that didn't make any splash. It looked like she just floated across the waves. She was someone I could have fun with, and, man, was she fast. Baby was so much cooler than I was at her age.

Lisa and Jenni started a lame version of the initiation process. They told Baby to run into the water as fast as she could. I watched her plunge face-first into the shallow whitewash. You see, there's a ditch at State. It's what makes for good waves, but it's also treacherous to run out unless you're a local and know it's there. And I guess Baby had forgotten. It looked like she was heading into the rip. Once she realized she could stand up, Baby inhaled and pushed off again without looking back. *Good for her,* I thought.

Lisa and Jenni were laughing. That was the dumbest dare I'd ever seen. They had taken very quickly to being nasty rulers.

When Baby got back, no one acknowledged her. So I gave her arm a little pat as she sat down. "That was good," I told her.

I needed to mellow out. I looked at Baby sitting next to me and realized that by that time the next day, Rox's baby would be gone.

CHAPTER THIRTEEN

(

That Day

The next morning, Jerry picked me up on his way to get Rox. It was weird, seeing him drive Nigel's van. He had replaced Jethro Tull with his favorite band and hung a coconut air freshener from the rearview mirror. As we drove to Rox's, he chatted incessantly about Marc Bolan, the lead singer of T. Rex, and the concert coming up. It was so trivial on a day like this. But that's what he did. All the way up San Vicente to Brentwood Flats, where Rox lived.

They hadn't seen each other since the day Jerry broke his board.

Rox looked good this morning. She'd dressed for the event in flowing, dark stretch pants with white sailor stripes and an oversized shirt. When she walked over to the car, I could see she was holding the dolphin necklace the lineup had given her between her fingertips. It was like she was sending me a message that said, *You are with me, Fiji girl.*

Rox's sister, Diane, followed closely behind her. Diane looked like Rox, but older. Same chiseled features and kickass body.

Before Rox got into the van, she said, "Wait . . . I have to pee again," and ran back inside.

Diane stood next to the van, glaring at Jerry. To say they were not getting along was an understatement. They were like oil and molasses. Jerry handed her an envelope of cash. Diane grabbed it. As she lunged forward, reaching across my body through the open window, I tucked down and crawled into the back of the van, afraid she might smack me instead of him.

"You asshole," she said.

I guess "asshole" is Jerry Richmond's new middle name, I thought.

When Rox reappeared, Diane quickly backed off and acted normal. As soon as Rox got her seat belt on, Diane handed her a moist towel to lay over her eyes. "I have such a headache," Rox complained.

I vowed never to let this happen to me. The only thing all of us could agree on, I thought, was that we hated Jerry Richmond.

Diane tapped the window. "Let's go. I'll be right behind you," she said, pointing to her car.

As we pulled away, Jerry looked at Rox. "I thought it was going to be just you, me, and Nani?"

Rox didn't dignify that with an answer, so he turned up the music and beat the dashboard loudly with his open palm. It made me nervous, with his temper and all. I looked down at my feet and saw Jerry's board under some towels.

He was planning to surf later. I shook my head and covered my face with my hair. Obviously today was no big deal to him. Maybe if Jerry was the one getting his insides scraped out, he'd feel differently. If guys could get pregnant, the world would change pretty damn fast.

—

The doctor Rox was going to see had an unpronounceable last name and an office on a tree-lined street in Beverly Hills. I prayed to Pele that Rox would get through this all right. But the truth was, I felt like everything was spiraling down. I was stuck in this weird love limbo, and everything was falling apart. I tugged my hair to one side of my head and bent low in the back of the van as it stopped, muttering, "Goddess, please bless Rox and me."

Diane had parked and gotten out of her car before Jerry even turned off the van. "Let's go, everybody," she ordered and motioned for Jerry to get going. Diane was determined to oversee every part of this unhappy expedition.

As Jerry got out of the driver's seat, Rox yanked me toward her and said, "You're going to watch him. He may be a jerk, but he's *my* jerk, and you're going to make sure it stays that way. Don't let him out of your sight."

Oh great, I thought. *Now I am babysitting Jerry Richmond, too.*

I must have had a blank look on my face, because she said, "Nani, please!" It was the slight tinge of pleading in her voice that made me agree.

Diane pointed to a deli on the lower floor of the medical building and said, "You two wait there." I hugged Rox goodbye, but when Jerry attempted to do the same, she turned away.

It was like she had slapped him with a big chunk of reality. Jerry put his hands on his head and turned so no one would see the look on his face. But I saw it. He knew he was screwed.

Jerry barely looked at the deli's menu before he ordered the first thing on it: pancakes with sausage wrapped inside, and two eggs.

"How can you eat at a time like this?" I asked him.

"I'm hungry. And besides, it's not all my fault, Nani."

"Why do guys always blame girls when they get pregnant?"

Jerry didn't answer. I thought about the poor little—what do you call it . . . tadpole?—swimming around in Rox, that was about to get sucked out. That's how it's done, someone told me. With a giant vacuum.

Jerry scarfed down his food when it came. He was a terminal, hopeless jerk in my eyes.

After a few minutes, he grimaced and ran outside. Was he leaving me with the check? I only had fifty cents in my wallet. After he didn't come in for a while, I peeked through the blinds and saw him curled over himself in the alley, throwing up. I jumped back so quickly, I spilled my coffee everywhere. But after I tidied up, I looked out again. He was leaning on the parking meter. He just stood there, for, like, ten minutes, staring at the ground. Then I watched him tuck his shirt back in and wipe his eyes and mouth.

I grabbed a newspaper from the empty booth next to us to look like I'd been reading the whole time. When he came back in, I looked up nonchalantly.

"I'm sorry, Nani," he said. He stared straight at me. "Look," he said, pushing his hair out of his face, "I feel really bad."

I could tell he was being honest. It didn't make the situation any better. In fact, it made it worse—more real, and even sadder. There was nothing I could do to fix it, so I changed the subject. "I hear you're going pro in Hawaii. You know, the drinking age is eighteen over there."

That kind of lit him up—almost back to his shiny self for a moment. "What's it like there?" he asked.

I don't think he realized he was jiggling his leg so hard under the table that our coffee looked like it was on the San Andreas Fault. I drew him a little map on the place mat of all the hot surf spots, from Waikiki to Pipeline. I reached over and grabbed one of his pancakes as I spoke, and before we knew it, two hours had passed.

Finally, Diane knocked on the window. She had Rox by the hand. "I'm taking her home. Hold on to her while I get the car."

I ran out so she could put Rox in my arms. Rox was holding her hands over her belly, not quite doubled over, but heading in that direction. Rox was so pale, and she smelled like rubbing alcohol. Jerry looked like he had just seen a ghost. "Hi, doll," Jerry said. He moved closer, and I let him hold her.

Rox seemed like she could collapse at any moment. She had tried to make her dream come true. I remember her saying, "We aren't like the others. We want babies and husbands." She had told me that when we first kissed. But today Rox melted away. Half awake, half asleep, she was half Jerry's. Half mine.

CHAPTER FOURTEEN

Upside Down

The next day, when I got home from State, the sun had already set. No one in the lineup had a clue what was really going on. They thought Rox was off being esoteric at Esalen and dismissed her absence as protocol.

At home, on the other hand, things were very weird. The dishes were clean, and I couldn't believe my mom had baked my favorite dessert: pineapple upside down cake. The flip was back in her hair, and she had an apron on.

"Don't touch that," she said. "Joyce is coming over any minute, and I want her to see it whole. But you get the first piece." And then she gave me a hug that made me feel better than piles of presents on Christmas Day.

She had placed a strip of fabric on the kitchen table to cover the water stains. On top of it were two little feeder fish in a mayonnaise jar. "Who are these little guys?" I asked.

"They're yours. I know nothing can ever bring back your aquariums from the Java Jones, but I thought, well, maybe having some new fish would make it easier to live without them." She put the jar in my hands, and I held it up to get a better look at them. "Do you remember when Mrs. Taniguchi's koi pond overflowed, and you and your dad collected those giant, foot-long koi and put them in the bathtub?"

"Oh, yeah," I said. "And you didn't know they were there . . ."

My mom finished my sentence. "And I screamed bloody murder."

"And Dad thought it was so funny." This was the easy-breezy way my mom and I used to be all the time. We were having so much fun, trying to think up names for the little guys, I almost forgot to call Rox. It was 9:00 p.m. by the time I grabbed the phone on my way down the hall. Hopefully her line wouldn't be busy, and Diane wouldn't answer. There was a heap of laundry on my bed. I switched on the TV and turned off the sound. Then I dialed Rox.

"How do you feel?" I asked.

"Oh, Nani," she said, disappointed. "I thought you were Jerry. I'm tired. Nobody told me that I'd leak so much after-ward. I've got old lady underwear on and—a pad," she said, slurping something.

"Are you eating?" I tried not to sound too surprised.

"Yeah, crappy applesauce and chamomile tea. It's good for the cramps. They're the worst. Hold on a minute." I heard Rox put down the phone and open a bag. "It's time for my pain pill."

I wasn't sure what to say, so I made something up, like you would for a kid about to get their first tooth pulled. Something that makes them braver and less afraid. "The worst is over," I said. "You're on the homestretch. You'll feel better in no time. And I'm in your corner." And then, just to make sure she understood, I said very clearly, "I'll be your shoulder to cry on, if you need." I wished I had someone like that tonight, someone into whose arms I could nestle my head and lumber off into a snooze, feeling safe.

When we were done talking, I felt closer to Rox than I had in forever, and I knew the sooner Jerry left for Hawaii, the better it would be for both of us. I waited for her to relax before I told her about Mary Jo's return. Finally, we could talk about something besides Jerry and the baby.

"Are you kidding me?" Rox said. She was furious. "I'll get that Mary Jo. You'll see."

Then I gave her some gossip about Lisa and Jenni double-dating with Coco and Johnny that night, and how Coco had been resting his feet on a little sand pedestal Jenni made him, and how Johnny kept holding Lisa's hand whenever he could.

Everything was great until Rox said, "By the way, I told Jerry you were suicidal without Nigel, so he's gonna keep an eye on you. Which means *you* can keep an eye on *him*, nonstop. Pretty good, huh?" Her language was looser than normal—unguarded, like her gates were down. I pulled the phone away from my ear and looked at it—as if she could see me through the holes in the receiver, mouthing "YOU DID WHAT?"

"I gotta go," she said. "The pill is starting to work." It sounded like she dropped the phone.

"Hello? Hellooo?" I said into the phone. When she didn't answer, I hung up, too.

I was looking at my David Bowie album cover when there was a knock on my bedroom door.

"Hi, Haunani. Can I come in?" Joyce had brought me a piece of cake. "Is it better if I call you Nani?"

I don't think a grown-up had ever asked me an intelligent question before. I tried not to look too stunned. "Yeah. Nani's good."

"Okay if I sit down?" That was two in a row.

"Sure," I said. I moved over so Joyce could sit with me on my bed while I ate the most amazing cake my mom had ever made. "Mom's doing good. Isn't she?"

"So are you," Joyce said encouragingly. "What do we have here?" She bent down to look closer at my new fish.

I named them in that instant. "Cecelio and Kapono."

"The singers?" Joyce asked. I couldn't believe she knew who they were. I nodded. Joyce said, "My husband and I saw them when we visited our son, Joseph, on leave. That was the last time I was on Oahu."

I let her hold the jar and pointed. "The gold one is Cecelio, and the one with the black spot is Kapono, 'cause he's a bit of a badass." Joyce thought that was funny.

"Do you miss home?" she asked.

"Every day. But I have good friends here now."

"Like Rox?"

"And these two guys." I took the jar back and carefully placed it next to my bed. It was kind of nice to have adults around again. We talked for about five minutes, and when she left I felt like I knew her better. Like, I actually *knew* Joyce.

CHAPTER FIFTEEN

The Elimination of Nancy Norris

Friendships spread as fast as flames in the lineup. Once again, candidates seemed to materialize out of the sand, and so, a few days after Rox's thing, we were hosting a potential SOS named Heidi Henderson, a model from *Teen* magazine. She even did a commercial for acne medicine once because her skin was like a baby's butt.

She was sprawled out in the prime guest spot next to Lisa. I closed my eyes to envision a lineup based on kindness, beauty, and love for the beach and each other. Maybe Heidi would lighten my load instead of adding to it. She was quite a catch.

She looked like the type of adorable girl who had a poster of a medieval unicorn tapestry on the wall behind her bed. Her voice was high, but up close I could see perspiration above her lip, meaning that she was nervous, which surprised me.

Heidi was a real jet-setter. Her dad was a pilot for Pan Am. She talked about seeing the Northern Lights, and what the sun looked like at midnight in Alaska. Her well-traveled tales included Rome, Copenhagen, Japan, and Paris. Jenni, who still wanted to be a stewardess for Pan Am, was stoked. Trying to impress us, Heidi said:

Je vais parler en français pour vous. Je suis mignonne. Tu es belle. Ceci est mon chien, mon chat , mon cochon, le ciel, le soleil, l'océan. Oui bien? Où est la banque?	I am going to speak French for you. I look good. You are beautiful. This is my dog, my cat, my piggy, the sky, sun, ocean. Yes, good? Where's the bank?

She was trying to convince everyone she was fluent in French, but I knew better. I was really into French history (another secret). In Mrs. Dupre's class I learned about the Celtics, the ancient natives of the land where France and Belgium are now. I liked the way they separated time by moons instead of months. It reminded me of home.

I watched in disbelief as the lineup bought her BS, hook, line, and sinker. On the beach, smarty-pants girls are banned. But Heidi definitely hadn't read the fine print of the never-ending dos and don'ts at State.

I just stared at her, wondering why nobody else seemed to notice she wasn't making any sense. I wondered why this blue-eyed Heidi—a graceful, Norwegian-looking girl—could act all stuck-up like she knew everything.

The lineup lay on their stomachs, oblivious to the crowds, screeching kids on skim boards, and the occasional gawker who was gaping at one butt more perfect than the next. They were concentrating on their back tans, and nothing could distract them—not even Glenn Martin from *Tubed*, who was standing in his assigned place, clicking away as the guys tried to out-surf each other.

Mary Jo's left elbow lay inverted, and her mouth was half open in the sand. She was comatose from a night of drinking ouzo, some Greek liqueur. She didn't see Nancy Norris descend and plop down the way a bird poops. And she didn't smell the zinc oxide that hovered around Nancy Norris's big grin as she cluelessly blocked the sun.

Nancy clasped her fingers to her chin and turned to Heidi, saying gleefully, "You aren't one of them. Are you here for the audition? Me, too. Hi!"

Heidi looked down the row of girls. The SOS lifted their heads, waiting for her reaction. She arched her chest and pulled her shoulders back. "And who is *that*?" she asked, shooting her thumb at Nancy Norris.

Nancy Norris wore a Day-Glo-green swimsuit and trolled around us, waving hello. Her eyes were a little too far apart, round, and sad like those Keane portraits of kids. Her forehead was unusually high, and the bridge of her nose was flat, but the tip was turned up. She had a thin upper lip that stretched into a permanent grin. Her frizzy, brown braids barely reached below her shoulders.

"Can't you make *it* go away?" Heidi demanded, looking indignantly at Lisa and Jenni. When they did nothing, Heidi turned to Nancy. "You know—you can feel your pulse if you stick your finger up your nose and hold it there."

Nancy happily did this. How could Heidi be so cruel? And why was she sitting with us? I was overcome with a feeling of disgust. If pretty is as pretty does, we weren't much to look at.

It seemed like poor Nancy was in suspended animation, with her finger up her nose, laughing because Heidi was laughing. Nobody else was. I closed my eyes the way I would to avoid witnessing something terrible and unstoppable. I thought to myself, *Haunani Grace Nuuhiwa, don't be a chicken shit. Defend Nancy, or tell her to run. Do something.*

But I lay back down and pretended to be asleep as Nancy Norris knelt next to Mary Jo and sang out, "Wake up, Jojo!" She stuck the tip of her braid in Mary Jo's ear. There was a reason Mary Jo had to be friends with Nancy Norris. She told me a long time ago. It seems back in the early 1950s, their mothers pledged Kappa Kappa Gamma together at UCLA. That freaky sorority bond meant a friendship for life. It was a cross Mary Jo had to bear.

Nancy had bands of steel on every tooth, with rubber bands crossed into an X over her front teeth. That made it difficult for her to talk—but not impossible. "Wake up, sleepyhead. Wake up, wake up."

Mary Jo groaned as she tried to come to. She signaled to Nancy Norris to be quiet, but once Nancy got going, she couldn't stop.

She turned to the lineup and babbled, "There was this one time when Jojo and I were in Westwood, and we were so starved we couldn't decide if we wanted fresh donuts from Stan's or a burger at the Hamlet—you know how good the Hamlet smells—and the onion rings . . ."

As she went on excitedly, Mary Jo stood, dizzily trying to navigate the treacherous terrain of hot sand and a pathetically out-of-control Nancy Norris, who swayed from girl to girl.

Nancy Norris talked on and on, fatally mistaking the annoyed looks from all the girls for positive attention. Nancy waved at everyone again and said, "Jojo told me your numbers are dwindling. Maybe I can join your group!"

Heidi let out a vicious laugh.

That heartsick feeling rushed back. I couldn't believe that no one, including me, was going up against Heidi, just because she was kinda famous.

Heidi counted, pointing to each girl as she did, "One, two, three, four, five, six—and with me, seven."

"That's more than enough," Mary Jo told Nancy Norris. "We don't need you. You're mental." Then she grabbed Nancy's shoulders, whipping her around so the rest of State couldn't hear as she exploded from asleep to crazy. She said, in one breath, "You're the one that still keeps your Liddle Kiddle dolls in your purse and blames your speech impediment on living in New Jersey when you were a baby. And you still wake up early every Saturday morning to watch *Yogi Bear* and *The Banana Splits*. Just the other day, you cried when I told you Beany and Cecil weren't real, and then I had to explain to your sorry ass that the Soviets and the Russians were the same people!"

I plugged my ears and thought about Hawaii, Parker Ranch cowboys, red clay dirt, and moss-covered boulders at the bottom of waterfalls.

"You guys should have seen her when she freaked out in third grade because she couldn't get her skirt over her big butt in a Drop and Cover drill," Mary Jo said.

Why wasn't I saying anything? What was I afraid of?

Heidi laughed.

I should have yelled out, right then and there, "LEAVE HER ALONE," but I didn't, so Mary Jo continued.

"And you still play tetherball at Canyon Elementary and stick your Water Wiggle sprinkler between your legs." Mary Jo closed her monologue by putting one leg behind Nancy Norris's ankles and pushing her on the shoulders, so she fell flat on her ass.

Nancy Norris scrambled up and ran off the beach, looking like a lab rat that had escaped with everything but its tail. She scurried away, tagged for life with imaginary pink elastic bands on her ankles that read REJECT.

Heidi applauded and stuck out her tongue.

Less than three years ago, Nancy Norris and I would have been geeks together. Me, the half-half with no friends, and her, the freakazoid. In the kinder world I longed for, Mary Jo would be gone, and the cruel Heidi would be jettisoned into another universe.

Anger exploded within me. Then came an overwhelming sadness. I ran toward the water and got under a wave before anyone could see just how upset I was. If only I could get underwater and find the peaceful place between a wave and air, maybe I could begin to forget what had just happened, and figure out some way to improve the person I was suddenly afraid I had become.

I swam out to the fifty-foot buoy and floated on my back, thinking about what my dad always used to tell me: actions speak louder than words. Floating made me feel a little better. I let myself drop down deep where the water was colder and darker. There, I let out a scream, which was the only way I knew how to confess my sins to Nāmaka, goddess of the sea, Pele's older sister.

The water tasted bitter, like a salt-rimmed drink. When I emerged on the surface, coughing, I saw that Jenni and Lisa had swum out to check on me.

"Are you okay, Nani?" Jenni asked, nodding at me consolingly. Lisa's control and beauty in the water was very Roxesque. It was kind of sexy. "Rox told us you're sort of suicidal."

Oh, great, I thought. *Why didn't she just take out an ad in the* Times?

"We're all upset, too. But let's just maintain, okay?" Lisa said.

We heard Heidi's unmistakable voice as she swam out to us. "Hey, you guys!" She seemed pleased with herself. Jenni and Lisa looked at each other.

"Can we vote about her right now?" Jenni asked.

"Hell, yes," Lisa said. "My vote is NO."

"NO," Jenni said.

"NO," I said, letting out a huge sigh of relief.

We had stitched ourselves back together. I thought, *I might not be able to reinvent the wheel, but I can reinvent the lineup. Enough is enough. You don't need to be perfect if you catch my drift, but the bottom line is:*

Hot girls don't have to be mean.

I was going to make this *pono,* make it right. I wasn't going to become a hypocrite who acted one way and talked another.

I would feel better if there was another girl with dark hair in the lineup. Someone who was darker, like me. That would really shake things up, tip the scales, shift the SOS gears. It's not like dark hair was the same as dark skin, but it's a start.

As our uninvited guest was about to join us, I told Lisa and Jenni, "I'm going to walk to the Pier and recruit." Before Heidi could say another word, we gave her a taste of her own medicine. All three of us submerged at the same time. With one deep breath, we ditched her and swam together underwater, all the way to shore.

CHAPTER SIXTEEN

Windy

I slid into my flip-flops and strolled onto the wide-open sand. I needed to hear myself think. Jerry Richmond chased me down the beach. "I'm coming with you," he said.

If only I could get off suicide watch. I wasn't sure whether having Jerry Richmond with me would be an asset or a liability. "I don't have any razor blades," I joked, holding up my uncut wrists. He didn't think it was funny. In fact, he looked concerned. So I told him, "I'm just going to the Pier."

"Ohhh," Jerry said tapping his forehead with his fingertips and looking up. "Lisa and Jenni thought you said you were going to *jump off* the Pier."

That was *so* not funny, but we both started laughing. Walking next to Jerry, I crisscrossed my feet into other people's footprints in the sand. The deep ones reminded me of my dad's.

Once we got past the green wall, Jerry said, "Even the gay boys check you out."

"I don't know why." I looked down. I wasn't wearing anything special: just my three-inch jean shorts sitting low on my hips, spiderweb-crocheted top with open sides, and my Levi's pocket purse slung down my back. I guess everybody looked at my hair now because it was so long it dangled past my butt. I tossed a Fireball into my mouth.

"Is that cinnamon?" Jerry asked, leaning a little closer.

"Yeah, Fireball." I backed away. Regardless of his faults, he was still Jerry Richmond, a sex god: six foot tall, with gleaming blue eyes that slanted just slightly over his high cheekbones. Majorly good looking. Not as pretty as Nigel but . . . a total babe. And totally off-limits.

"Smells good. Usually you smell like smoke."

I was flabbergasted. "You can smell my cigarettes?" I asked.

"Yeah. Nigel calls you his little smokestack." Then he scooped up my hair like water and held it to his face. "Yeah: smoke . . . and ocean . . . and—what is that? Prell?"

"Jeez, Jerry. What are you, some kind of bloodhound?"

"Yeah, I am. I have a very powerful sniffer."

I thought about how my mom smelled before and after a shower. Her permanent scent was *eau de* Benson & Hedges, Jergens lotion, and, just like me, Prell. That was scary.

I handed Jerry my cigarettes. "I'm gonna quit," I said.

The minute those words came out of my mouth, I regretted it. I watched him stick my Lark 100s in the back pocket of his trunks. I gave his little butt a tap, just like I did with Nigel. It was hard and round.

I thought, *I can never touch this guy again. If I do, I'm asking for it.* So I made up a new rule:

Keep your hands to yourself, and never touch a guy you want to be friends with.

As Jerry talked about the dangers of nicotine, my eyes wandered to a one-of-a-kind girl nearby, lying on her belly in the sand as she read a book. I read, but I'd never do it in public. She lay between two hunky guys who looked to be in their twenties—very impressive. The side of her face sparkled with suntan oil, giving her an otherworldly beauty, as if she was just visiting Earth for the afternoon. While Jerry rambled, I focused on her. Without moving, I stalked her like a jaguar scoping out its prey. She had caramel-blond hair with lots of highlights, not super long, but beautiful in the way it hung straight down to just below her shoulders.

The girl stretched, and a shiver of joy ran up my spine as I saw her muscles—not big like those of someone who swims the butterfly, but perfect and long, balanced and even. The best way to describe her was *toned*. Not only that, she had the kind of body every girl wants: a flat belly, narrow hips, firm legs, and a great tan.

She playfully slapped her boyfriend on the shoulder as she turned over. Then she squeezed his cheek. He looked like Mark Spitz, the Olympic swimmer, with his black hair and mustache. She had scored. But it was funny how she wiped her open palm on his arm, leaving clumps of tanning lotion fresh out of the tube. Their fingers interlocked. It wasn't like they were holding hands; this was more intimate and precise.

The other guy with a mustache had something in his lap. Jerry did a double take. "Nani, look. Is that a rat?" I couldn't stop him from turning me to face the group. I groaned internally. This was not the approach I wanted. He strutted past me.

"Jerry!" I squeaked. But it was too late. This was not going to be the most impressive introduction. But the two guys sat up straighter when they saw Jerry Richmond walking toward them, with his dark hair, six-pack abs, and red trunks slung low.

"What is that?" The two guys looked like meat packers, musclemen. Supermen. Not body builders, but impressive, like soldiers.

Tucked in the guy's mighty biceps was a white teacup Chihuahua with squinty, teary eyes. It was missing teeth, and it grimaced as it looked into the bright sun. Jerry said, "Give me a break. That isn't real." He moved to pet him, and the dog almost took his hand off. The guys laughed.

"His name is Ringo," one of them said. "We smuggled him onto the beach in this picnic basket." Inside the basket was a pink pillow embroidered with the Beatles' famous drop-T logo, and a small plastic container of water.

In the middle of the guys, the girl continued to read. Her eyes were peacock blue, and she smelled like graham crackers. Like I said, she was r-e-a-d-i-n-g.

"Want a beer?"

"Totally," Jerry said. They poured cold Miller into large Styrofoam cups for us. We clinked our glasses and said cheers like we were old friends.

The guy with the dog introduced himself as Pete. The other guy's name was Adam; I guessed he was the girl's boyfriend.

I looked down at her. "What are you reading?" I asked. She didn't answer.

Adam pinched her and said, "Wendy," to get her attention. But I thought he said "Windy," like that old song by The Association.

"Windy. I like that name," I said.

"My name is Wendy, not Windy."

"Well, you'll always be Windy to me," I said, just to see what she was made of.

"And you'll always be—" She held her palm open, waiting for me to answer.

"Nani." Our eyes met and locked for a little too long. I thought, *Right on*. There was an immediate sizzle between us. Maybe Windy felt it too, because she shifted uncomfortably on her towel and went back to her book.

"Doesn't reading in the sun hurt your eyes?" I asked. Her legs were freshly shaved, and her bathing suit was a rich shade of coral I had never seen before. I felt a push and pull between us, and I waited for her next move. She had strong SOS potential, and then some.

Pete held up Ringo. He had dressed the dog in a little terry cloth robe and hood.

"Who made the outfit?" I asked.

"I did," said Windy. I could tell by the look on her face that she was amused. She continued, "I make my suits, too." And then she showed off her bikini by twisting side to side, moving her hips this way and that and holding her hand up so I could admire the snug fit of her top. I felt my heart pound faster. Windy touched just below her belly button and said, "See how I put some extra elastic on the bottom so they don't fall off in big waves?"

"Do you surf?" I asked.

"Bodysurf."

"Yeah, she's gone out at The Wedge," Adam said.

"Are you insane?" I asked.

"It wasn't that big," Windy said, looking down at a ring on her finger and twisting it round and round, like she was slightly embarrassed.

I noticed the writing on the ring when she stopped fussing with it. It read MARYMOUNT.

"What's your last name?" I asked.

Windy sighed and said, "Davenport."

I knew that name. Wendy Davenport had a reputation. Rumor had it, she did something unthinkable, unbelievable, and unforgivable, and it got her thrown out of the fancy Catholic girls' school, even though she was their number one volleyball player.

"I heard Samo High and Pali were fighting over you."

She looked away, nodding, and said, "Where do you go?"

"Pali."

Windy hesitated and said, "Yeah, that's where I'm going, too."

"I'm on the team," I said, thrilled.

"Oh, cool." She smiled. In the same sentence she said, "What happened?" pointing to my Band-Aid.

What was I going to tell her? My girlfriend and I made a pact to be together forever? "Nothing," I finally said with a tight grin.

I could have sat with Windy for the rest of the day. She tossed me the book she was reading: *One Flew Over the Cuckoo's Nest* by Ken Kesey. "It's the third time I've read this. My life is better when I read about someone else's—even if it's fiction. Check it out."

I looked at it and handed it back to her.

"No. Read it," she said. "Give it back to me when you're done."

I couldn't carry a book down the beach. That was too uncool. So I asked her, "Can you hang on to it for me, until I come back?"

"Sure."

That set me up perfectly for later, when I would invite her to State the next day. She was interesting, not easy, and beautiful. But protocol was protocol. I couldn't be in too much of a hurry. It's like foreplay: if you want to get it right, you take your time. I had to finish my beer and wrap up this meet and greet, leave, and then come back and ask her to drop by State. That's the way it had to be done. Can't be too fast, too easy, or too clear.

I tried not to look back as Jerry and I walked away. He was talking, but I hardly heard a word he said. All I could think about was Windy.

CHAPTER SEVENTEEN

The Other Side of the World

Music was drifting down the beach. "Layla" was the song that wouldn't die. There it was again. Derek and the Dominos reverberating in my ears.

"How many years are they going to keep playing that song?" I asked Jerry. "I'm sick of it."

"Why do you take things so personally?" He laughed, and he started playing air guitar and singing it to me in his awful voice. I tried not laugh.

A moment later he was jogging backward and telling me what Pete and Adam had told him. "They're going to Morocco at the end of the summer," he said, "to ride camels and look for dinosaur bones. Those guys got the travel bug. And they said I'll have to run a couple miles a day to build up my stamina for the big waves in Hawaii."

How cool, I thought. *Windy's brother and her boyfriend are buddies.*

Jerry turned toward the pier and broke into a jog. "Come on, Smoky," he yelled to me.

"Don't call me Smoky."

"Okay, Smoky."

I tucked my Levi's pocket purse in the back of my shorts and placed my necklaces, both the Saint Christopher medal from Nigel and the coral one from my dad, under my left bathing suit strap so they wouldn't pound me in the face.

Running on sand is harder than on cement. The sand absorbed every step I took and made my calves burn almost immediately. It felt like I wasn't getting anywhere fast, so I strayed down to the water's edge, where the beach was firmer.

At Pali, we had to jog once around the field before volleyball practice. Our coach, Ms. Patterson, always told me to pretend I was holding a goose's neck in both hands to keep them loose, but I also had to position my wrists on either side of my breasts to anchor them so they wouldn't bounce. I wasn't as well-endowed as Rox, but things had definitely changed in the last year. I was determined to keep an even stride with Jerry, and I had to concentrate on breathing in through my nose and out through my mouth. No way was I going to lag behind.

When Jerry took off in a sprint, I did, too. It was a full-out race. He might have been taller, but I was fast and leaned into my stride before he ever knew what hit him. I had Jerry at first, but when he cut loose, the race was really on. We were neck and neck, just like those horses galloping to the finish line at Santa Anita. We tore through the sand, zooming around people, not stopping until we touched the huge wooden pilings that held up the pier.

He bent over, holding his knees, totally winded.

"You probably would have won," he said, "if you didn't smoke."

"Maybe you're right. Give them back." Jerry looked stunned as I grabbed my Lark 100s and unceremoniously dumped them in the nearest trash can.

This beach attracted a different crowd than the one at State. The families who hung out here definitely did not include Malibu blonds. They were working people enjoying their day off, swimming in shorts and T-shirts. No sexy bathing suits here. They reminded me of folks on Oahu, where the money doesn't flow easily, but families are stronger.

It was spooky under the Pier, and it smelled of rotting wood. Cars driving over wobbly planks echoed so loudly I couldn't hear what Jerry was saying. Then we noticed the unmistakable smell of pot.

A guy in a leather jacket approached, asking if we wanted quaaludes or speed. They were the new most popular drugs. I'd heard one slowed you down, and the other one cranked you up. Jerry waved him off. I could tell he wanted me to keep moving as we passed a sailor in whites ducking away with a girl in a sequined dress. This whole place reminded me of a place back home called Hotel Street, where guys go to get a girlfriend for an hour.

Stepping back onto the beach on the other side of the Pier, another world stretched out in front of us. I felt like a teeny speck of a girl. Looking at the sea, I felt like I really understood how massive the mainland was. Beyond Santa Monica was a succession of surfing meccas: trestles in San Onofre; Windansea in San Diego, where the great surfer Bob Simmons drowned; Mexico; then South America—and beyond that, the Panama Canal. It just went on and on—not like Oahu's beaches that curve around the small island and end up right back where they started.

We strolled by a faded cardboard sign that read TAROT READINGS. A woman in a Gypsy costume sat at a collapsible poker table. She looked like a cartoon. Who was she kidding with that patch over one eye? She pulled out a card and tried to hand it to Jerry and me: two naked pink people dancing arm in arm. "The Lovers," she said with a thick accent.

"No," we both insisted at the same time. The woman chuckled and pushed an offering bowl toward us. I gave her a Fireball. I didn't want to take a chance on her jinxing me, even though I was sure she was a complete phony.

"Thank you," she said. "You can touch my snake." A giant albino python twisted out from under her shawl. "Don't worry. She's already eaten today." The woman had a crooked finger, which she pointed at me. "You are on a slippery slope," she said.

I charged ahead and didn't look back. What did she know, anyway?

Past flocks of white doves, people rode bikes to a red shack with blue and yellow stripes. "What's over there?" I asked Jerry.

"Hot Dog on a Stick. When we come back from Zephyr, I'll turn you on to one of the best dogs in town."

I flipped my hair so he couldn't see that I was pissed off. Zephyr was kind of far away. Way farther than I'd wanted to go.

"Can you tell me more about Hawaii?" Jerry asked.

"I'll think about it." That's all I said.

Jerry Richmond looked really surprised that I didn't say yes. "You're such a badass," he said.

—

We'd hit the edge of Venice. A grassy hill led up to Bicknell and 4th, where the Zephyr store was. It used to be called Select Surf Shop, but now it was home to the notorious Z-Boys. I watched them skateboarding, zipping through orange cones only two feet apart, trying not to nick one or fall—but when they did, they'd roll down that hill like rubber balls and stand up laughing, bleeding from their elbows. Their toes were bleeding, too, and I thought that would make them slip off their skateboards, but it didn't.

"Why are they called Z-Boys?" I asked.

Jerry pointed to the shop sign over our heads that read ZEPHYR and gestured at me like, *Duh, you dumb girl.* It was humiliating, but I wasn't going to let him get the better of me. I decided to make what Jean said into a rule:

Once a mistake, twice a fool.

I wished she'd follow her own advice. And I decided that next time I'd ask a better question. I waited outside Zephyr while Jerry went in. When he came back, he was all charged up. "We've got to go to POP," he said.

Pacific Ocean Park, I thought. *The Cove?* Rox went there once, and she told me it was dangerous and smelled like a dead fish.

This is what I can tell you about POP: it was an abandoned amusement park, Santa Monica's version of Disneyland, and it had mostly burned down. Jerry lifted a portion of the chicken wire fence that surrounded what was left. Above it was another sign. Unlike the Zephyr one, this sign I had no trouble under-standing: No Trespassing. Violators Will Be Prosecuted.

"Let's go," Jerry said as he gestured for me to go first. I had never broken the law before, which made me so nervous I tripped on my hair as I crawled through. He followed without concern.

Jerry showed me where the Fun House had been, with its mirrors that made you look fat then thin. The seal tanks were now abandoned pools that stood across from the Whirlwind Dipper. The giant octopus ride was rusted, forever mid-spin. "Hang on," Jerry said to me as he climbed over a broken fence and vanished behind the tentacle.

I was the only girl standing on the balcony that jutted out above the ocean at the farthest end of the park. Most peo-ple never got this close to the railing. Guys below pushed their boards out from under the Pier. Then—talk about suicidal—the tide at this break sucked them right out. They soared through wave after wave, carefully realigning them-selves so they didn't get impaled by the metal pilings. Imagine eight-footers breaking in cornfields of solid steel. That's what it was like. If I compared this pit to State, my beach was like rainbows and daisies. I wished I had brought some sunscreen. By the time Jerry reappeared, my tan was two shades darker.

On the tiny strip of beach below, I could see him hand some cash to a really fine-looking guy. He called up to me, "I just ordered a totally cherry new board for Hawaii."

At that moment, I really hated Jerry Richmond again. He was smoking a joint and had some Mar Vista bimbo under his arm. When he came up to get me, I untangled him. After all, I had my orders.

As we slogged through the sand back to State, I punished him by talking about food nonstop. I could tell he had the munchies.

"I like sauces that explode in my mouth. Spicy and salty," I said.

"Yeah," Jerry said, his eyes lighting up. "Stuff that goes *boom* on your tongue and makes all the little taste buds stick up."

"Flaky and tender chicken."

"Deep-fried duck," Jerry added.

"Oh, and winter melon soup," I said.

"What's that?"

"All kinds of meats and fish, stuffed into a carved-out winter melon. And grilled peaches and butter corn. Handpicked Maui onions."

"I hear they have the best Filipino food in Hawaii," Jerry said.

"That's perfect for you, since you're Filipino."

"Well, half," he said. In the same breath, he pushed my shoulders down so I sat on the bench and said, "Wait here." I wondered if he was going to disappear for an hour again, but he headed over to the red-and-yellow-striped shack. When he came back, Jerry handed me a hot dog on a stick that was covered in batter and had mustard dripping down the side. "Don't call it a corn dog." He chewed in my ear. "See that guy back there? He's the owner. He's really proud of his creation, and he hates it when people say it's a corn dog."

I took a giant bite off the top. It was delicious. Better than any plate lunch I'd ever had. Jerry nodded, all happy. "And wait till you taste the lemonade," he said. "Go get it, huh? One of your friends is making a fresh brew." He bossed me around like I was his secretary or something. How did Rox stand it? But I went.

At the pickup window, I pointed back at Jerry and asked the Hot Dog on a Stick girl, who looked like a clown, "Do you have his lemonade?" She handed me a pint-sized container. I tried to take it from her, but she didn't let go. She had kinky hair shoved under her peaked hat. Her name tag read ANGELA. Her lipstick was too dark, too shiny. It wasn't until I heard the tiny Nepalese bells on her anklet that I thought, *Holy shit. Tinkerbell.*

"Does your pal know you snagged her boyfriend?"

It was the bitch who had attacked me and chopped off some of my hair last summer. I called her Tinkerbell, but her real name was Angela Espiñoza. She flipped me off as she dipped a hot dog in batter, turned it, and put it into the deep fryer. Then she slammed her palm down on the pump to a vat of ketchup, splattering red, drippy goop all down my legs. It was skillful, considering that her boss was right behind her.

She bent over the counter and hissed in my face. "Your kind make me sick. You're just a white girl wannabe. Brown hangs out with brown. White hangs out with white. Get your sorry ass out of Venice." She pushed the ketchup pump again, coating me with a second layer.

I held my hands together, clasped behind my back, so she couldn't see I was squeezing them so tight the blood stopped flowing. I knew just how to fix her. "Oh, thank you. I love that you call them corn dogs," I said loudly, looking at her boss and giving the A-OK sign. "Corn dogs. Great name." I felt a tinge of satisfaction as I quickly walked away, while her boss scolded her. That would shrink her a size or two.

After I finally got Jerry up and moving, I hosed off in one of the many showers lining the beach. Jerry was too freaked out to even ask what was dripping down my legs, but let me tell you this: he was relieved when I made it disappear.

I was in a hurry to get back to Windyland. I had to make sure my eyes weren't playing tricks on me. Was she really that foxy? But dumb old Jerry was walking so S-L-O-W. It gave me a chance to look for recruits, and boy did I find a couple winners. Two bookend blonds, sitting back to back.

I was feeling lucky, so I just went right up to them and asked for some matches. I was in the zone. Neither one of them looked at me. Instead, they looked at each other. One cocked her head and asked the other, "What do you think she is? Mexican or black?"

The other girl said, "I can't tell, really. They all look the same to me."

"Well, I think she's a little of both," the other said with a breathy laugh.

My back straightened and my knees locked tight. It was as if my whole life hung in the balance for a second. How tan I am—or am not—has always been an issue. Now, the question was, what was I going to do about it? Raise my fist over my head like Tommie Smith and John Carlos did at the '68 Olympics to declare black power? Or protest like the folks at Wounded Knee did earlier this year? The only problem is: I'm not black or Native American. I'm a breezy *hapa* girl, sparkling in coconut oil. Tans fade, but brown is forever.

You'd think after Mr. McBride and Tinkerbell, I'd have a fast comeback, but I just stared at them, paralyzed and speechless, until Jerry strolled up next to me.

Both girls coyly tilted to either side. One of them lowered her top and squeezed her arms together to puff up her boobs. "Oh, we know you."

"Hey, hi," he said, all friendly. "You might not know what *she* is, but I know what *you two* are." Their smiles turned up softly as they waited, anticipating him saying something sweet. But instead Jerry looked at me and asked, "Nani, do you think they're bitches or—"

Before he could continue, I stopped him. He was acting all sexy and loose. Jerry Richmond to the max. The girls choked back the rest of their rotten words, and we walked away arm in arm.

As we strolled, Jerry called back to them, "Do you know who this is? You two just made the biggest mistake of your lives. And don't ever come to State. She'll make you wish you were never born." He bit at the air like a mad dog.

While he did that, I tapped a bit of pink gloss in the center of my lips, then pursed them together, puckered up, and blew them a kiss. When we were out of sight, I patted Jerry on the back. "Thank you. Or should I say, mahalo. It's about time you learned how everybody talks back home."

I was so disgusted, sweaty, and tired. I tapped him on the arm, hanging my purse over his shoulder and sticking my shorts in his hand. Then I waded into the water for a while to perk myself up.

How humiliating had that been? It was one thing to have to deal with people's stupid racism on my own, but having it happen in front of Jerry Richmond made it worse. When I finally came out of the water, pushing my hair off my face and twisting it to one side, squeezing it as I looked up, Jerry was standing where Pete and Adam had been. I looked up and down the beach, jerking my head back and forth so quickly I got a kink in my neck. I grimaced, grabbing where it hurt.

"Are you okay?" Jerry asked.

"Where are they?" My hope vanished.

"You didn't expect them to wait?"

"Yeah, I did," I told him. I felt shattered. "What time is it, anyway?"

"It's after six, Nani. You should wear a watch."

"Never. Watches are for *haoles*." I had decided not to use that word anymore, but I was so pissed. I fell into a cavernous space inside myself, where all my regrets waited for me. I still felt Windy's presence. Where she once sat, she had left three paperback books: *Rubyfruit Jungle* by Rita Mae Brown, *Through The Looking-Glass,* and *One Flew Over the Cuckoo's Nest,* sticking out of the sand like tiny tombstones.

I was so disappointed. In that instant, the loneliness I always tried so hard to avoid returned. But I straightened up again and walked back to State, determined to find Windy. Even if it took all summer.

CHAPTER EIGHTEEN

Roses for Rox

Jerry hovered over me as I reached into the mailbox at 33 Sage. Still no letter from Nigel. I tried not to look bummed. Inside were the usual third and fourth requests for bill payments. My mom told me she liked to stretch her pennies until the final notice came. I was sure they'd be coming soon.

From inside the house, I could hear the phone ringing off the hook. I left Jerry right there on the street, racing up the porch stairs.

"Hello?" I huffed.

"Haunani Grace Nuuhiwa, where have you been?" My mom's voice was sharp and angry. I could hear her so loud and clear that I held the receiver away from my ear.

"State," I said, keeping the phone in front of me as if it were a microphone. What did she think? That I had a supersonic secret telephone with an endless cord that I could plug into a moveable socket and carry around in my pocket so I could always be at her beck and call? The truth was, I liked the way she had started to notice when I wasn't around. It felt like someone was holding me tight again. As if I were found after being lost.

"Diane brought Rox into the ER this morning. She's been asking for you."

"What?" I clutched the phone and pressed it harder against my ear.

"How quickly can you get here?" There was an urgency in my mom's voice that I rarely heard.

"I'm on my way."

"Room 315. And . . . I love you, honey."

Jerry strolled into the kitchen. "Can I have some water?"

"No," I said. "We have to go. Rox is at St. John's."

I felt a lump in my throat. My lips went dry as I thought about Rox. It seemed like everything always caved in on me.

Jerry was swerving around in his lane. "Do you want me to drive?" I snapped.

"This is all my fault." Jerry was no longer cloaked in the masculinity that protected him like muscles around a bone. Now he was fluid, like the ocean.

I refused to feel bad for him. I crossed my arms. I thought Jerry might start to cry. I'd like to see salt stains permanently on his face, and I wouldn't comfort him. I was tougher than Jerry Richmond.

When we got to the backstreets of Santa Monica, where St. John's was hidden away, I told him, "Wait here." He parked, then started to get out of the van anyway.

I said, "Stay," and pushed him back. "Diane's inside."

I blamed him for all of this, and it gave me great satisfaction to have the upper hand. He had no choice but to listen to me.

The smell of St. John's slammed me in the face. It stunk of overcooked carrot medallions, peas, and ammonia. I used my last five dollars to get some end-of-the-day roses for Rox in the gift shop. There was no time for a bow; I had to jam. I raced down the hall to the elevator. Next to the doors was a small statue of a crucified Jesus and a large gold-plated photo of the boss of St. John's. Underneath the photo were the words SISTER MARY HELEN O'SHEA. She was the one in charge of my mom's peer review—and the one who always called.

There is a strangeness in hospitals. People try to act normal despite the fear and sadness. In a hospital, nothing is arbitrary. The nurses wear different types of hats, which tell visitors who is important and who isn't. Every bell ringing and floor number has a meaning. Rox was on the third floor. That's where the emergency patients go—car crashes, kids with high fevers, and broken bones. The second floor is where the babies are. And up top—well, that's isolation for patients who are contagious or terminal.

The second I stepped off the elevator, I wanted to run into Rox's room, but my mom motioned to me. She was standing with Diane at the end of a shiny, white hallway. They were talking to a nun who had a newbie by her side. Their voices lowered as I got closer, until I could barely hear the words coming out of their mouths. When we were finally face-to-face they went silent. Getting the whole story out of this group was going to be hard.

My mom hugged me. I hated the starchy way her clean, pressed uniform felt, but her arms were warm.

"Sister Mary Helen, this is my daughter, Haunani."

"Oh, how are you feeling? Better, I hope?"

Jean gave me a quizzical look.

Let me tell ya: this nun was not pretty like Julie Andrews; she was a frowner like Rosalind Russell in *The Trouble with*

Angels. She was stout, thick, and dense, with rimmed glasses and crooked, tea-stained teeth. No wonder my mom was terrified of her.

She said, with a bit of a brogue, "By the way, Jean. I think it's wonderful that you adopted." Her voice was crisp and tart.

I thought, *Are you kidding me?* But I knew Sister Mary Helen was important because her picture was next to the one of Jesus, and because she was the one charge of my mom's job. So I zipped my lips and just stood there.

"Well no, Sister," my mom said apologetically. "Nani's father was from Hawaii."

I wish I could describe for you how nasty that nun looked when she pursed her lips and said, "I see," then walked away. The nerve. I love Jesus, but I was really beginning to wonder about some of the people who work for him.

I turned to my mom. "I've got to go see Rox."

"Look," she said. "Rox has had a really hard time, but she's going to be fine. You get five minutes." She held her hand up in my face, and she spread her fingers wide as if to make sure I understood what the number five meant. "I'm going to take Diane downstairs to get her some coffee and food."

Rox's sister was stiff as a board, staring down the hallway as if she was possessed. Her eyes darted back and forth. Obviously she was looking for Jerry. It was as if she wanted him to show up so she could tear him apart. Diane was consumed with hate. Like a river after a flood, she had changed beyond recognition. Grown-ups are so tragic in stressful situations.

I gave a little knock on Rox's door. Inside her hospital room there were three beds, but the others were empty. Rox was lying down as a nurse took her pulse. I stood in the doorway, feeling squeamish. A male orderly rushed a bedpan to the bathroom and I heard the toilet flush. Then he dashed past me, nearly knocking me over.

"Watch where you're going, Willie," the nurse commanded as she adjusted the bed. *If I ever have to work in a hospital,* I thought, *better to be a doctor than a nurse or some Willie cleaning up piss.*

"Sallow" is a word I have never used in my entire life, but that is the only one that described the way Rox looked. I gasped. She sat up in the bed and tried to strike a pose, then withered back into her pillows. I shuddered at the sight of my true love, who was too shaky to sit up. The person I knew as an immortal and unconquerable leader was now white as a sandstone fossil with some deepwater creature embedded in it, an imprint of something long gone.

"Hi, Nani." Her voice was weak. She wore a shapeless smock with a checkered pattern. Her own clothes were folded on a chair, and I could see she had been taken to the hospital in her pajamas, the striped ones she wore whenever she was sick. There was an IV hanging above the bed. I wished my memory wasn't so Virgo sharp. It was going to take me forever to get this picture out of my head.

A little hope came into her puffy, sad eyes when I pulled the roses from behind my back. "Are those from Jerry?" Rox asked.

I felt a sharp pang beneath my ribs. "Yes," I said. "He told me, uh, to tell you—that he—loves you . . . a lot!" I didn't want to say it, but I did it for Rox. And it was worth it. She lit up like a firecracker.

The nurse finally finished her paperwork and pulled the curtain around the bed. She told Rox, "Turn on your side.

I'm going to give you a shot of morphine for the pain. Do you want your friend to wait outside?"

"She's seen my butt before," Rox said with a sly smile. Luckily, the nurse didn't get the joke. But I wished I had turned away before seeing the long needle plunge into Rox's backside.

"You rest now, dear." And then, as if Rox wasn't in the room, she told me, "She'll be asleep in a few minutes." She placed her hand on my shoulder. "Try not to upset her." She whisked off to see to another patient. I gave her the stink eye as she walked away.

Rox grabbed my arm. "You've got to keep an eye on Jerry," she said. Her words tumbled out, swift and urgent.

"I haven't let him out of my sight. He's waiting outside."

"No, no. Don't let Diane see him. She'll kill him. Really—she will."

"It's okay. He's hidden away on a side street."

Rox looked out her window, searching for Jerry all the way down 20th Street. It looked like her eyes were scanning as far as the new Promenade, past the Lawrence Welk towers, and on to the ocean, which seemed to be holding up the sky as the sun began to set. Finally, she came out of the daze and shook her head, turning away.

"I can't feel my fingertips." She clutched a barf bag to her chest like it was a teddy bear.

I tried to speak in my calmest voice. "Do you need to use that?" I asked. "Do you want me to get the nurse?"

"No!" She shifted around, trying to sit up again. I worried as she winced and rolled onto her side. "I need to tell you something." She paused, then said, "What I did was not patriotic. What if another war breaks out? Who is going to fight in it?"

"What does any of this have to do with being patriotic?"

"Oh, Nani, you wouldn't understand. You aren't even American."

I leaned closer to make sure I heard her correctly, clutching the cold metal railing of her bed. She had dismissed me in her meanest Rox way with her last bit of strength.

"What?"

"You're not really American."

"How do you figure? Hawaii is part of the United States," I said, grinning. I really hoped she was joking.

But she continued more seriously than before, "It wasn't a state when you were born, Nani. Think about it. You're not really American. And this awful little nun named Helen Mary or Mary Helen something told me stuff. It's making me worry." I put my hand on her forehead. She was blazing hot with fever. She didn't know what she was saying.

To cool her down, I fed her tiny, chipped pieces of ice with a small, pink plastic spoon. She licked her fingers like a kitten. I asked, "What did the nun say to you?"

She looked up at me and whispered, "That I'm going to go to hell." The morphine was kicking in. She sounded really stoned.

"Well, you're not."

She gestured for more ice. "Yeah, you don't know what I did," she said as she slurped the spoon dry.

"Making a choice is your right. As an American." I tried to tie in the patriotic theme somehow, but Rox was too far gone.

"Do you know what happens when a guy gets gonorrhea?" Her sultry blue eyes were fixed on mine, but they began to close. "His balls swell up, and it feels like his dick has been set on fire. But it's not like that for a girl. Do you know . . ." She signaled for me to give her more ice. "Women have no signs. Zippo."

Then she caught me off guard, pulled me in close, and whispered in my face with her stale breath, "I have gonorrhea. That's why I got this infection. I'm sick, Nani."

Now I knew I really would kill Jerry. I wasn't going to leave that pleasure to Diane. I was going to incinerate him. "So Jerry got you pregnant *and* gave you the clap?"

"No." Rox was trying to wave her hand in my face. She couldn't keep her eyes open. "No," she whispered again. "It was Scotty Ward—you know, that actor guy who surfs? But I love Jerry."

I remembered that the nurse had said not to upset her, but I talked right into Rox's face. "What do you mean?" When she didn't answer, I said it a little louder. "What do you mean, Rox?"

I wasn't going to let her fall asleep. She couldn't—not yet. I tugged at her gown.

She opened her eyes. "A couple days after we went to Fiji, I met Scotty at my Chart House interview. He's a waiter there. Well . . ." Her head drooped to one side, and then the other.

"Well, what?" I gave her another nudge so she couldn't doze off. I was not going to let that morphine knock her out until she told me.

"Well, I figured I was pregnant already, so when one thing led to another, I thought I was safe." She covered her face and shook a little. "Diane thinks it was Jerry." Her voice trailed off as she said, "Nani, you have to know . . ." but she didn't finish her sentence.

She never would finish that sentence, so I tried to end it for her. Nani, you have to know: I love you. I'm sorry. I beg your forgiveness. I will never lie to you again. You are the most important person in the world to me. I need you more than ever.

I felt an invisible force materialize between us—something that would wreak havoc for a very long time. I fell back into the chair, looking down at my arm. Then I ripped off the Band-Aid. A scab had formed over the burn spot that was supposed to be the symbol of our love. Looking at Rox passed out, I had a hard time mustering up any more sympathy for her. It was like she used Jerry and me to filter out all her dirty secrets so she stayed pure, while telling people I was a suicide case and Jerry was a total dirtbag.

I sat up suddenly. My thoughts were going too fast for me to keep up with them. I gripped my fingers together and felt a tightness in my chest.

Did I have it, too? Can girls give gonorrhea to girls?

But before she had trailed off, she had said "a couple days *after* Fiji." So I was safe.

Wait a minute.

A couple days after Fiji? A couple. Days. After. Fiji?

I had to angle myself close to the wall because of the dizzying effect of so much adrenaline pumping through my head. It felt like all my love for Rox had burst, as if my heart was an egg that someone had cracked and emptied into a sizzling frying pan. A couple days after she slept with me, she had a—what?

A fling? With some guy? She had two-timed me, which meant she had triple-timed Jerry.

I wanted to get away from Rox as fast as I could.

I grabbed the flowers and threw them in the trash just as my mom poked her head into the room, Diane following close behind. Jean looked back at Diane and said, "Oh, good. She's asleep." She turned to me. "I'm going to do a double shift and stay here with Diane. Will you be all right?"

She was so focused as she took me out into the hall, closed Rox's door, and gave me a big hug. She pulled my hair back like she used to, then took my face in both her hands.

"Are you okay, honey?"

"Yeah." I let her hug me again before I said, "Mom, that Sister Mary Helen said some bad things to Rox."

She shook her head. I thought she was going to sympathize with me, but I should have known better. "It's a Catholic hospital, Nani," she said. "I don't care how many laws are passed. What Rox did is against our faith."

Our faith? Great, I thought. My mom was getting all religious on me, like she did when Dad died. What a joke. *Don't say anything*, I told myself. I repeated it silently, again and again, *Don't say anything, don't say anything, don't say anything.*

We walked to the elevator in silence. Then she stared me right in the eyes. "Look, I don't want you to get in trouble. You and Nigel aren't . . ."

"Oh, no. No. No." I couldn't deal with her. Just the fact that she asked made my head explode again. "No," I said one more time, cutting her off before she could say another word.

"Good." She was satisfied. "Don't forget: men only want to marry a virgin, so always leave a little room for Jesus when you're with a boy. Because if he feels the urge—"

"Mom!" It was like she was reading from some parenting book.

Luckily for me, a young candy striper distracted her. The girl was holding a steaming baked apple, the brown kind with the skin still on it. It looked pretty gross, sitting there in its own juices. My mom told the candy striper to keep her hands tucked under the tray.

"After all," she scolded indignantly, "it's a patient's food."

Sister Mary Helen slithered by us and gave Mom an approving nod. Yeah, she was definitely going to get a good review. She might not have been the greatest mom, but as far as I could see, she was an amazing nurse.

CHAPTER NINETEEN

(

Spam

When I hopped in the van, I told Jerry almost nothing. The truth is, for the very first time, I felt sorry for him. We'd both been fooled by Rox.

He was such a wreck after the hospital, the least I could do was cook him some dinner. I sat him at the kitchen table while I cooked. To cheer him up, I decided to continue his lessons on Hawaii. First, I reminded him that it was the fiftieth state. Then I gave him a little quiz: "How many islands are in Hawaii?"

He shrugged his shoulders. I couldn't believe he didn't know even the most basic information, so I wrote down the names of the islands in their traditional spellings, hoping that would give him a bit of an edge when it came to becoming a local. But at home there were so many different spellings for each island, I just had to give it my best guess. He wouldn't know the difference.

"First there's Hawai'i, the big island. Then comes Maui, which was named after a real demigod—kind of like Hercules. Story goes: Maui dragged all the islands out of the sea. Anyway, off of Maui is Lana'i, the pineapple island. Across from that is Moloka'i the friendly island. Then my home, Oahu. Kauai is the garden island, and Ni'ihau is the forbidden island. Don't ever go there. There's also a couple of tiny islands off of Maui. One of them is Kaho'olawe, but people from the mainland don't count it as an island, which is lame."

I decided I was going to splurge on him, so I cut up the last bit of butter we had in the house. As I made some delicious Spam and grilled cheese on Wonder Bread, I could feel Jerry come up behind me. He was standing too close and caught me off guard when he pushed my bangs away from my face with just his fingertips. I quickly grabbed a bowl and moved away.

I made a tasty mixture of mayonnaise and soy sauce to dunk our sandwiches in. When I pointed Jerry back to his chair and sat the food down in from of him, he gobbled it up and then asked, "Is Spam ham?"

"Sort of. It's part ham. Part pork shoulder. And it has lots of salt and sugar mixed in. You can cook it just about any way you want." I showed him my dad's favorite Spam recipes, which my mom still kept on index cards in a tin box. I was surprised when a black-and-white photo fell onto the floor. Jerry picked it up.

"That's my dad. It's from one of our hikes to the Akaka Falls." I remembered that day so well. Dad had told me about the *Menehune*, little people who lived in the hills and built temples and roads that still exist. I wish he had told me more. In the picture, bright sunlight was angling across his face, and his eyes were closed. But, like always, he was smiling.

"Wow," Jerry said. "He was a big guy. Did anyone ever tell you he looked like Duke Kahanamoku?"

When I didn't say anything, Jerry asked, "Are you upset? You're fiddling with your hair. I noticed you do that when you're bummed out."

I was surprised when he put his arm around me. I wanted to curl into him instead of pulling away. He felt too good. Jerry Richmond was like a sunbeam I didn't want to land on me.

I painted a blank expression across my face; it was like a curtain blocking me from the world. The last thing I wanted to be with Jerry was romantic. "Spam goes great in lasagna," I told him in my spunkiest voice. "It's also good with panko." I wriggled out of his arms to show him the box of Japanese breadcrumbs, so he'd know exactly what it was. Then I carefully put my dad's photo back into the recipe box.

"I guess you don't want to talk about it," Jerry said. He stood up and went into the other room. I heard him turn on the TV, then yell, "Where did Spam come from?"

"In World War II, the food ran out on Oahu. The army turned us onto it."

Then we ran out of things to say, and it got quiet except for the show Jerry was blasting. I kept drying the same dish, just so I wouldn't have to go sit down with him. It was a relief when the phone rang.

"Your phone goes off nonstop," Jerry said.

"It's probably my mom," I said, running down the hall to the phone table. Before I even choked out a hello, Rox yelled, "Where's Jerry?" She sounded stoned and crazy.

"In my living room. I have him watching TV."

"Well, make sure he goes straight home."

Then she hung up on me. The nerve!

I went back into the living room. Jerry asked, "What did your mom say? Is everything okay?"

"Everything's great," I told him. "Rox is doing much better."

But as he moved toward me, I felt a tickle down my spine. An alarm went off in my head when he hugged me and said, "Thank you—I mean, mahalo—for everything. You're really sweet, Nani." And even though it was a friendly hug, the warning whistle went off louder. Hugging Jerry Richmond was like playing with fire.

Quickly I asked, "Can we talk tomorrow? I'm kind of tired."

"Oh, yeah, for sure, for sure," he said, grabbing his stuff and letting himself out the back door.

I watched him drive away. My thoughts went to the sky. I needed the moon. Something bigger than being brown. Bigger than Rox, America, and nuns. I imagined that I could see Oahu out in the ocean, instead of the faint lights from Catalina. I didn't belong here, and I would have risked shark-infested waters to swim home.

CHAPTER TWENTY

Hit and Run

I was getting home later and later from the beach each day. What was the point of being home, anyway? Rox wasn't calling, and I wasn't about to call *her*. The sun was almost down when I got home one evening and found Joyce leaving a small saucepan at the back door.

"Hi," she said. "In case you're hungry."

"You want to come in?"

"For a minute."

Once again, I was impressed with what Joyce was wearing. She had on a cardigan and plaid skirt. Even at the end of the day, she still looked fresh and groomed.

"How are things going?" she asked.

I tried to keep a nonchalant look on my face, but, like I said, that Joyce is a sharp one. I could tell she could see through me. "I haven't talked to my best friend in a week. We're not getting along. At all."

"Is this the one who had an abortion?"

"Yeah." I wasn't going to BS with Joyce. She knew the deal. "Rox said some really . . ." I was trying to find the word for it. "Lousy things to me when she was in the hospital."

"Was Rox feeling all right?"

"No. She was sick as a dog."

"Do you think that was why she said it?"

"I don't know."

"Can you give her one more chance? I mean, if she's your best friend."

I liked the way Joyce asked me questions to help me figure things out. I wasn't going to say yes, and I wasn't going to say no, so I just said, "I'll think about it."

After I had a big bowl of the clam chowder Joyce had left, I thought more about what she had said and decided she was right. I shouldn't throw away Fiji—at least not yet. I put on something cute, slipped a Fireball in my mouth, and put the pot, still holding what was left of the soup, into my bike basket. Then I rode up San Vicente to her house. With each pump of the pedals, I felt better. Joyce was probably right. This was one big mix-up. I was worrying about nothing.

And sure enough, when I looked in the front window of her house, I fell in love with Rox all over again. She didn't know I was watching her walk through the living room, turning the lights off as she went. She was wearing pink, her feel-good color, and playing with the necklace the SOS gave her.

I snuck around to the back of the house with the pot of soup, making sure none of it spilled. Her room was dimly lit, and the ruffled canopy over her bed matched the butterfly wallpaper. I loved that bed. I knocked on the sliding glass door with my foot.

The second she opened it, I said, "Are you going to kiss me, or what?"

Rox shoved me back into the patio. "Hey, watch it!" I said. Luckily, I didn't spill a drop of soup because my hot pads were firmly on both hands. She shushed me, so I said quietly, "You look good." She really did. And she was wearing her special, sexy Chanel perfume, so I joked, "Let's have a hit-and-run."

"Did I invite you over? What are you doing here?"

That's also when the bathroom door opened. A guy came out, and a shock wave went right through me. Rox hissed under her breath, "Scotty and I are making up."

"You're together?"

"Almost."

The porch light turned on and Scotty came to the door. Rox said curtly, "Scotty, this is Nani. She's one of my little friends from Pali."

He looked at me and said, "How's it going, sweetheart?" Like I was five or something. Before I could say another word, Rox had me halfway down the driveway.

"Be right back!" she called to Scotty.

Because I was still holding the soup, I couldn't fight off her tight grip on my forearm. I must have looked like an idiot. My hot pads were slipping, and I had to use my knee to push up the pot before it fell and dumped soup all over me.

I forced the soup pot into the bike basket and whirled on Rox. "Are you kidding me? Really?" I got right into Rox's face.

"Keep your voice down."

"What about Jerry?" And then I thought, *Screw Jerry.* "What about me? What about us? We made a pact!" I held up my arm and showed her the scar. Rox had a blasé look on her face. It was clear, but I said it anyway, "You don't care, do you?"

"Not really."

She started to freeze me out and shut down. I told her, "Don't you treat me like that. How can you be with a guy when you're a lesbian?"

"I am not a lesbian. *You* might be one, but I'm not."

"Yes, you are."

"No, I'm not, and don't you ever say that disgusting word around me again."

"Lesbian. Lesbian. Lesbian. Lesbian. Lesbian!"

"You're so gross!"

Rox kicked over my dad's bike, and the soup went spilling into the driveway.

"I don't want to go to Fiji anymore," I said.

"Only I decide that."

"No, you don't." I froze her. And then I said, "You may be right. We're not lesbians. And since you don't want Jerry anymore . . ."

"Don't you dare."

I jumped on my bike and kicked up some dust. Like head-lights on a dark highway, Rox's eyes lit up the night—she was that pissed. She went off like a pinball machine, banging around in the same place—ricocheting *DING, DING, DING, DING*. I had stuck it to her.

"I'm going to follow your order," I called back at her, all happy, "and not let him out of my sight!"

As I rode home, I thought of her waking up next to Scotty and how she would kiss him, parting her lips slow, then hard, against his. I wanted to scream. How could Rox fall for a guy like *that*? How could she leave me and Jerry?

And that's when it really hit me: Jerry Richmond was all I had left of Rox.

II

July 8–August 4, 1973

Thunder Moon

*PUT BAD TIMES
BEHIND YOU.*

CHAPTER TWENTY-ONE

The Birds and the Bees

Sitting on the beach, I looked at the empty space on my right and tried not to think about Rox. It had been two weeks, but I still felt shell-shocked.

I forced myself to think of something wonderful, and Windy was the first thing that came to mind—even though I still had no clue how to find her. You know, I don't like fairy tales or rhymes, but despite that, I got into reading *Through the Looking-Glass* at 3:10 a.m. the night before. Maybe just because it was Windy's pick. And also because I liked the way Lewis Carroll checked his readers into another world filled with magical creatures.

When I got to the chapter in the garden with the talking flowers and the bossy Red Queen, I again tried not to think of Rox. I had been her pawn. I wished I could shake Rox into a sweet, little kitten like Alice did with the Red Queen. But I wasn't going to let any waterworks drip over her.

The world had changed so much since I had last seen her. David Bowie announced that he was never going to perform Ziggy Stardust again, and Tom Bradley had become the first black man to be elected mayor of Los Angeles. Jerry and I went jogging every day, and it was a lot easier now that I wasn't smoking. Lots of girls had come by as recruits, but the lineup had nixed them all. The Topangas and the SOS were five and five. But still, I was in no mood to recruit, until the gossipy Mary Jo brought up rumors about Windy to the lineup.

It happened when we were swimming out to the buoy. She was backstroking and suddenly swam over to me. "Do you know why she got expelled from Marymount?" she said. "She was kissing a girl."

"There's no way that's true," I told them. "I met her boyfriend. His name is Pete, and he's, like, twenty, buff, and has a mustache." I lengthened my stroke and glided toward Jenni and Lisa. It was kind of ironic: the *Funny Kine* girl defending the non-*Funny Kine* girl.

When we got back to our towels, somebody picked up a copy of the *Palisadian Post* that had been left as trash. On the second page, it said that Wendy Davenport was transferring to Palisades High and entering the eleventh grade in September. It said she was such a great volleyball player that she would almost surely be starting on the varsity lineup.

What a weird coincidence. The whole lineup took it as a sign.

And that's when it hit me: If the State lineup was also the volleyball lineup, we could turn the Pali High Dolphins into she-heroes. I liked the idea of the lineup becoming a team instead of just a bunch of beach babes. Then we'd have a purpose that went beyond getting tans and watching our hair get lighter. We could be winners. With the way I set, Windy's notorious spikes, and Mary Jo throwing herself at every ball low to the ground, we could totally dominate.

Especially with the two towering six-footers on the team, our impenetrable blockers. I called them the No-Fly Zone. Michelle and Mindy were like twins, even though they weren't related. I knew that guys called them something else, something awful. They called them the Double Baggers because they weren't pretty. But to me, Michelle and Mindy were goddesses because they were Amazon-strong.

Jenni said, "Wendy Davenport is like a prodigy."

"What's that?" Baby asked.

I told her, "A prodigy is somebody really young who can do things better than adults. Like Mozart."

"Who's Mozart?"

Lisa jumped in. "He's this guy who lives in Malibu." Jenni laughed. They were the perfect team. Lisa made the jokes, and Jenni laughed at them.

These rulers were getting way too predictable, and I didn't like them teasing Baby. She couldn't help it if things went over her head.

I had never had a little sister, but I had heard that they require a great deal of patience. Baby moved her towel between Lisa's and Jenni's. She gathered us into a small circle. I thought she was going to ask more about Mozart, but she said, "Since you guys know so much, I've got to ask you something. My mom told me not to do it with a guy, or even ask her about 'it,' until my honeymoon night."

"Ask about what?" Mary Jo said.

"You know. Losing my virginity. My mom said men are supposed to do it a lot to practice before they get married. But girls are just supposed to kiss. So when men get a virgin to marry, they know what to do to make the virgin feel comfortable on her honeymoon."

Lisa and Jenni weren't even trying to keep a straight face—but Baby was serious.

Before the laughter got out of hand, I said, "You know, I heard the same thing." Somebody had to come to Baby's defense.

I was surprised when Jenni joined the conversation. Lately, she had been hinting that something might "happen" between her and Coco. She seemed to be on a permanent high—downright giddy. So I wasn't too surprised that she eagerly explained, in great detail, how to have "intercourse."

When she finished, Baby looked like she might throw up. But out of curiosity, I wanted to know if Jenni was following the rule:

Don't sleep with a guy until he's officially your boyfriend.

So I asked, "Jenni, do you still have your V card?"

"Oh, yeah," she said reassuringly. "I just got all that info from this book *The Joy of Sex*. My parents had it hidden. Those little drawings in it tell a b-i-i-i-g story. Nothing like the sex-ed Disney cartoons we watched in fifth grade."

"Oh, I remember those," Lisa chimed in. "Jiminy Cricket said, 'Hey, boys and girls.'" She imitated his squeaky little voice. "'Let's talk about your bodies.' Then he danced and flung himself around."

I didn't see those cartoons in Hawaii. After Bambi's mother died, I never wanted to see another Disney movie in my life. For sex education I got old Mrs. Kobayashi, who talked about the birds and the bees, flowers and pollination.

Jenni continued, "I love the way the princesses talked about not going horseback riding or exercising too hard when you have your period. Then the teacher showed us what a menstrual pad and belt looked like."

"Scary," Lisa said.

Mouthy Mary Jo latched on to Jenni and asked, "Can you bring that sex book to the beach sometime?"

Jenni didn't dignify her with an answer.

Baby turned to me. "How old were you when you had your first real kiss?"

I wasn't going to tell her last year, so I wove another mini braid down the back of her hair and changed the subject.

The VPMs were playing concussion ball—like football, but rougher. There were no goal lines or end zones; it was just tackling and hitting. It hurt just to watch them, and they didn't stop until someone had to hobble away.

Jerry had been hanging out with them because they idolized him. He was like the Che Guevara of surfing, a revolutionary do-or-die type. Even on land, Jerry Richmond was always in motion, unburdened by day-to-day things like getting a job. He was a Taurus, so he liked risk and uncertainty.

That's why girls adored him. Of course, I wasn't one of them. I had just said I was to hurt Rox. Jerry and I were friends. Just. Good. Friends.

I knew love was a dangerous thing, like the ocean. Most people don't understand this, and if they did they'd be really cautious before jumping into it. Think of it this way: Nāmaka is a sea goddess—not a playground but a giant entity with a mind of her own, foamy and bubbly, turbulent and surging. The fishermen back home use her traditional name,

Namakaokahahi, and they have a rule: don't get near a woman when she's angry, or the ocean when she's stormy. State's ocean wasn't stormy on the top, but she sure was underneath. Kind of like me.

CHAPTER TWENTY-TWO

☾

Party in the Palisades

We had been recruiting for almost a month, but the only potential SOS besides Baby was Julie Saratoga, who had been sitting in our guest spot. Let me tell you: she had charisma. Mojo in her stride. She smoked Shermans, which are brown cigarettes that look like long, skinny cigars. They were dark and mysterious—just like Julie. She had a body that impressed us all, too. She wasn't thin, but she wasn't fat. She was *lush*.

Julie Saratoga was from Ventura, a small, sleepy beach town up north, and she used to hang out with the Raw Surf Commandos at C Street. They were the only ones who could coexist with the town's large community of Hells Angels. She wore a straw hat that went with the pink in the chevron design of her bikini, and a hip-long macramé purse, the kind with beads jingling on the tassels.

Word of mouth was, her boyfriend had just broken up with her. So she was single and sort of temporarily misplaced. That happens to girls when they get dumped. They realize they spent so much time with the guy that they lost all their girlfriends. What interested me about Julie was how unfazed she was about going solo. That's something you can't fake, but here's the rule:

Never give up your friends for a guy, because you'll need them someday.

Julie was going to hang with us later at the VPMs' big party at Coco's house. We'd know pretty fast if she was ready for the big time.

Lisa and Jenni put her to the test by making her tell the Topangas the wrong address. Julie confided in me, rather pleased with herself. "I gave them the address in Kenter Canyon. Lisa told me they won't know it's the principal of Pali's house until they ring the bell or sneak around the back. Either way, they'll miss the party." She had a funny, high laugh that was contagious. I really hoped we could keep her.

I was determined to have fun tonight. Here's how I did it: I put on extra Whiplash mascara (the kind Alice Cooper wears) and lip gloss with a tinge of red. And this was the really extreme part: at a garage sale the week before, I had gotten Jerry a top hat and myself a black ostrich-feather boa. I wore that boa like I was Marlene Dietrich. I wanted to be a cabaret girl with garter belts over my bikini, but I knew the Palisades wasn't ready for that yet. So I went for my signature look: a blouse, unbuttoned and tied, matching suede hot pants, pale pink socks that went over my knees, and three-inch platforms. Once I put on my thick, black eyeliner, I felt like an exotic bird.

I wanted to show Jerry Richmond that I could be on time without wearing a watch. Long before his van pulled up to 33 Sage, I sat on the steps, legs crossed, leaning to one side, like I was bored and had been there for hours. When Jerry arrived and saw me, he drove the van up over the curb and started howling like a wolf.

"What?" I said.

"What?!" he said back.

"What?"

"I kind of want to make out with you; you look so hot," he said matter-of-factly.

The truth was, I would have gladly stuck my tongue into his mouth, but I didn't—even though he looked as pretty as a girl.

I surprised him with the top hat and he stuck it on his head. He pulled it right off again, but I flashed all my pearly whites and said, "Leave it on. You look so cute." He was all clean and silky, no sand between his toes, wearing dry, navy-blue trunks and an open tuxedo shirt with ruffles down the front. He leaned toward me like he wanted to kiss, but I just looked out the window and played snotty.

"Not an option," I said. "Let's go."

Of course we listened to T. Rex: "Electric Warrior," "Telegram Sam," and "Children of the Revolution," which was my favorite.

He shifted over again and asked, "Are you sure you don't want to make out?"

He was such a pain in the ass. I had to change the subject, so as we passed Marquez Elementary, I said, "Bet you didn't know there was a really powerful Mexican family named Marquez, who owned everything from the Palisades to Santa

Monica. They were proud, and now their relatives live totally unrecognized in the Canyon."

It was the same exact story as in Hawaii, just different names. Once-powerful families who couldn't get anyone to pay attention to or hire them. Before Jerry left for Hawaii, I would make a point to teach him about Queen Emma, the last Queen Lili'uokalani, and King David Kalākaua the Merrie Monarch, who brought hula back.

"Are you suuure?" Jerry gave me a couple winks and a goofy grin.

"Did you know Pico Boulevard was named after Pío Pico, who was the last Mexican governor? And Sepulveda was named after Don Francisco Sepúlveda?"

How do you know all this?" he asked.

"I go to class." That made him laugh—actually more of a chuckle. He barely made a sound. His smile was so beautiful it made me slouch forward to get a better look.

I could see why he unhinged Rox. He was totally genuine. In the rearview mirror, the scattered lights of the city flickered below. There was something beautiful and serendipitous about all of this. I could have just driven around with him for the rest of night.

"Hey!" he said, thumbing the steering wheel. "Is there a Señor Lachman, too?" he said, pointing to the Lachman Lane street sign. He was making fun of me. That's what happens when girls are smart and know something guys don't. He was back to his annoying self. I let it roll right past me. At least he didn't want to kiss me anymore.

Then, out of nowhere, he said, "You know, it had never been better with Rox. Now all this."

I could have said the exact same thing. As awful as she was, I missed waking up looking into her eyes. I bet he did, too. I wondered if she let him put oil on her hands or if he kissed her slowly, like I did. Did they tell each other their dreams? I doubted it. Jerry cranked the music. It's funny: I never thought Rox and I were two-timing him. I didn't see it that way because we were girls.

The van kept chugging up the steep, winding road. It was pitch black. Jerry had to put on the brights. He told me, "We're looking for a carport and a flat, white roof."

"They all look that way," I said. Then, luckily, we smelled pot wafting down Lachman as we rolled into a traffic jam. Vans were double-parked, and there were guys with towels over their shoulders and dripping wet hair walking in the middle of the road. There must be a pool. Obviously I had my bikini in my Levi pocket purse, along with a few Fireballs. That was a rule.

Jerry clapped his hands. "I hope they're playing Rod Stewart tonight."

"Why?" I asked.

"Because maybe then you'll get up on a table and go into a hula craze again. That was so hot."

I would never live down that night at the McBrides when Mary Jo dosed me with Blue Cheer, a.k.a. LSD. It gave me a one-of-a-kind reputation, but it wasn't something I would ever do again.

"Hula is not some girly show to turn guys on," I snapped at him. "It's a prayer, a sacred story, and a way to live life. It has mana, spirit—energy."

"You know what?" he said. "I still want to make out with you."

"How can I teach you anything if you keep acting like a sex-crazed mental?" I banged the dashboard.

"Hey, watch the van!" Jerry said.

"Nigel won't mind if I dent it up a little bit." I hit it again.

"Okay, okay, you never have to do the hula for me. It's okay."

I had to accept that Jerry Richmond was a typical surfer. I couldn't expect too much.

"Stop the van," I told him. I jumped out, slamming the door. "I'll see you in there."

I merged into a flow of people walking toward the party house. It was small, but sort of stately with its well-manicured lawn, perfectly even hedges, and pretty, little daisies. Mary Jo stood on the roof directing traffic in just her bikini and cowboy boots. The VPMs sat next to her. Their bare feet dangled past the rain gutter as they shared a joint.

Mary Jo pointed to a girl below and called out, "Looks like she's gonna hurl!" Whenever somebody threw up this early, you knew it was going to be a good party. Too bad it was always a girl with long hair.

The VPMs handed Mary Jo a bucket of water balloons. It's not very heroic to throw that stuff at defenseless people, but I never claimed Mary Jo was a hero. She started chucking them at anybody without a tan. People scattered. I ducked out of the way, but the two girls in front of me, wearing leather-patched miniskirts, weren't so lucky.

They screamed as Mary Jo soaked them.

"Alriiight. It's a party," Lord Ricky shouted. I hated how he stretched out each word he said like it was sooo important.

I had somehow found myself standing all alone next to him and his psychopathic friends. It looked like a pool man's convention. I call these scrappy old guys "Hunters." They like to look at women through peepholes and come to parties in search of underage girls. This party was a mecca for that: there were young girls everywhere.

They immediately formed a circle around me. Someone struck a match. I didn't recognize any of them except for Lord Ricky, who identified me as the girl from Hawaii. That's when I remembered the rule:

Never walk into a party alone.

Lord Ricky growled, "Let's have a ball," as he passed around a bottle of tequila, the kind with a worm at the bottom. Disgusting. His pals had already gone through the medicine cabinets inside and were handing each other pills like they were Milk Duds. They had a stash of other things too: silverware and a whole bunch of jewelry they had stolen. It made me cringe. Lord Ricky was holding a baggie of quaaludes, and a wad of cash stuck out of his pockets.

"Busy night," I said.

This one guy, who was just wearing trunks, slunk toward me. He looked like a swamp rodent with a long neck, pointy nose, and limp arms. He held up a shrunken head, probably convinced it was real. But up close I could smell the plastic. "Hey, foxy lady," he said. Then he took the bottle of tequila and chug-a-lugged the rest of it, showing me the worm on his tongue before he chewed it up like a piece of gum. I gagged.

"Where's my kiss?" Lord Ricky said. I felt my legs tremble as the circle of creeps closed in even more. They had me surrounded and were moving toward a windowless van. I felt dizzy and cold. My fingers went moist. Lord Ricky's expression darkened as he slid the side door open. "Don't worry your pretty little head over anything. This'll be over in no time."

I looked into the unlit van, and saw there were two faceless men already in there, waiting.

"Hi, Nani!" Jerry walked by, completely clueless. I was terrified. I wanted to call to him, but I couldn't. It was like a nightmare I've had where I try to scream but no sound comes out. Thank God he turned around again and saw the look on my face. In a completely different voice he said, "Come on, Nani. Let's go inside."

The circle broke open for him to pull me out. Jerry was too famous for these guys to mess with.

I immediately followed him.

"I need a smoke," I said.

"No! You've been doing so great!"

I was mad at myself, at him, at Rox, and at Nigel for being in Calcutta and leaving me here alone. I grabbed the first cigarette I saw and waved to the lineup standing outside by the pool. I didn't care what brand I smoked or if it was menthol or regular. I just needed to clear my head, and a deep inhale would make that possible.

Then I saw Windy standing by a glass door on the other side of the living room. I dropped the cigarette into this girl's beer as she walked by, and popped a Fireball into my mouth.

Windy looked amazing. She was wearing the same wedges as me, plus cutoffs and an oversized T-shirt. I liked the fact that she didn't have big boobs. I didn't want to be around any girl who reminded me of Rox.

Our eyes locked. We rushed together and just about fell into each other's arms.

That was when Ellie Katz, the feminist from Pali, almost slammed into us. She was wearing baggy denim overalls and an off-the-shoulder peasant blouse, and she was quick on her feet—a real smooth sailor, who impressively held two plastic cups filled with beer.

Windy and I laughed as she almost drenched us and then walked by. The music was too loud to talk, so we danced. I wanted the rest of the lineup to meet Windy, but I didn't dare risk leaving her side ever again. She raised her voice as loud as she could, "Did you get the books I left you?"

I nodded.

"Have you read them all yet?"

"*Alice*!" I yelled back.

"What about the others?"

I shook my head. "Not yet."

"I like what you're wearing," she said as she touched my feathers. I wanted to bite her finger and keep it between my lips. Windy was better looking than I remembered, with her shirt hanging off one of her shoulders. She bumped her hip into mine, and I nudged her back.

She told me, "I'm going to Pali."

"Yeah, I know."

Some VPMs tried to pogo between us, but Windy and I dodged them. You'd think after all this time, I'd have a clever conversation-starter ready, but I was so nervous my mind went blank. Maybe if I could get her outside I could gather my wits.

Just as we were moving, Pete appeared and signaled her to the door.

I grabbed her hand. "No," I said. I didn't let go. I had just found her. She pulled a pen out of her tiny suede purse. It gave me chicken skin as she unfolded my hand like a piece of paper and wrote her number gently on my palm.

"Call me."

Pete urgently tapped her, nodded at me, and said in one breathless sentence, "Hi—hurry—let's go."

"Cops!" Coco yelled. And a stampede broke loose.

I watched Windy sneak past the police like some ninja, while I walked right into them, blinded by a stream of light. Officer Walzcuk and a few other cops were on the street, busting people. The party bolted in a million different directions. Jerry surprised me as he grabbed my hand and pulled me along. He said, "Let's get to the van." But Lord Ricky stopped us just long enough to stick the baggie of quaaludes down the back of my shorts, hiding it under my hair. He gave my butt a pat.

"I'll get my kiss later," he drooled.

"Like hell you will, Rick," Jerry said, pushing him back into the shrubs, which, of course, got Officer Walzcuk's attention.

"Run!" Jerry yelled as he took off. As if running were even possible on the damp grass and three-inch wedges. *What a bonehead*, I thought. I could see Lisa, Jenni, and Julie hiding in a thick gardenia bush across the street.

"It's after curfew, missy," said Officer Walzcuk, stepping in front of me and blocking my way. "You're going to come with me. And why are you the only one wearing a costume tonight?"

"These are my regular clothes," I said, grateful that he didn't recognize me from the notorious bust last year.

He looked at his partner and said, "Doesn't she look like Gypsy Rose Lee?"

"The stripper?" his partner asked.

As Officer Walzcuk took me by the elbow, I told him, "I live right there," and pointed to the house directly across the street.

"Really?" he asked skeptically. "Let me see you go in that front door. Once I see your mother, we'll say good night."

I walked away, clasping my hands behind my back to hold my hair down over the baggie. I knew people got sentenced to years in jail for pot. I couldn't imagine what would happen to me over this many pills.

Officer Walzcuk kept his flashlight on me while I walked through a smushed bed of daisies toward the house. I opened the mailbox to make it look real. "Guess Mom already got the mail!" I gave Officer Walzcuk a thumbs-up.

Out of the corner of my eye I could see Lisa, Jenni, and Julie crouched low in that bush, all of them looking terrified.

I marched up the front porch and rang the bell. An old Buick was parked in the driveway, and the house smelled like it had been sprayed for termites recently.

I saw the lights turn on upstairs and then in the living room. I tried not to look scared. There were chimes by the front door just like at my house. Maybe that was a good omen. I looked over my shoulder. Officer Walzcuk was still watching me.

When the door finally opened, an old lady peeked out. I waved at Officer Walzcuk and called, "It's my grandmother," and pointed to her.

"May I please use your phone?" I whispered. The old lady was confused, but she opened the door a little further. "That party is too much for me. I have to call my mom to pick me up." That did it.

"Oh sure, sweetie." She ushered me in. I waved at Officer Walzcuk triumphantly as she closed the door behind me. The house didn't have very good ventilation. It was like no one had visited in a long time. It made my eyes itch.

She handed me the phone. It was an old model: clunky, big, and black. I pushed the receiver button down with my thumb, and dialed my number. I waited, pretending it was ringing.

"Hi, Mom," I said. "Uh, could you please pick me up at Coco's house? Thank you." I pretended not to even let my mom finish her sentence, so it sounded natural, and put down the phone. I glanced out the window and saw Officer Walzcuk herd a few unlucky kids into his patrol car and drive away. Looking around the old lady's living room, I gasped at what I saw.

There were cats everywhere: short-haired, long-haired, some cats with tails and some without, spotted tabbies and striped tigers, even a Siamese with crossed blue eyes.

"Honey, would you like some tea while we wait for your mom?" The old lady had a nasally voice, white hair, and a terry cloth robe wrapped tight. A litter of kittens were meowing in a laundry basket at the bottom of the stairs.

"Oh!" I couldn't help myself. I went over to the basket and picked one up. He was a creamy shade of white and purred as he curled into my arms.

"These little fellows are Maine Coons. They're gonna get really big!" The old lady touched her fingertips to my forearm and said, "Elliot likes you. I think you should have him. Let me get a box," she said, shuffling into the kitchen.

I wanted Elliot more than anything in the world. He could be something to love and have for my very own. But how would I take care of him? I couldn't ask my mom for money. She had enough on her plate, and so did I. Carefully, I placed Elliot back with his brother and sister kitties, all mewing and licking their paws. I didn't want to leave him, but I forced myself to walk out the front door and not look back.

Outside, Lisa, Jenni, and Julie grabbed me from behind. They were laughing so hard I thought they would pee in their pants as they picked leaves out of each other's hair. I could see that Julie fit right in.

"That was so bitchin'!" Jenni said.

"Don't we smell good after being in that gardenia bush?" Lisa asked.

"I think I'll start wearing gardenia perfume," Julie said.

They pulled me forward and started skipping down the street. We didn't stop until Jerry and the VPMs came into sight. Jerry tipped his hat at me. We all laughed. I was having fun.

CHAPTER TWENTY-THREE

Honey Girl

Jerry Richmond seemed to know every hot dog place in LA. His other favorite, The Hot Dog Show, was in the Palisades— not too far from Coco's. It was crazy crowded. Jerry squeezed the van next to the VPMs'. We were about to have a major tailgate party. The lineup set up backrests and towels. One of the VPMs had a kerosene lantern and an oversized umbrella.

Since Jerry was buying, I ate two chili dogs with tons of onions and fries. I chewed with my mouth open, pushing ostrich feathers out of the way, and gobbled up french fries. "This is living," I told Jerry.

I loved breaking The Rules. As far as I was concerned, girls *can* eat in front of guys. And besides, Jerry and I were just friends. Being kind of gross was how I kept it that way.

Between you and me, I was on such a high after outsmarting the cops that when Jerry finally drove me home, I took my shoes and knee socks off and placed my feet strategically on the dashboard. The rule is: always smell good, but I say:

**Let him get a whiff of these babies with that
super sniffer of his.**

This was the beginning of the New Rule Revolution. My tootsies reeked. I spread my toes wide to let the wind tickle through them, and I kept a beat to T. Rex as we curved down Chautauqua. I even stuck one foot right in Jerry's face and laughed, shifting my weight to avoid the lump of the pills still in my shorts.

It dawned on me as we drove toward 33 Sage that no one but Lord Ricky knew about the stash I had. The question now was: What was I going to do with it? I sure as hell wasn't going to give it back to him, so he could dose some other unsuspecting girl.

"Julie is kind of neat," Jerry said. "Do you think she'll make it in?"

I couldn't believe he was asking about the lineup. But he was right. Julie *was* cool. She had passed with flying colors.

"It looks really good for her."

"I like her butt," Jerry said. I slapped his shoulder and pushed him to one side. He continued, "I never noticed how much you guys, I mean, you girls, have to go through. It seems like you have to deal with so much. I'm not going to take my eyes off that Ricky Lord. And don't you either. Deal?"

"Deal."

I wasn't looking forward to going home. I felt that irreversible sadness when I thought about 33 Sage. It made me feel empty.

When we got there, I noticed a shady-looking Mustang parked in front of my house. A guy was slouched down in the driver's seat. His bare arm dangled out the window. A cigar burned bright between his fingers. It smelled good. I was jonesing so bad for a cigarette. I would even have smoked a stranger's stogie.

Jerry, being Jerry, pulled right up to the car's bumper with his brights on before he even realized there was someone in there. The guy kind of waved us off.

"Do you know him? Are you expecting someone?"

"No," I told him. "Go check him out."

I was definitely not getting out of the van. From now on I had to be cautious to a fault.

Jerry slowly got out of the van, all the while burping nonstop. I waved the air around me; it stunk of sauerkraut.

I told him, "If you need to get rid of him, just go burp in his face. That'll do it."

He approached the car, shuffling sideways with his hands in his pockets, then dropped his head down to look inside the car. I watched him just stand there for a minute, like maybe something was wrong. I was locking the doors to the van when Jerry grabbed the sides of his head and shouted, "No way!"

I riffled through the glove compartment, looking for something I could use as a weapon. There was comb, a can opener, and a roach clip. I wished Nigel were here.

Jerry came running. When he couldn't get into the van he knocked both fists on the front window. "Nani, Nani, come out. You've got to see!"

He practically dragged me to the car and pointed inside. "Look! It's Solomon Kekahuna from Mākaha!"

"Wassup!" Solomon's voice bellowed like thunder.

When I saw the tattoos on his arm and the single shark tooth dangling from his ear, I knew it really was him. He had traditional tattoos—the kind that were hammered into the skin with bird bones. When he got out of the car I could see he was giant, like Buffalo Keaulana. He looked one hundred percent Samoan with his thick, black hair and had to be six-four and at least three hundred pounds.

Solomon surfed the monster waves of Mākaha. That was his break. He was born and raised at the foot of jagged mountains with a magic that haunted intruders. He had just been on the cover of *SURFER* Magazine, and up close he was solid as a rock. Those crushing thirty footers that blew other people up like bombs probably slid right off his back. What was he doing in front of my house? I kept my mouth closed so the ostrich feathers from the boa wouldn't fly up and stick to my lip gloss. Maintaining was of the utmost importance, since Jerry was losing his mind.

The west side of Oahu is different from the rest of the island. Its slogan was: "If you don't live here, you don't belong here, so don't go there." That's what we told tourists—except when they wanted to watch the big waves breaking in the winter. The long paddle out will kill most surfers, but not Solomon.

From what I could smell, Solomon was stoned on Swipe, a local home brew made illegally from fermented pineapples and other stuff. It's the strongest drink in the world. One sip would fry even my dad.

"Eh, Honey Girl. You must be Haunani?"

I flipped my boa and then my hair. A thrill exploded within me. It had finally happened. A surf god called me a Honey Girl. I felt the words melt deep down into my bones. This was the greatest moment of my life. It was a triumph. A dream come true, granted by none other than the Mākaha god, Solomon. And my witness? Jerry Richmond. A sweeter success in girl land there never was.

Jerry grinned at me. "Honey Girl?" he said, nodding as if he had just really seen me for the first time.

"Eh, Nani," Solomon said. "You *Nohea Lady*." I knew that meant I was dressed real pretty. He was tanked. He held up a flask and looked at Jerry. "What's up, *cuz*? S-w-i-p-e?"

I backed away. That stuff was so scary. One sip and you were blasted.

"Annie's up there," he said, thumbing toward the house. All the lights were on. I could hear voices.

Annie Iopa was here?! I couldn't believe it. I jumped up and down. Then I smoothed my hair around my face, pinched my cheeks, and wagged my finger at Jerry. I warned him, "Don't drink that stuff!" and hauled up the stairs.

Annie was the one who had told me all the secrets of what it means to be a Honey Girl—not just a sweetheart, but an immortal priestess of cool, who can rule a beach without ever having to state a single verbal claim. When you're a Honey Girl, all your power comes through an inner beauty that shines on any place with sand. I might not agree with the cold way Annie treats *haoles*, people who aren't brown like us, but there was no denying her magic on the beach. I picked up my pace as I dashed up the stairs—happy, happy.

I thought my mom would be at work, but she was home. Maybe she was sick. Quickly, I took the pills out of my shorts and tucked them behind a potted plant. The nearer I got to the house, the louder my mom's voice became. Annie's shoes were outside the door. Everyone in Hawaii takes their shoes off before coming in, but Jean and I stopped doing that long ago.

"Take it," Jean was saying when I walked in. It freaked me out when I saw her. She was furiously ripping twenty-dollar bills from the bottom of my dad's urn and throwing them at Annie's bare feet. It must have been over two hundred dollars. "Get out! That's the last of it. I don't owe you anything. Get out!"

Jean was leaning in the doorway of the kitchen, face red as a beet, lips stretched tight over her teeth in a blind rage. The veins in her neck raised, and her hands gripped the wall like talons. She screamed over and over again at Annie, "Get out, get out!" She was wearing the kimono my father gave her. It was falling off one shoulder, and she had spilled something down the front of her nightgown. The damp silk clung to her belly.

It was obvious—she was drunk. She swayed and tipped back and forth, holding the urn loosely under her arm, then she kicked a chair into the kitchen table.

Annie pulled me to her.

"*Mo'bettah* outside," she said. I had never seen Jean touch the urn, and I didn't like how pissed she was.

"You don't need to see any more of this," Annie said as she guided me back down the stairs. "Your *muddah's* a crazy *pupule*."

I wasn't going to argue with Annie Iopa.

"What are you doing here?" I asked.

"Oh, you'll see," Annie replied, patting my back.

She was being so nice, I put out of my head the fact that I hadn't heard from her in almost a year. I had forgotten how graceful Annie was. As I followed her down the stairs, she counted the money and talked over her shoulder. "Mike Kei is such a *focka*. He wouldn't pay me, so your mom owed me. I'm the only one who kept the Jones open. *Memba*?" She kept slipping between Pidgin and English. I forgot how she did that. It made me homesick.

"Where are my fish?" I asked.

"Gone."

"What about the tikis?"

"Gone. *Tanks* to your Uncle Mike." She tucked the money and something else into her purse. Then Annie looked down the street and saw Jerry leaning on the car next to Solomon. She pinched my arm and said, "Eh, all right, Haunani. You made that local boy your own. You give him sauce?"

"Sex?! No."

"Good, 'cause he's da bomb. Make him wait."

I let Annie think whatever she wanted about Jerry and me. I could tell by how Solomon and Jerry were moving, their arms stretching and twisting, that they were talking waves. Jerry had a gleeful bounce as he chatted with the Mākaha elite. He was laughing so hard, his face was streaked with tears.

"Aw, he's all *buss'up*."

Great, Jerry was drunk. He stopped in his tracks when he saw us coming down the stairs. He gawked at Annie's thick waist-long hair, tan legs, and short skirt.

"Honey Girl!" he yelled at her.

Solomon nodded. "Big time, *brah*," he said.

When I got close enough to Jerry, he wrapped his arms around me and said, "Nani, you're a Honey Girl, too."

He was hugging me too close, with a tender touch. For the first time, I could feel how soft his skin was, and I could hear Rox's voice telling me how it made her cum. Jerry pointed to Annie. "She's a Honey Girl," he repeated.

Solomon was cracking up at how drunk Jerry was. Too loaded to drive home. I untangled myself, walked over to the van, and took the keys out of the ignition.

"Didn't I tell you not to drink that?" I said, stomping back with both my hands on my hips. I looked Jerry right in the face and wagged my finger. I enjoyed scolding him.

"Hey, you *nuha*?" Solomon said.

Yeah, I guess you could say I was bent out of shape over Jerry getting drunk. But, as was typical with guys as ridiculously fine as Jerry, his mellow demeanor had wooed not only Solomon, but Annie, too, who stepped in closer to get a better look.

She sniffed him like he was a dog, then had him do a little spin so she could appreciate him from every angle. She took the top hat and put it on her head, then said, smiling, "You partying?" We all laughed. Annie squeezed Jerry's cheek. "*Maika'i.*" That meant she thought he was hot.

"Yeah, I love you, too," said Jerry, as he kissed her hand like a real gentleman.

That's when Solomon kind of rolled between them and said, "Eh, no *bugga* my wife."

Did he say *wife*? He couldn't have.

"Oops, sorry, man." Jerry crawled into the back seat of Solomon's car and said, "Well, good night, everyone." He almost put his head down, but before he could, something snapped him out of his drunken stupor. I literally saw the color drain from his face.

"What's wrong?" I asked.

He tilted his head and stared into a dark corner of the back seat. I followed his eyes. In a plastic laundry basket, on top of a blue blanket, lay a teeny sleeping baby. My jaw dropped. Jerry looked numb. *Where did that come from?* I thought. He stretched his hand out and touched the little body wrapped in a dish towel.

"Is it a boy?" he asked.

"Yes," Annie emphasized, "*It* is."

My eyes popped open. "Whose is it?"

Annie looked like I had snapped a rubber band on her butt. She whipped her hair to one side and tied it in a knot on her head in one motion. "Mine," she said, like I was some kind of idiot. She shoved me to the side with a hurricane force and quickly reached past Jerry to get the baby.

Then Jerry got all drunk-acting again. No one can fight off Swipe once it's got your brain.

"I was gonna have a son," he said. "Teach him to swim and surf. Get him little trunks and a baseball bat." He held his hands over his mouth, closed his eyes, and shook his head back and forth, slower and slower until he drifted away.

Annie was instantly blissed out when she got the baby in her arms. I peeked at her through my hair as she gazed at him. "How old is he?" I asked.

The lights went on in her eyes as she leaned down to kiss his forehead gently. "Six weeks," she said.

It was clear there was no space left in her life for me. I had been erased.

"Look, we came to the mainland to introduce this little guy to the Kekahuna family," Annie said.

I got it. I wasn't even part of the plan. Annie and I weren't going to start hanging out again. She had gotten what she had come for, and it wasn't me. It was money. Once and for all, I was pushed to see her for who she was, and not who I wanted her to be.

"I named this little guy Jimmy Star," Annie said. "After your dad, Nani."

Just like that, my mood flip-flopped. I was so happy to hear my dad's name was going to live on, I didn't care who had it. I wanted to jump in her arms, but they were full.

"You get it now, don't you? We need the bucks to get Jimmy home."

I was going to say, *Sure, yeah*, but Solomon interrupted, and the smell of cigar smoke—and what must have been a dirty diaper—made me back up as he said, "Guess we're giving Jerry a ride." He swooped down and took Jimmy from Annie.

"Easy!" she demanded, looking like she could have bit his head off. Solomon gingerly squeezed into the passenger seat.

"I'll see you back home someday, yeah?" Annie asked, never taking her eyes off the baby.

"Yeah, sure," I said, without thinking. I didn't want to ever go back upstairs and see Jean, but I didn't want to stay where I wasn't welcome either. I was stuck between a rock and a hard place, and I knew I'd never find my way back to the kind of kindness I'd once had—especially from Annie.

"Where dis guy live?"

"Rustic Canyon."

"Where?"

"Just go that way," I said pointing. "Aloha." I looked Annie in the eyes and waited until she finally said it back.

"Aloha."

And then they were gone.

CHAPTER TWENTY-FOUR

☾

The Big Picture

I was just about to go inside when Annie put on the brakes and backed up. She got out of the car and looked at me long and hard. It weirded me out.

"What's wrong?"

"Eh, Haunani. I gotta give you this."

I hoped she was going to hand me back some cash, but instead she pulled a crumpled newspaper clipping out of her purse. "Since you're gonna come home someday, you gotta know."

It was from the *Honolulu Star-Bulletin* and had a big photo. Annie unfolded the clipping. The moon was so full, I had no trouble seeing the headline. It read, "Landmark Java Jones Demolished for High-Rise Condos." And there, right next to the article, was a picture of a proud Uncle Mike standing in a vacant lot.

After a second, I realized I wasn't breathing. I sighed and clasped my coral necklace. My mouth went dry, but I didn't make a sound. It was a total shocker.

All I could muster was a joke. "Wow," I said sarcastically. "My fish really *are* gone."

"Sorry, Haunani." Annie tapped my shoulder with just her fingertips. "I really miss your papa. He was *ohana*, real family, to everyone who worked at the Jones."

I wondered if she really meant it. The whole subject hurt too much to even think about, so for the second time in the night I found myself changing the topic.

"Can you do me a favor?" I asked her as I looked at Jerry in the back seat, his arm around the empty basket. He was so sweet and peaceful. "Jerry is going to Oahu to surf and—"

"Solomon will take care of him." She finished my sentence for me. "He'll be *ohana*." She gave me the *shaka* sign, thumb to the sky, pinky to the earth, connecting them both. At least I knew one of us would be taken care of.

As Annie drove away, one thing was for sure: she was never coming back, and I'd probably never see her again. The smell of her red ginger perfume lingered in the air.

Jerry would leave next, and I bet he'd never come back, either. I stood looking up at the stars, trying to remember which constellation was which. The V-shaped stars were the tips of Taurus's horns, about to smash down on Orion.

Snap. My reality broke. It would never be whole again. Too many had said goodbye. Too many were gone for good. I uncrumpled the newspaper. Here's what it said:

> Developer Mike Kei is turning the location of the once-popular Java Jones into a 20-story condominium. "Hawaii is on the rise," he was quoted as saying. "But we must preserve our culture." He credited the tourist boom for the increased housing demand.

Preserve Hawaiian culture? I thought. *As if.* He was the one most responsible for destroying it.

The Lurline steamship used to be the only way to get to Hawaii, but now, planes were shoveling tourists into Waikiki nonstop. Honolulu was growing faster than any other city in the United States. Thanks to folks like Uncle Mike, I wouldn't be surprised if Oahu sank from the weight of so many new people. I ripped the article into tiny pieces. I stomped and spit on them.

33 Sage was quiet. Suddenly I remembered Jean, still drunk inside. If it weren't for her and this stupid house, Uncle Mike would have never been able to get the Jones away from us. I charged up the steps, two at a time, and cleared my throat so I could scream louder. I felt like a loaded gun, cocked and ready to fire.

I was not going to take Jean's drunken BS. She was a despicable person. A liar and loser like her pal, Nixon. I was going to make her take responsibility for getting drunk again and destroying the Jones—and my life. Even if I had to kick it out of her. This time I was taking no prisoners.

I threw open the door. Jean was kneeling on the rug in the living room. A portion of the urn's contents had spilled out in front of her. She was hysterical, trying to gather everything up by grabbing at the green shag rug.

My need to annihilate her deflated as a flash of horror replaced it. I couldn't look at her and be unswayed. I was watching my mom disintegrate—and now she knew the awful, despicable thing I'd done.

I knew saying sorry wouldn't cut it, but I *was* sorry. So sorry. I stared down at her and told myself that when she disowned me I'd never be able to escape the memory of this moment. I would be completely alone. She'd never talk to me again. And I couldn't blame her.

What could I say to make her forgive me?

She looked up, sobbing, the rough sand filtering through her fingers. "Some of Daddy fell out. He smells like the ocean. I didn't know ashes were so gritty."

"Oh, Jesus." She was so wasted she didn't know. The truth was right in front of her—she was literally holding it—but she couldn't see it. She tried to funnel a handful of sand back in the urn. "I'll take care of this," I told her.

I felt sick inside, but so incredibly relieved. I hated myself for that.

Snot dripped down Jean's face. I helped her up. She bumped against the wall as we moved toward her bed. I had to be the grown-up again.

Finally, I got it, loud and clear: no one was coming to rescue me. If I needed something, I would have to make it happen. No one would ever do it for me. I had to take care of myself.

Jean collapsed onto the bed. I had never realized how drunk someone could get. So drunk that she didn't notice the wrinkly little leaves, tiny shells, or cherry pit scattered through the sand I'd used to replace Dad's ashes. I picked up the wineglass and half-drained tumbler of vodka from beside her bed.

I would have given anything to come up with some way to explain what I'd done. But there was no excuse. For the first time ever, I understood that there is no way to sugarcoat shame.

I told myself:

Don't cry. Don't cry. Don't cry. Don't cry. Don't cry.
Don't cry. Don't cry. Don't cry. Don't cry. Don't cry.
Don't cry. Don't cry. Don't cry. Don't cry. Don't cry.
Don't cry. Don't cry. Don't cry. Don't cry. Don't cry.
Don't cry. Don't cry. Don't cry. Don't cry. Don't cry.
Don't cry. Don't cry. Don't cry. Don't cry. Don't cry.
Don't cry. Don't cry. Don't cry. Don't cry. Don't cry.

I hated crying. It was like throwing up to me, and I avoided it at all costs. Even so, this was hard to swallow. My jaw went tight, and the back of my throat felt too narrow.

I ran into my room and curled into a little ball. When the first tear fell down my cheek, I wiped it away. But in no time, I was sobbing. When I finally stopped, my lower back hurt and my throat was sore. As soon as I could see straight, I headed into the kitchen to get a mop and pail.

I cleaned to repent. I cleaned to make my mom healthy again. I cleaned to change. I cleaned to fix the mess I'd made. I cleaned to make it better, until the whole house smelled like Ajax.

Only then would I allow myself to think about the Java Jones. It had just been a dark cocktail lounge with low-slung bamboo chairs. A cave, really. But a special cave, with timber floors and curtains of beads that shimmered when you walked through them. It was a place where you could be yourself and forget time. All that was left of it were a few Mai Tai mugs, some swizzle sticks, and a couple tablecloths from the Rendezvous Room.

I gathered up my food and plates and hid them farther back in the cabinet, where I kept my unopened pack of cocktail napkins from the Jones with the words: AIN'T NO BIG TING.

I was panicked by the possibility that Jean might actually find out that I had stolen Dad's ashes someday. Since she was totally passed out, I snuck into her room, grabbed some Super Bonder from one of her drawers, took the urn, and sealed it up. It would never spill out again. Then I put it back on the table next to her bed and tiptoed out of the room.

I needed to make a fresh start. Reclaim my summer, and my life. I stood over the kitchen sink holding Jean's bottle of vodka. I had found it hidden in the freezer right after I discovered a fifth of gin floating in the toilet bowl.

I was just about ready to pour them down the drain when the thought occurred to me: I could drink this stuff and—*poof!* Nothing would hurt as much, and the chatter in my head would stop.

I could literally feel my mom's sickness churning inside of me. I wanted a drink. I needed a drink. And then I remembered the quaaludes hidden outside. I took a flashlight and went to the rock they were hidden under. I laid them in the palm of my hand and counted out twelve. As I looked at my hand holding the pills, I saw that Windy's phone number had blurred into a single black circle. Everything in me just went *thump*. It was a terrible feeling. Losing her number was the last straw.

I really wanted to take the pills, but I put them back in the baggie.

I locked the door and looked at the Benson & Hedges butts, stained with Jean's orange lipstick, in an overflowing ashtray by the sink. I picked one up and straightened it out. There was tobacco still inside. I needed this cigarette. The only problem was, I knew when I was done smoking it, my bad thoughts would still be there, and I would just hate myself more.

The bottle smelled stronger than a full tank of gas. I put it to my lips, but another thought came to me: if I took one sip, I would end up like Jean—passed out in a room with the TV on. No matter how much I drank, the memories of tonight and the lies I told would just keep coming back.

I poured the contents of both bottles down the drain, stuck the quaaludes in my purse, and emptied the ashtrays into the trash. If I didn't stop before I started, I was doomed.

I paced the kitchen. I'd have to get a job. If Jean got a bad review or was fired, I'd have to be able to buy food for myself. Cigarettes were thirty-five cents in the vending machine. If I didn't smoke, I could save lots of money, and with five dollars a week, I could get more than a dozen eggs, a pound of sugar for sixty-five cents, and bacon for eighty-five cents, and a lot more—like peanut butter and bread. I'd have to take those babysitting offers seriously if I was going to support myself.

I repeated, "Everything will be all right," as I patted the side of my face gently like my dad used to do. That made me sad, too. I could feel tears starting to trickle down my face again. *No crying.* I was furious with myself. *Get tough, cream puff.* That's what the soldiers used to say.

I closed my bedroom door and prayed to Nigel's friendly version of Jesus to protect me from Jean, from all the cigarettes I wanted to smoke, and from the vodka and gin I hated but would drink by the quart to make the hurt go away. I paced some more and pounded the bed. I held the rosary I kept pinned to the wall, but there was no relief. I was desperate for salvation—anything. Then I got really hopeless, dropped to my knees, and threw myself onto the carpet, praying big time.

Instantly, I knew what to do.

I knew the one thing that would save me.

I reached under my bed and pulled out my board.

CHAPTER TWENTY-FIVE

Caught Inside

I ran to State Beach clutching my board, wet suit, and a change of clothes. I didn't stop until my feet touched the water. I threw my stuff under the lifeguard station. State was deserted at night—except for a few gay guys and Lōlō, the local bum. He was talking to himself. His weird, stocky dog lingered by his side as he stood over a trash can like it was a buffet, eating something that looked like potato puree from a Dixie cup.

Hurriedly I pulled Nigel's wet suit up over his trunks. It felt cumbersome and heavy. I'd never worn one of these things before. But it was so cold out there, I knew I had to. Then I tucked my hair tight into the baseball cap, the one with the faded S that was unreadable, so the cap just read DODGER. No one could know I was a girl.

With Dad, I had always surfed longboards, but nobody took longboard surfing seriously. And obviously he thought I could handle the speed of a shortboard, which was more like a Porsche than a cheesy Pinto. This board was exactly like Gerry Lopez's. Only a few people in the world had one. It was a major sign of respect that Dad got it for me.

I had night surfed at Queens, but the full moon in Hawaii and lit-up hotels made it easy to see. Not so at State. It was so dark I couldn't make out the takeoff zone in the distance, even with the full moon. It was spooky out there.

What made it possible to paddle out was feeling my dad's thumbprints embedded in the wax he had melted on top of the board. He had made them deep, so my toes would have something to grip. Eventually, I'd want to be more sure-footed, so I could maneuver my board tip to tail. I'd need to get some Mr. Zog's Sex Wax to coat the slippery spots. But for now this would have to do. It felt like he was with me.

In the water, it seemed as if I was swimming into a crypt. The ocean smelled saltier than normal, and the foam was fluorescent white. The tide led me out, as the whitewash fizzled in front of me. I would have chickened out right then and there, but I didn't have anywhere else to go.

Santa Monica Bay is crescent-shaped. But there is no coral reef, so the paddle out is much shorter than in Waikiki. *Easy breezy*, I thought. The only catch was, the ride in wouldn't last very long. I had waited for this moment ever since I got to State. I wanted to max out my high and savor my first wave in almost two years.

But as the waves got closer, I felt a rush of fear. I flipped my board to get under the first one. It's called turning turtle, but it was a mistake. Without the weight of a longboard, I ate it.

When the next wave came, I didn't lift up enough over it, so the whitewash couldn't pass around me. It was so strong. I ended up back on shore with my board on top of me.

When I used to surf, my dad would help me through the foam. But without him I kept getting caught inside. It was pathetic. I had to remind myself of what he'd say: just keep your chest up. But I had boobs now, and they hurt and threw me off balance.

The board was so light it was like paddling on a feather. Actually, it felt incredible. It was quick, but the waves were quicker.

At home, the ocean had wide sections of turquoise and clear shades of blue. Even at night, you could almost see through the waves. But in this part of the Pacific, colors didn't separate. Everything was smoky gray. Finally, there was a break in the swell. I went for it and paddled hard past little two-foot waves, which seemed like ten-footers to me.

I had to find the takeoff zone or else I'd never get a wave. Except the current kept shifting, sticking me in the ditch. Waves have their own frequency. Each one is different. I had to find the right spot, but I couldn't find it in the dark. I paddled deeper inside, got in position, but fell off my board and got sucked under. The feel of a shortboard was so different, I couldn't pop up. I got chased down by another wave and wiped out.

I decided to use Mrs. Kinski's house on the bluffs to orient myself. She had a light on in her giant front window. I went for the next wave I saw. I wanted it. I wanted it more than anything in the world. I needed it more than a cigarette. As it lifted me up, I thought, *I've got you.* I popped up quick but came down the lip too fast. The board flew out from under me, and I windmilled forward. The ocean twisted me around. Dad used to call it getting stuck in the washing machine. Kelp and sand swirled around me. It's a good thing I was alone. I was so out of control. The waves pushed me down until I floated back, breathless, onto land.

I wanted to whine like a little kid alone in the middle of the night. This was bogus. I knew how to surf. I dug in and paddled out again. State was not going to get me. I was going to get *it*. I thought, *You watch me. I will bend, and you will never snap me in two.* I didn't care how big or powerful the ocean was. No matter what, I was going to surf.

I used all my weight and pushed the board down over the whitewash. I plowed through a wave with a rush of excitement. My necklace splashed up against my chin. I was tired and wired—good—until another wave caught me off guard. It was so big it blocked the moon.

Darkness. It was violent under water.

I had slammed the curl of the lip so hard it jammed my board up, and I fell backward again—totally tossed. I didn't even know if I had hit bottom. My eyes stung from the salt when I opened them, and I finally floated up, gasping for air. I was smack dab in the middle of an enormous swell.

A slight wind had picked up. I tried to catch another wave. I told myself, *Paddle, paddle, paddle.* "*Wiki, wiki,* faster, faster," my dad would have said. I popped up quickly, but again I came down the lip too fast and fell. I tried and fell again and again and again until a thin pink line on the horizon warned me: *sunrise.* I'd lost track of time. Like Cinderella, I had stayed too long at the ball.

CHAPTER TWENTY-SIX

(

Dodge the Devil

As I dragged myself out of the water, I saw the VPMs driving into the lot. As soon as they parked, Lisa and Jenni slipped sleepily out the back. News flash: the tailgate party had lasted all night. When more vans started chugging in, I grabbed my stuff and ran into the tunnel that led directly to the bluffs.

I was waterlogged and exhausted. Every bone in my body ached, and my calves were so cramped I could barely walk. Where was I going to stash my board?

Mrs. Kinski's back gate was cracked open. I made a dash for it, just as Lord Ricky rounded the corner in his mom's station wagon. Brad and Stu were sitting shotgun. I crouched behind a rusted old car that had no front seat or wheels and was raised up on bricks. Through the splintered fence, I could see Lord Ricky guzzling a Mickey's big mouth, the breakfast of champions.

I searched for somewhere I could hide my board before they noticed me. There was a shed—sort of like a storage bin or closet. I separated two rotting planks of wood and looked inside. It was like a museum of broken surfboards cluttered together. Rumor was, Mrs. Kinski had fifteen grown kids. Talk about a baby machine. It made sense that some of them surfed.

I set my board alongside the slabs, replaced the planks, and pushed the tall grass up back against the sides. This was a good hiding place, and I'd have easy access to it for my next session. As quietly as I could, I rinsed my wet suit with the garden hose and hung it on a hook to dry. There was a rusty stove and boxes of pots and pans littering the muddy yard. I rolled my trunks and hat into my towel, and exchanged them for my signature look: a tied-up blouse and low shorts. Lord Ricky's pills fell out of my purse. I was so over it. I undid the baggie. I'd never pulled an all-nighter before, and I was really feeling it. If I took one of them, I'd get some sleep. The question was, where?

I tried to sneak past Lord Ricky and his two buddies, but I startled them instead. They must have jumped a mile, and they dropped the joint they were sneaking. After the night before, I knew better than to laugh. They were talking about their new surf shop, Amphibian. It sounded like their business was more about dealing drugs than selling boards, and the second they saw me, Lord Ricky threw what was left of his beer at me.

He yelled, "What are you, *Bewitched*? Where'd you come from? Where's my kiss?" I stumbled backward and fell over Mrs. Kinski's low fence. My legs lifted up from under me, and I slammed down onto the ground. Lord Ricky, Brad, and Stu laughed. As they stood above me, I felt my skin getting tight like a wet wool sweater that was shrinking. "Where's my kiss?" Lord Ricky spat again.

I threw the bag of pills at him. I had forgotten it was open. Quaaludes went flying into the street. Brad and Stu ran after them as they rolled in every direction. Lord Ricky said, "You're not a little witch. You're a little bitch, and I'm gonna get you."

I didn't need a broomstick to fly down those stairs, and as I ran, I yelled across the highway, "Hi, Jenni. Hi, Lisa." Everybody in the parking lot turned and looked at me, as Lord Ricky slid back into the bushes.

CHAPTER TWENTY-SEVEN

(

Black and Blue ERA

I wasn't awake, and I wasn't asleep. I was stuck somewhere in between, and I had no idea what time it was. Lisa and Jenni were talking in that hush-hush tone Rox and Claire used to use. "Have you seen the way he looks at her?"

"Yeah. Good thing Rox hasn't."

I knew they meant me and Jerry. I slid back into my dream state. I wasn't ready to explain anything, or to open my eyes.

In my mind I was still surfing—steady and in slow motion, like Gerry Lopez in *Five Summer Stories*, my fingers stretched out like his always were, guiding me through a wave as big as a house. I was fluid and seamless, and I knew one thing for sure: I didn't want to marry Gerry Lopez anymore; I wanted to *be* Gerry Lopez.

I squinted my eyes open. Julie Saratoga was chatting away and making Lisa and Jenni laugh. She was definitely in. Jenni and Lisa had also invited some pampered Palisades girls, who lived in cliffside mansions. They were pool blonds, who'd stayed in the chlorine water so long their hair was turning green. Good breeding wouldn't help them get in the lineup. Their voices floated right past me.

I mean, why come to the beach when your own pool is the size of a lake and the palm trees on both sides of your street are planted in straight lines, same as the ones in Hawaii that mark where kings once walked? When they trotted away, their gold loop earrings and Tiffany rings glimmered in the near-blinding sun.

Lisa shrugged them off, saying, "It was really dark at that party."

"For sure," Jenni said. "You never know what you've got to work with until daylight."

They inspired me to write a new rule that even locals need to know:

Never, ever join any circle without an invitation.

Here's the point: it will save you unnecessary doubt and the humiliation of feeling unwanted. Seriously. Go where the *aloha* is.

I had been asleep so long I felt like I was actually getting sunburned. It was the first time I had totally crashed out at State. When I finally managed to sit up, I realized how sore and hungry I was, and that the Topangas had moved their towels dangerously close to ours. They had added another girl, too, so now it was six to six. The lineups were even. I had no time to waste. I had to get recruiting.

"Hi, sleepy." Baby curled into my side. She was wearing a periwinkle-blue bikini. It made her eyes look like two small, blue, Mediterranean flowers. It was going to be her color for sure.

Lucky for me, Baby's mom had packed her a lunch. She gave me her bologna sandwich, potato chips, and one of her four Twinkies.

"Hey, how'd you get that?" Lisa asked, tapping her finger on my leg.

I looked down at my calf. Like any surfing bruise, it didn't hurt when I was in the water, but now that I looked at it, it was a real humdinger. "Uh, I rearranged my room last night."

"Look at the one I got," Lisa said.

"Me, too," Julie chimed in.

It turned out they had all gotten scratched up the night before, while hiding from the police. They wore their marks proudly, like badges of honor.

"When do I get to go to a party and get bruises?" Baby asked.

"When you go to Pali."

Baby looked like she was going to lose it. "But that's not for over a year!"

"Don't worry. Ninth grade goes really fast," I told her. Then I said, "O-M-G."

Lisa pointed at a girl with an amazing body walking slowly down the beach.

Jenni whispered proudly, "I told her to stop by today."

It was Ellie Katz, the girl from the party who'd nearly drenched me and Windy with beer. No way did I imagine that, under those baggy overalls, Ellie had an explosive body. She wasn't very tan yet, but that could change. She was making a statement by walking onto State wearing her feminist T-shirt that read: "A woman without a man is like a fish without a bicycle." Unfortunately, I don't think one guy read the words

across her chest. They were too busy gawking at it. 34-24-35.
Not a combo to a locker. They were her measurements, from
my guess.

I struggled to make sense of her as she came closer. It was
original that she wore a tight T-shirt with her bikini bottom.
She seemed savvy, like an Aries, which meant she was probably
short-tempered, since they're ruled by Mars, the war god. But
most likely she could hold her own. Sun signs are like that.

As Ellie situated herself, Lisa couldn't help but stare. "Hard
to believe you're only going into eleventh grade," she said.

"Why?"

"Because you're so smart," said Jenni. "Get cozy! Sit next
to me!"

We all knew that Claire had dubbed Ellie Ms. ERA, after
the Equal Rights Amendment. She came up with that diss
because on January twenty-second, when Roe v. Wade was
decided and women were assured the right to have an abortion, Ellie tried to get school closed. She wanted it to become
a national holiday.

Ellie was really big on women's rights, and calling her Ms.
ERA was meant to be a put down. It was how Rox and Claire
made fun of her behind her back. But when we saw her in that
bikini, the nickname started to seem more like a compliment
than an insult.

"Is it okay if we call you Ms. ERA?" Lisa asked.

"Ms. anything is good by me," Ellie answered cheerfully.

I could tell she was the type who fought for what was
important and let the small stuff slide. I bet she even read the
newspaper. And I got the sense that Ellie wasn't obsessed with
boys the way Lisa and Jenni were. I needed someone depend-
able. Maybe Ellie was it.

"Guess what?" Jenni said, looking at Lisa for approval. "Tonight we're doubling at Chart House."

"Just the two of you?" Ellie asked. "Sounds romantic."

"No, us and our boyfriends," Jenni said defensively.

"Wow, sounds serious," I said.

Lisa chimed in, "Yeah. Rox is getting us a table by the window for sunset."

I tried not to react, but Jenni saw something in my eyes.

"What's wrong, Nani?" Jenni asked.

The last thing I wanted was for them to know Rox wasn't talking to me. It hurt to be excluded. I promised myself that when I was a ruler I wouldn't do that to anyone. "Red Baron," I told them. My period was always a good excuse.

I was starting to notice how often I made stuff up.

"Anyway," Lisa said, "Rox's new hostess job is in full swing."

I wished I could have hidden behind the smoke of a cigarette. Funny that no one had even noticed I wasn't lighting up.

"What do you want to be when you graduate?" Julie asked.

"What do *you* want to be?" Lisa countered.

"I want to start my own bikini line," Julie said.

This was met with great approval. Jenni still planned to be a stewardess and see the world. Lisa said she hadn't thought too much about it, and Baby wasn't sure if she wanted to be a wife or a mother anymore after hearing about that dirty book, *The Joy of Sex*.

Lisa, Jenni, and I laughed. "What about you, Nani? What do you want to be?" Ellie said.

I couldn't tell them I wanted to be the best surfer in the world, but I knew the truth, and that's what was important. I had to figure out a way to stop lying, so I told them, "I want to be something in Hawaii. That's all I know."

Ellie was satisfied enough with our answers to enlighten us, "You know what I want to be?" she asked. "The first woman president."

"Oh, right." Lisa sort of laughed, but Ellie was serious. She wanted to be the first skirt in the Oval Office.

"Why not?"

Jean always said Republican men in their sixties or seventies make the best presidents. Like Ike. But maybe not anymore. Even so, the idea of a woman president sounded way too far-fetched. *While we're at it,* I thought, *why don't we just get a president who is brown, like me? Some guy from Hawaii who'd show up for diplomatic dinners in a Spooner shirt with sand between his toes. A guy with full lips and a big, bright smile, who looks totally primo in shades.*

No doubt he'd serve poi and pig from an *imu*—which is an underground oven—he dug himself. And he'd set up a real luau, so all those uptight white guys would have to eat with their fingers and sit on mats. There'd be flame torches on the White House lawn, pupus, hors d'oeuvres like Spam-and-pineapple kabobs, and coconut chips, and mai tais with rum and lime juice, crushed ice, and a cherry on top. "Mai tai" means "good time," and I bet those politicians would be having just that. Plus, anyone would be better than the faker in Washington *now*.

Ellie was a real pistol. She talked about how Phyllis Schlafly, the number one enemy of the ERA, was trying to screw up women's lib by getting housewives to hate it.

Ellie said, "I guess those women want abortion to be illegal again because they still want men to be in charge of every-thing—including their bodies."

Mary Jo blurted out, "Where would you be if your mom had had an abortion? Nowhere. Plus, I don't want to get drafted. So who wants equal rights? Do *you* want to fight in Vietnam?" she asked the entire group.

Ellie gave her a flabbergasted look. She said, "Regardless of what you want or don't want, laws are changing for good. And as far as women's lib is concerned, I personally don't want to be a baby machine and cook and do the laundry all day. I want to have a job, and a purpose beyond my husband's agenda."

Ellie's boobs jiggled when she got worked up. *That was quite a speech,* I thought. Ellie was the most openly brainy person the lineup had ever hosted. She left the SOS silent for a moment. Then Lisa, our fearless new leader, chimed in, "Yeah, look at Mary Tyler Moore. She has a job."

Baby got all excited. "Yeah, she has her own TV show and, like, in the TV show she even has a job at a news channel. So she has *two* jobs."

I rolled my eyes, but nobody noticed except Ellie.

Jenni nodded enthusiastically. "Saturday night is the best on TV!" she exclaimed. "You've got *The Mary Tyler Moore Show, Bob Newhart*, and *Carol Burnett*. You don't even have to get up to change the channel. It's all on 2."

I dropped my shades down. They didn't get it; they were talking about TV while Ellie was talking about real life. Intelligence was hard to find at the beach, and I was determined to keep Ellie around.

Lord Ricky was looking super scrappy today as he lurked around the beach. He was furry and unshaven. His beard grew in patches that looked like brown shadows on his face. Obviously, he was stoned. When he walked by, he sneered at me. "Where's my kiss?"

"He's a real existentialist," Ellie said. It made me laugh. I liked her sarcasm. I knew she'd be a great addition to the lineup, though I worried that, because she was Jewish, Claire would put the kibosh on her. It was a non-issue to Lisa and Jenni but, tragically, Claire still had a deciding vote. She had an attitude with every person who wasn't Bel-Air Bay Club material. It bugged me that she thought that way.

Bob was about to raise the no swim flag when some kid I'd seen him warn for the umpteenth time got caught in the rip with his raft. He should have known better; he had to be at least ten. The kid's head was so low in the water, you could barely hear him screaming for help. By the time Bob got past the waves, I could see the kid's eyes weren't in focus. I wanted to look away, but I had to make sure Bob got there in time.

It was weird to me that someone could drown so close to shore. The fear on his face stained my mind as he tried to open his mouth to yell. He swallowed ocean instead of air. The kid jerked back and forth, struggling helplessly as he was yanked farther out to sea. His mom started screaming.

In the seconds it took Bob to get his rescue gear around him, the boy got pretty far out—spasming. That's what happens when your airways fill with water. And it can kill you fast. Lucky for him, Bob got there before it was too late. Bob jimmied the kid onto the raft and body surfed him in as rapidly as possible. The whole beach stood to watch as the boy's mom came running to meet them. When they got to shore, Bob immediately pumped his chest until the kid started chucking up watery food. Maybe there *was* something to that saying: Don't swim for a half an hour after you eat.

Lord Ricky walked unceremoniously right past the drama. He was schmoozing Glenn, trying to get the photographer to take some pictures of him. The VPMs followed, and once the kid sat up, everything at State continued as though nothing had happened. Nobody seemed to care. But my hands were trembling.

—

Jerry was telling the VPMs, "I'm getting a new board. It's going to be thicker and longer for big waves." They listened attentively as they lined up. "I'm heading to Oahu in a few days." They hooted. "Going to live with Solomon Kekahuna and his Honey Girl." The VPMs went wild. I knew that Jerry Richmond was just another mouth Annie would have to cook for. It was unreal that he was going to get to live with her, and I was stuck on the mainland.

I was short of breath and felt like I was floating around like Major Tom, high above the flickering lights of the Earth, looking down on my sorry ass life. As the guys paddled out, Glenn adjusted his tripod and clicked away. I watched them attentively, squinting toward glittering waves. I memorized where Jerry positioned himself as he peeled into the first curl from top to bottom without a second thought. He never missed a takeoff. Neither did the VPMs. For sure they would all be in the article. They found the sweet spot every time, just to the left of Mrs. Kinski's house. I studied every move Jerry made: the smooth strokes that took him beyond the break. How he got to his feet so quickly. Speed was the ticket. I knew I had to be faster when I popped up.

Jerry was like poetry in the water. Surfing was always an improvisation, but not random. He had form like no one else; the magic was that he didn't try to control it. He surrendered to the wave so each move was completely new and spontaneous—like sand drawings by the ancients, which existed only for a moment before the wind blew them away.

Bob let the locals have an hour in the water before he raised the blackball flag, which meant no more surfing. Then the biggest event of the day happened: Jenni handed Coco a towel when he came out of the water. That was significant, and everyone knew it. If you give a guy a towel, it means he's yours. And if he takes it, it's official.

The guys lingered near us little longer than usual that day. Yeah, their stuff was right by us, but that wasn't why they hung around. The reason was Ellie Katz. She was a guy magnet. Not that she was trying; it's just who she is. I think most guys at State were actually scared of her, she was so gorgeous. I was relieved when Lisa and Jenni adjusted their towels, leaned back on their elbows, and relaxed. That was the sign of a green light. If you can kick back with a girl, you can be friends with her. All we would need now was Windy Davenport and a floater.

CHAPTER TWENTY-EIGHT

Return of the Prodigal Son

Later in the afternoon the lineup was sitting on the railing overlooking State. "Whoa!" Lisa said.

A brand-new, black Ferrari screeched to a stop and backed into a parking space as if its driver owned the world.

Jenni stopped licking her Popsicle. When a car you've never seen before pulls into State's parking lot, it's news.

We watched as none other than Shawn McBride slid out of the driver's seat. I knew it was him by how he walked. Nigel didn't strut like that. Shawn's hair was still super short, but it was darker. It made him look a little more dramatic.

Wait a minute, I thought to myself. *He isn't supposed to be back for another week. And why isn't Nigel with him?* That was weird.

Lisa called out, "Hey, Shawn, how was Calcutta?" as if he had been on a leisurely cruise. Her newfound friendliness toward a McBride was the sign of a true ruler.

He spun around and told her, with a forced laugh, "I'm not planning on going back."

Then he noticed me and practically tripped as he hurried away. I wanted to ask him where Nigel was, but for the longest time he focused his attention on the guys in the volleyball courts, on Bob, the VPMs—anywhere but on me.

Finally, he waved me over. I turned to Lisa and Jenni. "Will you guys come with me?" I asked nervously. They were more than happy to oblige, and we walked in unison toward the Ferrari.

"Do I have a railing mark?" Lisa asked out of the side of her mouth.

I peeked at the back of her thighs and reassured her, and then of course Jenni wanted me to do the same for her.

In keeping with her ruler status, Lisa was the one who spoke first. "Where's Nigel?" she asked.

Shawn didn't answer. Instead, he reached down into his shiny new car and grabbed an envelope from the dashboard.

"Sorry, Nani," was all he said as he handed it to me and quickly got back in the car. I took it from him and plunged it deep into Jenni's purse. I knew this was very bad and, from the looks on their faces, so did Lisa and Jenni.

Nobody said another word as we watched Shawn's Ferrari tear out of State, make a screeching left turn, and head back up the coast.

When the sun started to set and everybody began packing up, I knew I couldn't avoid what was in that envelope another minute. And since I didn't want to be alone when I read it, I said to Jenni, "Give it to me." Everyone gathered in a circle around, one towel touching another, shoulder to shoulder.

When I looked at the single piece of paper with words on both sides, I couldn't bring myself to read it. I handed it to Jenni, knowing her sweet voice would make whatever it said less painful. I covered my face with my hands as I listened.

> Dear Nani,
>
> I have been called to Christ.
>
> Serving God is the only thing greater than my love for you. Because your mom works at St. John's, I know you'll understand the hardships of the sick. I had no idea of the suffering of humanity before I came to Calcutta.
>
> I push myself from sunrise to sunset, as I am being trained for various tasks alongside the Sisters of the Merciful. They wear their habits all day in the heat but never complain. Sister Mary Margaret has taken me under her wing.

"She better not be cute," Lisa interrupted. Without looking up, I tapped Jenni to continue.

> She has been serving the poor in Calcutta for 23 years.

"Well then, that's okay . . ." Lisa said. "Go on."

I have joined her staff as a volunteer until I can begin Seminary School. Today I fixed her sewing machine and had culinary duties. I baked bread for the children. Some days I help out singing and reading, sometimes even assisting Father Mark with altar services.

"Did I hear that Nigel McBride is baking bread?"

Lisa shushed her.

I had hoped that Mary Jo had left for the day, but there she was sitting down, uninvited, drinking something that smelled like whiskey. Since I had no choice, I asked Jenni to continue.

It's going to take eight years before I am called to the Bishop to receive my Holy Orders.

Mary Jo interrupted again, "What the fuuu—"

"Maintain," Baby told Mary Jo in the most adorable way. "This is hard for Nani." She had become the voice of reason. I signaled Jenni again to continue.

Becoming a priest is something I've known I wanted to do for a long time. Please forgive me for not being honest with you. I hope that, in the future, you will celebrate this bright beginning with me and receive me with open arms once I overcome my earthly desires. But Nani, please know I will never stop loving you, ever!

Jenni was choking up now as she read. It should have been me crying, but Jenni dabbed her cheeks with the edge of her towel, composing herself, and said, "This is so beautiful."

I think Julie Saratoga teared up, too, but I turned away and slipped my shades down over my eyes.

Everyone here is brown like you, which is probably why I care for them so much.

Please pray for me, and for those who suffer, as our faith in Jesus Christ Our Lord moves the mountains ahead.

In the spirit of Christian mercy,

Nigel

P.S.: You can have my van once Jerry is done with it.

And then, just to seal the deal, I read aloud the last line he had written:

The light shines in the darkness and the darkness has not overcome it.

John 1:5

I dropped my head in my hand and didn't look up until Mary Jo said, "Jesus. He already sounds like a priest."

When I think of a priest, I picture a big man reading a small Bible, reciting prayers to himself, moving his lips as he reads. He's wearing a black jacket and white collar; on his lapel there's a gold pin supporting some noble cause. His black plastic glasses are thick and square and sit low on the bridge of his pink nose. His white hair is receding, and he has a double chin, dark eyebrows, and a billowing strong voice.

That is not Nigel McBride, with his long, willowy limbs and soft blue eyes that twinkle when he gets close to me. That is not a surfer who gets so deep into a wave he disappears.

One thing I definitely know is that a *kahunapule*, a priest, isn't a good kisser or a bonghead. It's not someone like my boyfriend, Nigel.

CHAPTER TWENTY-NINE

(

Through the Looking Glass

Rox had taken to stopping by State on her way to the Chart House. She'd visit the parking lot, hang over the railing in her tube top dress to say hi to the guys at the volleyball court, and make sure I saw her by whistling through her teeth and waving at the lineup.

When I rode my bike home, Joyce was in her silver Eldorado, just pulling away from the curb. She put on the brakes and waved me over.

"Come with me, Nani. Let's go get an ice cream." I thought, *Oh, great. First a letter and now an ice cream.*

"She's drinking," I said, tossing my bike into its secret hiding place.

Joyce didn't even raise her eyebrows. "I know." She turned off the car and got out. "You know it's not your fault, right?"

"Oh, yes, it is." And out of my mouth spewed every secret about the urn and Jean, and the entire story of the night before. I told Joyce about Nigel's letter and how Rox and I hated each other now. I wasn't going to cry, but when Joyce reached into her alligator purse and gave me her crisp handkerchief, I took it and paced back and forth in the middle of the deserted street, slamming my fist in the air.

"Why aren't you my mom?" I asked. Joyce gingerly put her arm around me, moving me out of the street. When I was on the sidewalk, she opened the car door and gestured for me to get in.

As she put the key in the ignition, she said, "Kids like you have to grow up faster. And you need to be good to yourself."

Joyce talked the whole time she drove. I liked the way she steered with one hand and smoked with the other. It calmed me down, somehow. When I had settled into Baskin-Robbins with my triple scoop of Rocky Road, Chocolate Mint, and Coffee and smashed down so I could lick it 'round the small sugar cone, Joyce said, "Isn't grief hard?" She scraped the last little bits of ice cream from her cup.

I nodded in agreement, then asked, "What do you mean, *grief?*"

"You know, my son, the one I blamed the car crash on? His name was Joseph. We lost him in Vietnam."

"I'm sorry. I have a friend, Mary Jo, whose brother died in Vietnam."

"Oh, yes, the Stevenses. I know her mom. Another Gold Star family in the Palisades. There are too many of us." She threw the cup into the trash can with the precision of a professional basketball player. She looked pissed. "You know, when we got the news, I didn't drink. That's how I know what I know. Grief changes. It did for me, and it will for you, too, Nani. Not every day is awful, and yet, I can't predict the pain. Some days it just comes. But I'm here, and I'll be here for you. If you want."

The words came pouring out of my mouth. "My dad was a pothead and let Uncle Mike run the business because he was too stoned. He supported Jean and me by getting people drunk. He never got up before ten in the morning, and he partied himself into an early grave."

You know how it is when you say something and immediately know it's the truth? That's what happened to me when I said all that stuff.

"I'm so sorry, sweetheart. But as I said, none of this is your fault. You are a wonderful girl, Nani." And then we just looked at each other. That was the big difference with Joyce. We could be sad together.

"I was going to leave this at the door for you, but—"

"What's this?"

"Twenty dollars. I want you to get yourself some food. I hope I don't sound too preachy," she said, "but there are always going to be obstacles, and none of them can blow away your dreams unless you let them."

"I wish you were my mother," I said again.

When Joyce dropped me off, she didn't hug me. She was toughening up, getting ready to say goodbye. "If you're in trouble, you can call me anytime," she said.

I asked, "Can I call you if I'm not in trouble? Like if I get an A+ and have no one to tell?"

"Anytime means anytime."

I watched Joyce drive away. I had a feeling that if she looked at me in her rearview mirror it would prove she was sincere. If she didn't, I knew I'd never see her again, and it would be one more awful loss.

My mind was racing. Up was down and down was up. I was Alice on the other side of the mirror with cookies crumbling and tea sets cracking, where caterpillars smoked hookahs and rabbits in coats chased time. I had to cross the chessboard. I would not be anyone's pawn once I reached the other side. I would be the queen. I forced myself to come back to Earth, and as I did, Joyce looked at me in her rearview mirror.

CHAPTER THIRTY

☾

Make it *Pono*

I stood in the doorway to my room, shaking my head in shock. It had been ransacked. Everything was scattered everywhere: shirts I had just folded, my tenth-grade notebooks, seashells I had collected with Rox. It looked like a tornado had hit it. But judging from the slippers and beer spilled on my rug, I knew there was only one person who could have done this. Jean had totally raided the top shelf of my closet, too. Thankfully, my copy of *Playboy* was still hidden in an issue of *Seventeen*.

The first thing I noticed was gone were my dad's buds. The whole, giant jar. But even worse, my turntable looked like it had been jumped on. There was no way the arm was getting reattached, and the plug was never going to connect to the wall socket again. Having no music was a fate worse than death.

I charged into Jean's room. As I expected, she was passed out drunk, *'ona*. I guess she had called in sick to work. I shook her until she woke up. "What happened to my room?"

She took the pillow and placed it over her head, mumbling, "Sorry."

"Sorry?" I screamed at the top of my lungs. I grabbed the pillow and threw it on the floor.

Jean pounced up onto her feet. She came at me with a killer force and screamed in my face, "I'm sorry!"

She was ferocious and primal—like when Annie was here. It completely freaked me out. I backed into her TV tray, which made her laugh in a wicked way.

That's when I saw Dad's stash next to her bed. "You shouldn't have that," I said.

"And you should?" she laughed again.

Then she pushed me and said, "Stay out of my room. You're not allowed in here."

It was the taunting sound of her voice that finally made me leave. Nobody's mom should ever scare them or treat them like that. Like I said, up was down and down was up. I couldn't switch off the bad thoughts in my head that billowed through my mind all at once. When I got this angry at Jean, my instincts told me to push back, hit harder, and hurt more, but that just made the storm worse. It fed the flames. Why did I have to behave when she didn't?

Then I barricaded my room. I looked out the window, saw the spectacular moon, and thought of Hina the Moon Goddess. She got tired of carrying her kids' crap to the other side of the island every day, so she ran away to the moon to take care of herself. That's how she became one of the great goddesses I pray to. Right then and there, I decided I had to be like Hina and stop trying to take care of my mom.

"I am going to move to the moon," I said, cuddling with Mrs. Beasley, my doll.

I decided to pray to David Bowie. I pressed his new album to my chest. It had his picture on it, with a red-and-blue lightning bolt painted down his face. I got on my knees, folded my hands tightly together like a little girl in a pew and prayed, *Help me, David Bowie. Please, pretty David, lipstick man. Ziggy boy, star traveler—I pray to you. Give me something beyond hope. I need your voice to protect me. I can't touch your spirit without the music. Swallow me whole. Please take me away from here. Show me where to go. Please help me.*

It was a mantra entrusted to me from the great beyond, not something inspired by somebody else's religion.

I put my headphones on, even though there was nothing to plug into, and sang along with an imaginary Bowie, remembering his deep voice and the saxophone on songs like "The Prettiest Star." I sang like a soprano, snapping my fingers as if the two of us were creating a vinyl harmony. Then I crawled into bed and waited for sleep.

CHAPTER THIRTY-ONE

No Panic in Detroit

At exactly 3:10 a.m. on the dot, my eyes opened. I don't know why, but it's been like that since my dad died.

I left my room barricaded and squeezed out the window. I was so sore from surfing the night before. It hurt to bend or lean forward. Even when I arched my back, my neck tensed up.

But I didn't let it stop me. I definitely had the jitters, but I was ready to try again. I had to get back on my board. It was like what the cowboys on the Big Island say about riding a horse: when you get bucked, you have to get right back on.

I slipped in and out of Mrs. Kinski's backyard without making a sound—hair up, hat on, with my wet suit and board tucked under my arm.

The waves sounded bigger tonight. I walked out until the water reached my chest, then paddled slowly. Once I got past the white water, I hoped that I could calm down. *Paddle, paddle, paddle,* I told myself as crashing waves replaced cricket sounds. But it was grueling. My arms felt like they were going to fall off.

I was determined not to get stuffed—pushed under by a wave. I don't know if it was luck or skill, but I made it past the break. I lay flat, arms stretched forward, gripping the tip of the board until my knuckles went white. Waiting, wondering if I really belonged out here. My dad used to say there were lots of ways to surf. You could be on your belly or your knees. But I knew I had to stand to make it real. Not in a wide-legged survival stance, but smooth and silky. I wanted to surf like Jerry Richmond.

I tried to catch the shoulder of the wave but chickened out. The next one had to be at least four feet high. I caught it, but didn't pop up. I let it glide me to shore, doing a full-on belly ride through the foam balls. How pathetic. Still, I refused to let anything stop me.

I inhaled loudly and exhaled deeply, pointing my board back into the surf. The current was changing and moving. I extended my arms to make long, stretched-out strokes, and paddled as hard as I could.

As I cleared the break, I could almost hear my father's voice saying, "Attagirl." That's when I realized I was inside his unmarked tomb. The ocean was his coffin, and I was floating in it alone.

Thousands of people had been lost at sea. The dead outnumbered me. It was as if I could see ghost gods scattered out in the clouds. I felt winded and creeped out until I got my dad's smiley face back in my head.

From my vantage point, I could see the bluffs. I tried to line myself up to the left of Mrs. Kinski's window, but my vision was blurring from the sting of salt water. I had a good feel for State on land, but being out in the ocean was a different thing altogether.

I smelled something extra fishy. *Of course you do*, I told myself. *You're in the ocean, for crying out loud. Concentrate!* I sat back on my board. I had to stay sharp. Waiting was the hardest part.

I kept my eyes peeled as something swirled upward in the ocean. I flinched. It bobbed up again. *Sharks don't bob like that*, I reminded myself. I had no idea what it was, but it left me feeling suspended between heaven and hell. I had to handle my panic, so I sang to myself, "No Panic in Detroit," rewriting Bowie's song.

Waves are shadows at night. You can't really see them, but you can feel them. When I saw a shadow coming, I paddled as hard as I could, popped up, then lost my balance and wiped out. I didn't like swimming in the ocean with something else out there. But I found my board fast and went for it again.

When I sat up, exhausted, I realized Mrs. Kinski's house wasn't where it should have been, and neither was I. The riptide had me. My instincts were wrong, like every other bozo's: I wanted to go against the tide. The pull was relentless where I was, and if I didn't catch the next wave, I'd be halfway to Catalina in a few minutes—sucked out for good, and no one in the world would know what had happened to me.

Though I was getting really tired, I knew I couldn't drown while I was holding onto my board, so I started paddling diagonally toward shore, as hard as I could. I heard somebody scream before I realized it was me.

Then I heard a second voice on the wind. "Are you okay?" A guy stood on the bluffs, waving his arms over his head.

What is he doing up there? I thought. *I must look like a bumbling idiot. How long has he been watching?*

There was no way I was going to get rescued. I had to get myself out of the rip. I held on to the sides of my board for dear life, resting my head to the side and making sure I didn't swallow any water.

When my dad was a beach boy he found a dead lady. She had been eating lunch at the Royal Hawaiian in the rich people's dining room, and she choked to death on a tiny shrimp. The story goes: she swallowed wrong and excused herself from the table. Maybe she was on her way to the bathroom, but she didn't make it. When my dad told me the story, I had asked, "Why didn't she get someone to help her?" He guessed she was too embarrassed to ask. And he told me to never be ashamed to ask for help. Since I didn't want to be like that dead fancy lady, I sat back on my board and swung myself into position, never looking back. I could feel it behind and underneath me: water surging. I caught the wave and popped to my feet.

I stayed low in a crouch; with my knees bent, I almost got tubed. I had my balance and managed to build up speed and keep it. The wave would tell me what to do next.

That's when I understood: I needed to take what Nāmaka gave me and go with the flow.

I didn't try to carve back or do anything special. I just floated and faded in closer to the curl. Then the magic ride ended. I hit a flat spot and glided all the way to the shore. I felt like I was floating on air—until I fell on my face, thanks to wobbly legs.

I rolled in the sand. I had done it. It was like I was waking up from a deep sleep, and every light in the world had turned back on. I fell to my knees and bowed, thanking Nāmaka for blessing me with a wave.

The guy from the bluffs came trotting down the beach. Clumps of sand were lodged my ears so deeply that I could barely hear him at first. He set his board at my feet and said, "You're awesome." He pointed up and said, "I heard singing. I thought there were mermaids. Then when you yelled, I thought you were in trouble, but you were cranking."

Unbelievable. It was Jerry. He had no idea it was me. I adjusted the baseball hat low to cover my face, and I slumped a bit as he began waxing his board, moonlight dappling his shoulders.

He continued, "You can surf, man. I never had the balls to go out at night."

As he introduced himself, he fixed his eyes on mine. I smiled, which I do when I'm nervous. Nothing could disguise the space between my teeth or the color of my eyes. Jerry jerked his head forward. His eyes almost fell out of his skull. "Nani! What are you—suiciding?" If I hadn't been holding my board, I would have slapped him.

"How do I go from a guy who could surf to a girl suiciding in one second?"

Jerry was visibly mortified. I stepped back, carefully, into the water.

"It's going off," I told him.

He looked at me like I was from another planet. "I've heard rumors about girls who surf, but I've never seen one."

"Well, now you have. Can I use some of that?" I pointed to Jerry's wax. He gingerly placed it into my hand, still looking at me in this weird way. There was no sand or anything in his wax, and it smelled like coconut and mango.

"Keep it," he said. "You've got a lot of bald spots." He pushed his hair back. "That looks like Lopez's board."

"It's identical," I told him.

He touched the board with great reverence, and a smirk spread across his face. This was the second time my world had split open when a guy smiled at me. It was the same as Nigel McBride last summer—but this time, with Jerry Richmond, it was even better. I waxed my board, knowing it would be a brave new world surfing on something that didn't feel like a Slip 'N Slide. "Follow me." Jerry Richmond led the way.

"You're heading into the rip," I warned him.

"Exactly," he said.

After just barely surviving the rip, the idea of jumping back into it did not appeal to me. But I knew to trust Jerry. He moved confidently, steering himself into the rough water, which instantly pulled us out. I didn't even have to paddle. My fear fell away as I followed him right out of the rip.

He paddled up next to me. "See? That way you don't wear yourself out. You need to hold on to your strength."

That was an understatement.

As we waited for a set, I asked him, "What were you doing on the bluffs?"

"I was thinking about Rox." He looked away and slapped the water. "You know, you shouldn't surf out here alone. How long have you been doing these night sessions?" he asked.

I knew I could either make it *pono* and tell him the truth, or start another web of lies. I chose to tell him everything— right down to how my dad bought the board for me before he died. When I was done, Jerry Richmond was looking at me differently. There was genuine respect in his eyes, and I could tell he understood.

I didn't even see the set coming, but Jerry turned his board and effortlessly dropped into a wave. I watched him sail away. He was more than a surfer; he was a promise of good things to come. And next time I would be right behind him. In the water, a girl is just like a guy and has to earn respect. The playing field was leveled, and I liked it.

Jerry was watching my every move, just to make sure his eyes hadn't played tricks on him when he saw me surf.

"Come on! These are just ankle busters." Jerry was paddling out toward the looming shadows.

What he saw as little waves were huge to me. Maybe because in Hawaii we measure a wave from the back, and on the mainland they measure from the front. Regardless, I had to follow him. I turned in on the shoulder of a wave that was about to break. I was committed. I dropped in and held my balance. Once again, I didn't think; it just happened. Energy jetted out the tips of my fingers, and my hands felt like wings as I stretched my arms out as far as they could go. Putting my weight on my back heel, I cut deep into the wave. It felt like I had just been saved—as in: saved by Jesus, saved by Pele, saved from falling off the edge of a once-flat world. I knew what I wanted: I wanted to be fluid. Far from the brittle, solid, Earthly Nani. I looked over at Jerry, who raised two fingers to his forehead as if giving me a little salute. He couldn't see the singe of heat rushing into my cheeks. I felt a thrill of finally being seen for who I really was: a surfer. Not a girl or a boy, not *Funny Kine*, gay or straight, white or brown. Out here I could just be myself.

CHAPTER THIRTY-TWO

The Oscars

Jerry and I waited for waves. It had been quiet for about a half hour. I traced the patterns of stars in the sky. Mars actually looked red. It must have been closer to the earth. Venus shimmered and twinkled so much it looked like it was changing colors. The glassy reflection that mirrored the moonlight on the water seemed to come from inside the ocean, rather than from the sky.

As I sat on my board, I told Jerry the story about waves, and how Dad said they are the last breath the ocean takes as she travels into shallow waters. It's as if their final desire is to reach up to the sky before the weight of eternity forces them to disintegrate on the sand.

Jerry responding by telling me that each wave has its own vibe. Like girls, some are sharp and serious, others loose and playful. We floated side-by-side, weightless, bumping into each other every now and then as we kept watch.

I had lost that feeling of dread until something swished, and the water crested over. It looked like something skimmed the surface just a few feet from us. It was the same unusual shape I'd seen before, and whatever it was, it was getting closer. I pulled my feet on top of my board and told Jerry, "Try not to freak out but—"

He didn't let me finish my sentence. "Yeah, I can smell them," he said. "It's the Oscars."

He pointed in the direction of two small heads poking out from a thick bed of kelp. One was wiping his face with flipper-like paws. The other was peeking out with just his nose above the water.

"Oh, '*ilio-holo-i-ka-uaua*!" I said, relieved.

"What does that mean? Seals?" Jerry said.

"No, it means 'dog that runs in rough water.'" I splashed him.

"They're the real locals," he said. "Want to meet them?"

The last time someone asked me if I wanted to meet the strange local creatures of State Beach, it was Mary Jo talking about Rox and Claire. I hadn't thought about them or Windy or the lineup for hours. The similarities between the Oscars and Rox and Claire made me laugh. They were all unapproachable and yet totally inviting, cute and lovable, but biters if you got too close.

"Here they come." At first I thought Jerry meant more seals, but then I saw him paddle forward as fast as he could and align himself to catch a wave.

I followed into the set. I had to maintain my grip and dig in. There was no way I was going to let him get this one without me. Paddle, paddle, paddle. *Please, wave,* was all I had time to think before it lifted me. I felt strong and popped up faster than I ever had.

Jerry looped gracefully into the wave and tucked low, sailing past me so close I could have reached out and touched him as he glided by. As he crouched down, I did the same, locked in right behind him—until both of us got closed out. The wave just collapsed, and we fell into it. Underwater we each held tight to our boards to keep them from hitting the other.

As Jerry paddled back out he said, "You rip."

I felt heavy chains break apart, and I was free. With Jerry, I knew all the answers.

I dipped my hand into the next wave. It was a full-on overhead. Inside the churning ocean again, I didn't think. There was a sudden peace and quiet. Then everything shattered into water pounding all around me, until my speed picked up and thrust me into the sparkling foam. I could almost imagine the lineup in front of me, on their feet, cheering, as I walked off the tip of my board onto land again.

I felt a giddy sense of euphoria swishing down my back as I paddled out again, meeting Jerry as he moved at a breathless pace to the takeoff zone. He would only take the best waves, so we waited. He reached for my board and pulled me close, both of us sitting with our legs spread.

"I didn't know it was so sexy surfing with a girl," he said. Jerry Richmond was strong and secure; he did not fear a girl invading his ocean. He seemed to actually like being out here with me.

The current drifted us closer and closer. We could talk without shouting over the break. I told him about Jean smashing up my room and destroying my turntable. I cringed as I thought about it again. "No music," I told him.

"That's the worst," he said.

Then in one gentle move, he took off my cap and put it on backward. My hair fell past my waist. He watched the tips float in the water, while he put his hand around the back of my neck and dipped his lips into mine. I liked the taste of ocean on his tongue. And when the kiss became more intense, I felt like I was part of a new solar system, filled with planets to be discovered, surrounded by liquid, in the presence of the gods.

A swell lifted our boards. We pulled apart. I took back my cap.

"We can never do that again," I said.

Jerry kissed me and said, "Okay. But Rox and I aren't good. We haven't even done it since the time that got her pregnant."

I was relieved. That meant he couldn't have the—you know—the clap thing. Regardless of whatever mind-bending conversation we were starting, when we felt another swell lift our boards, we turned and paddled out.

In the water, just like on land, Jerry Richmond was like love potion—only more intense. I wasn't sure I could keep my distance now that he had touched me.

CHAPTER THIRTY-THREE

☾

Genesis of a Secret

Rox held one secret.

Jerry held the other.

And I held them both.

I'd never noticed what gravity felt like before. I walked with Jerry through the squishy sand as if there was nothing to it. We were so blissed out that, as we passed hundreds of seagulls huddled together, they didn't seem to mind us.

In the showers, Jerry held my board as I hosed off. I knew he was looking at me—the way I untucked my hair from the cap and rinsed it under the water, then unzipped Nigel's wet suit and let the shower jet down the two tiny triangles of my bikini top that were exactly where they should be. No girl could recover her status if her boob sticks out of her bathing suit. He was watching me so closely; I couldn't dig the sand out of my butt. That would have to wait until I toweled off alone.

Of course I returned the favor and held his board, but I made a point to look another direction. I already had an idea of how good he looked; seeing more could be hazardous to my *Funny Kine* self.

When we got to the van, Jerry opened the door and said, "Ladies first." I figured I had made it clear that I could handle opening my own doors, but I kept my mouth zipped as I climbed in the back to change. For the first time in hours, I was alone.

When I came out changed, fresh and nice, the sun was up, the air was warm. The VPMs didn't see my wet suit top or my board hanging in the racks. But they *did* see me tying up my shirt and zipping up my shorts. I tilted my head down and let my hair fall over my face as I muttered, "Oh great."

Jerry was oblivious—again. He was on his usual happy high from surfing, but I could sense the impression all this was creating. Jerry at Nani's? Nani getting dressed in the back of the van? Nigel gone? It was a disaster, and from the look on Lord Ricky's ugly mug, one that was only going to get worse.

He went all singsong-y and he said, "Jerry and Nani, sitting in a tree. K-I-S-S-I-N-G. B-U-S-T-E-D."

"You stink like the Oscars," I told him.

Lord Ricky went ballistic, kind of like he did last summer when I touched Mary Jo's brother's dog tags, not knowing why he wore them. "How do *you* know about the Oscars?"

Jerry came to my rescue. "I told her, man."

"That's not chick stuff, Richmond." Lord Ricky hocked a big loogie and swung his board a little too close to me as he charged toward the water.

Jerry gave me the stink eye.

"I know, I know," I said. "I'm sorry."

He took my arm and pulled me aside, again sparking unwelcome attention from the VPMs.

"Nani, what happens in the water can never, ever be talked about when you're on land."

I nodded. I totally got it. It was just like the unspoken rules the SOS had on the beach. Except this was a rule *guys* lived by.

Jerry continued, "And I want you to keep your board in the van. It's safer."

"But what if I want to surf when you're not around?"

"If they found out, it could end really bad for you—and me," Jerry said.

It had never occurred to me that I was putting Jerry at risk by surfing with him, but if he were to lose the trust of the guys he surfed with, they wouldn't watch his back anymore, and that would make it very dangerous for him, too. So I agreed, as long as he promised to meet me again tonight.

CHAPTER THIRTY-FOUR

(

The Bet

For the rest of the week, I barely heard the lineup and recruits talking. The only thing that made me feel good was the ocean, so I concentrated on it. I was clear-eyed and in flow with the universe when I was in the water. Once, everything was the ocean. Most people don't know this, but all of us come from the sea. I had to be in Nāmaka's world.

The lineup sunbathed like topless girls on a yacht. We had that much attitude. They checked their ring tans and admired that they were getting darker. I was doing just the opposite, wearing sunscreen and making sure I didn't get too dark. Regardless, we were looking good. Our towels lined up evenly, starting with Ms. ERA, then Julie, Jenni, Lisa, me, Baby, and Mary Jo.

The Topangas were trying to get Glenn's attention. They still didn't know about the No Girl rule in *Tubed*. It amused us to watch them try, again and again, to get Glenn to take their picture.

The whole lineup was smoking—except me and Baby. Every five minutes somebody lit up. But I hadn't stolen, bummed, or snuck a single cigarette. I wasn't worrying about finding some guy to buy me a pack of Larks in the morning. And falling asleep next to my abalone ashtray was much nicer when it wasn't full to the brim with old butts. The stink that had once made Nigel call me his little smokestack was leaving me for good—along with the constant craving for more.

The VPMs had the break to themselves for the entire week. The wind picked up in the late afternoon, and it looked radical out there. I felt a camaraderie with the guys, now that I'd be out there. I studied how they dug in super strong, took off deep and steep, and never rag-dolled. I knew I couldn't sit among them in the takeoff zone, but I was gaining a lot more understanding of what they were doing out there. That's all I really wanted to think about—surfing.

The lineup didn't talk about the rumors they heard about me and Jerry, but I knew they were saying stuff behind my back. Lord Ricky told everyone at Roy's—I mean Patrick's—about me coming out of the back of the van. The VPMs told Lisa and Jenni, and the way it spread from there was pretty easy to figure out. Everyone was getting way too interested in my private business. That's why it kind of annoyed me when Jenni asked, "Are you really going to drive Nigel's van, now that he's gone for good?"

Her point was: girls don't drive that kind of car. They were supposed to be in convertibles, or VWs. That was another stupid rule I was going to break.

I was tired of taking Jenni and Lisa's sass. "You make it sound like Nigel's dead," I told her.

"He may as well be," Shawn said, appearing out of nowhere with his board.

I looked at his sad face and guessed that Nigel really did denounce all his earthly ties—including his family. That must have made Shawn feel pretty alone. I knew what that was like. Shawn's eyes were the same blue as Nigel's, but his had become hardened by the constant awareness that half of him was absent.

"Hey," was all that needed to be said.

"Hi, Nani."

Baby, Julie, and even Ms. ERA looked like they were going to swallow their tongues. They had never seen a McBride in the flesh. His beauty had somehow grown over the summer. There was a little hair on his chest, and his shoulders were broader. Even his voice was deeper. I wondered if Nigel's body was doing the same thing as he baked bread for the poor.

Jerry stood by Shawn's side, wearing drawstring trunks, untied, hanging low, which revealed a treasure trail bleached from sun and salt. He balanced on one leg, held his surfboard with one arm, and stretched his quads with the other.

Everyone looked away uncomfortably as he tried to get my attention by making funny faces. Lisa broke the awkward silence by shyly asking Shawn, "When does Claire get back?"

"Few days. She's spending some extra time in Paris." Shawn didn't sound too excited. He also had a hickey on his neck— so, obviously, he wasn't as lonely as one might think.

I refused to look Jerry in the eye with so many people watching us. But it was like this: if someone tells you not to think about sugar, all you think about is sugar. And Jerry was sugar to me. One big piece of candy I wanted to bite into but couldn't. I didn't want to be like Rox, a *Funny Kine* who does it with boys, so I was putting myself on a Jerry Richmond diet.

When I tuned back in to the lineup, Julie was saying that her parents had just signed divorce papers. Her mother was calling herself a divorcée now. She said, "My dad found somebody else. That's how come we ended up in LA."

Baby turned to me. "Do you mind if I ask what happened to *your* dad?" she asked with concern. Everybody moved in a little closer.

I guessed it was time to start telling the truth. Letting the lineup in. At least about some things. I slowly rolled up until I sat tall.

"He had a heart attack. He pretty much died in front of me."

I was surprised when Julie came and sat on my towel and slipped her hand into mine. Not like, *Let's get together.* But like she cared. The tough ones are always the sweetest.

We all sat in silence, listening to State: radios playing, waves, and seagulls.

"Do you get homesick, like I do?" Julie asked. "I miss the Ventura Pier, the penny arcade, and the kiddie merry-go-round. All the little stores with wind chimes, stained glass, and tiny, freaky animals made out of driftwood and shells."

"You know what I miss?" I said. "Flowers. Oahu has its own sweet scent." I told them about the smell of white pikake and jasmine. "We used to make leis out of plumerias," I said, but I didn't tell them that plumerias are also the flowers planted in graveyards. "I love the plants that come in clusters of trumpet shapes and cling to walls and twist into vines. Sort of like morning glories on the mainland. Then there's anthuriums that look like hearts with yellow beaks."

Baby laughed. She thought that was so funny.

"They're red," I continued. "Shiny and waxy. There's also this flower called heliconia. It's pink, and it's nicknamed the Lobster Claw. And then, of course, there are birds-of-paradise." Julie said, "We have birds-of-paradise at my house. You can come visit them anytime."

That kind of nice cracked me open. Julie, Baby, and Ms. ERA were just the combination I needed. They balanced and sheltered me from the wild card, Mary Jo, and they neutralized Lisa and Jenni.

A feather flew past me. The breeze picked it up and made it float slowly enough for me to catch it. This was a sign, I knew it—an omen meant to remind me that there was something gentle inside me. Calmer seas. Call it hope. There was a place I had forgotten to tap into. That's when I realized: I had been so caught up in Nigel, Rox, Jerry, and my mom's drinking, that I hadn't been to my dream chamber in days. The place inside me where I felt things had disappeared. But thinking about flowers and making new friends unlocked that place in my mind.

Out of nowhere, Melanie Clearwater stood over me, blocking the sun. She dropped her hand into my face and opened it, gesturing.

"Can I have it back?" she asked, pointing to the feather I was tickling my leg with. "Nicole gave it to me."

"How do we know it's yours?" Lisa demanded.

Melanie put her hands on her back and arched it forward. "Who else's would it be?" she asked.

"A bird's?" Baby asked innocently.

That sent a titillating ripple through the lineup, who were blocking their eyes from the reflection off Melanie's sparkly, gold, see-through shirt.

"Taking this sun virgin thing a bit far, aren't you?" Lisa said, annoyed.

Melanie was waiting. Staring at me. She was serious, and I worried that the long-overdue turf war between the SOS and Topangas was about to happen. Luckily, since the beach was crowded and Glenn was snapping away at waves for *Tubed*, it would have to be a low-key battle. No raised voices or fists.

In her most Zen, cool-girl voice, barely moving her lips, Melanie said, "I'd just like my feather, please." She was so pissed she was twitching.

I was about to hand it to her, but Mary Jo stood up and snatched it away from me. "You're too nice, Nani." Mary Jo was at her best during a conflict. She needed trouble every day, like the regular world needs vitamins. Chaos was the only way she kept herself taped together.

Suddenly I *got* Mary Jo. The riddle was solved. She was a person like me, whose world had been torn apart—doors knocked down, windows blown to smithereens. Like mine, her life was about trying to avoid getting cut on shards of glass. The more we tried to get the broken stuff out, the worse it got. Mary Jo and I knew what it was like to have wounds no Band-Aid could keep from splitting open. Joyce called it grief.

I got it. Mary Jo *had* to use. She was stuck in a world without her brother. She had the same pain as I did. It lived in her every day. Every day she woke up with only one goal: to forget Ray and the fact that he had been blown to bits in a stupid war. Forget that, like my dad, Ray was gone without a goodbye.

"Hold this." Mary Jo handed the feather to Lisa and dragged Melanie back to her towel—which, by the way, was almost touching the SOS's. They talked quietly.

Mary Jo was acting as our liaison. That made me nervous. But as I watched her, I felt my prison doors open. In my mind's eye, I saw myself walking away from the ball and chain I let other people attach to me.

Mary Jo gathered the Topangas in a circle. They peeked at us over their shoulders with plastic grins. As she talked, they nodded.

Melanie Clearwater looked happy again. Her voice had a sinister twang to it as she said, "Deal," and drank from Mary Jo's thermos, passing it around. Downwind, the brew smelled like rum.

Then the most amazing thing happened. The Topangas moved their towels ten feet back, to their usual spot.

"How did you do that?" Lisa asked as Mary Jo strolled back to the lineup.

Mary Jo sat down, pulled out a cigarette, and lit up. "Well . . . I made a bet with them. If they lose, they permanently—as in FOREVER—stay put."

"And if WE lose? Jenni asked.

"They get our spot," Mary Jo said.

"Shut up."

"What?"

Lisa and Jenni were talking at the same time.

"Don't worry, we're going to win." Mary Jo was tipsy again—to say the least.

"What's the bet?" I asked.

"Wendy Davenport joins the SOS." The whole lineup looked relieved. Mary Jo continued, "By August fourteenth. Baby's birthday."

I blinked. That was in exactly one week.

"So when do you think we'll meet Wendy Davenport?" Mary Jo continued. Everyone looked at me.

I wasn't going to tell any of them I had lost Windy's phone number and had no idea how to reach her. So I lied. "Soon."

"Better be sooner than soon." Lisa grimaced.

How would I find her? I didn't know if Windy was playing me, or just playing hard to get. When it came to Windy Davenport, I had more questions than answers.

CHAPTER THIRTY-FIVE

T. Rox

Over the next three days, I went through the yellow pages twice, calling every Davenport from Santa Monica to Malibu. Nothing. I tried spelling Davenport with an "i," too—just in case. I was desperate; I even called Davenport Pets in Culver City. But still no Windy.

At State, I acted like nothing was wrong. I sunbathed and I listened to the lineup preparing for Baby's birthday, which was coming up fast.

On top of all this, I didn't have money for the T. Rex concert later that night, so I had to make up one of my BS excuses. I could have used the twenty dollars Joyce gave me, but I needed to stock up on food for the rainy day I knew was coming. To cheer myself up, I headed to the fancy market in the Palisades. Jean was on a binge, and taking care of me wasn't exactly a priority.

Hughes Market was deserted. As I walked in, I saw on the front page of the *Times* that the Senate had subpoenaed Nixon's private tapes. He was so busted now. I was sick of Watergate this and Watergate that.

My stomach growled. I grabbed a rotisserie chicken. It smelled incredible. It was going to be my reward for being so mature and taking care of myself.

I wanted everything in that market. It all looked so amazing. But I got good stuff—you know, peaches without bruises, cheese without mold, and a dozen eggs.

I headed straight for the exotic canned foods: SpaghettiOs, artichoke hearts, olives, and, last but not least, shiitake mushrooms. Then soap and toothpaste. And finally, I went looking for my favorite cereals.

In front of my shopping cart full of treats was a pyramid of Cheerios boxes carefully stacked, corner-to-corner. Next to it was a tower of Frosted Flakes. And there, between them both . . . was Rox.

A surge of fear jolted through me. Rox looked different but the same. What were the odds that she would be standing in the middle of this section, inspecting her nails for chips?

Like any startled predator, she went right on the attack. "What are *you* doing here?" Her tone was sinister, and her eyes narrowed. Her stare made my short hairs stand on end. "Tell me about you and Jerry."

She was seething, and much too close for comfort. What was I going to tell her? That I kissed him? That we surfed together? That I loved Jerry's style and how he could come out of the barrel clean and untouched? That he knew how to read waves like a mystic and that sitting deep in the takeoff zone with him was as good as any trip to Fiji with her?

I fiddled with the tips of my hair.

She pointed her finger at me and said, "I trusted you."

Rox bore a striking resemblance to a dinosaur with her claws stretched out, mouth wide open, and her hair whipping around like a giant tail.

"Why are we acting like this?" I asked.

"There is no more 'we.'" Rox tore open a box of Frosted Flakes and poured the contents on my head. I was going to stop this before it turned into an atomic bomb dropping on both of us. I pushed the box out of her hands.

A manager lady came rushing over. "Are you girls all right?"

I covered my face. The cereal stuck in my hair. I don't know why I even left my house. Rox shape-shifted into a sticky sweet girl—like the kind of candy that makes you gag, it's so full of sugar. "My friend just got really hungry," she said.

"Well you're going to have to pay for that," the manager scolded.

I handed the box to Rox and said, "Oh, yeah, she will." As I ran toward the door, I saw tons of ice cream in Rox's cart. Not one quart but five.

"Breaking your fast?" I asked, hurrying away, leaving my rewards and any hope of a friendship behind.

CHAPTER THIRTY-SIX

The Red Queen

In the parking lot, I put my hands on my knees and dropped my head further down. I felt sick to my stomach. What a god-awful mess.

Now I saw Rox as the Red Queen. Just like the Red Queen with Alice, she outranked me and would forever be someone to avoid. Because no matter what I did, she always had the advantage.

What happened in the market was like a game of chess—the only good thing I ever got from slimy Uncle Mike. How to play it, that is. He would always say, "You're only as good as who you remove. Get rid of your opponent fast as you can, and never get captured." Well, Rox was my opponent now. Our pact was so over.

If I wanted to be a Queen, a ruler, someday, I had better start acting like one. Like I said, soldiers used to say, "Get tough, cream puff," or "Suck it up." Not like Don Ho's audiences suck up drinks, but like a warrior. Despite everything we had done and said and promised, Rox and I had nothing in common anymore.

I was not going to give up my position on the board. There would be no more sacrifices in this girl game. I was not going to protect the Red Queen ever again. I looked at the scar on my arm and picked off what was left of my scab.

I felt dizzy as Rox walked around the corner into the parking lot. She stood in front of me, slowly lighting a cigarette then tossing the still-lit match at my feet. I shivered when she said, "Everybody has put two and two together." I wondered if she meant about us. I felt a pit in my stomach.

Then there was *maluhia*—silence—and everything went slow. Rox had gone into Obliterator Mode. She was taking aim—like in Vietnam. Soldiers said the *maluhia* just before an ambush was the most terrifying part of battle. It meant the Vietcong were coming up through tiny tunnels to drag soldiers down by their boots into a hell no religion could prepare you for.

I saw nothing but hatred in her eyes. I was taking my love back, and there was nothing she could do about it. I felt a volcanic rage that almost brought me to the point of tears. But there was no way I'd ever spill a tear over her again.

I feared if I didn't do something, I would get stuck right here—in a parking lot of heartache with a lump in my throat. I turned to walk away.

Rox raised her voice, "You screwed Jerry, didn't you?"

"Do you really think I'd do that?" She'd never come to her senses.

She just went off. Rox *had* to be right, even when she was wrong. "You're a liar, a cheat, and a two-timing bitch."

I was glad to finally tell her off. "If *I'm* a two-timing bitch, and you two-timed on Jerry with me, Scotty, AND a fellow Sister of Sand before me, that makes you—what?"

Rox didn't answer. So I answered for her, "That makes you a four-timing bitch."

"Only guys count. Which means you don't count for anything." An Obliterator like Rox could make cruelty so deliberate, it was an art form.

I felt like she'd slapped me. Her fury was inexhaustible. Even though I deserved some of it, I didn't deserve it all. Rox sank her teeth into me with one unholy word after another. It was as if her mouth was synced up with someone else's mind— or maybe this was the real her. I wanted to cover my ears and sing loudly. But it was Rox. So I couldn't.

"We don't use words that start with *c* and end with *t*," I yelled.

"How many times do I have to tell you? There. Is. No. We." Her cheeks were blotchy red with the anger of an Obliterator coming in for the final kill. "I'm going to tell everybody about you," she said.

This time I knew she was talking about girl love. I felt shattered. And then—set free. Because I had the same dirt on her. She couldn't hurt me. I matched her fire with fire as I told her, "Then I'm going to tell everybody about *you!*"

I froze her without saying another word, and I circled round with a polar freeze. I gave her the stink eye the way she had given it to so many others. Like a sailboat in a windless sea, she waited before me, motionless. She would not meet my eyes. Her sizzle and sense of self-importance were suddenly gone.

"We're *pau*," I said.

"Speak English."

"Why? I'm not American."

Rox held up her middle finger in my face, and then with a fast jerk of her hand, she ripped the dolphin necklace off and threw it as far as she could. She turned and stormed away.

She really was the Red Queen, and she had lost. That's how it works in chess when everything you did to screw up somebody else ends up screwing you.

As I looked down at my arm, at the scar I'd carry forever, I noticed her cigarette smoldering on the cement, like one last memento. I wanted to pick it up and touch my lips to where hers had been. Instead, I dug the heel of my sandal into it and rubbed side to side until *it* was obliterated—not me.

III

August 5–August 14, 1973

Red Moon

NEVER GIVE UP.

CHAPTER THIRTY-SEVEN

Little Lightning Bolts

Jerry cancelled our surf session. We were planning on hitting State after he got back from the concert, but like I figured, Rox didn't waste any time before officially getting back together with him. She probably went right to State from the market, so everyone would see that she and Jerry were a happy couple again. It freaked me out to think of them together; now they both had a secret about me, and I wondered if they would tell. The question was, who were they more loyal to: me, or each other?

I absorbed every mean word Rox had said the way a sponge soaks up dirty water. My lower back had stiffened up, and my face felt like my skin was breaking out. I had survived a sneak attack—nothing like they have in Vietnam, but something more personal.

At 3:10 a.m., I did the only thing I could do: I retreated into the ocean. I needed to clear my mind of how much I despised Rox. Jerry stood me up–and I knew, somehow, that she was behind it. Surfing would make me whole again. It would rekindle my faith in myself and the universe. It would heal me.

I liked the dark water now. It forced me to be more focused and determined. The break at State had become really shallow; if I fell, I'd have to be careful not to crack my neck. As I walked out, floating my board to my side, I bowed under a little two-footer and let Rox wash away. I emerged baptized and cleansed. I imagined that all her hatred had gotten caught in the rip and was lost forever at sea.

I gave thanks to my protectors: Nāmaka, Mahina, and the stars. I could see they would not leave or change their direction because they are immortal—not man or woman, dad or mom. In the stillness of the water, they always returned, and I knew they forgave me and loved me just the way I was.

The ocean was pierced by dim moonlight and a white mist that lay beyond the break. Real Sweethearts is what I called the small waves I walked out into. There is a holy silence in the ocean when each wave moves delicately and barely breaks when it reaches the shore.

I sang "Lady Stardust" to myself, just loud enough so the Oscars could hear. I knew now they were State Beach's 'aumakua, spirit protectors. My song drew them so close to my board, I could have touched their noses. I knew better, but still, I reached my hand out.

A flash from the beach, like an angry spirit or ghost, surprised me, and then there was another one—like little lightning bolts. The Oscars dipped away. I lay low on my board and paddled quietly.

Everything was blurry. I wasn't sure if it was a car in trouble on the highway, or maybe fireworks. And then something ran across the beach. There was another flash and a beam of light, this time from the lifeguard station, and that's when I knew for sure: it wasn't a ghost; someone was there watching me. I'd been spotted.

If they were going to murder me for surfing, at least I would die on a wave.

I saw the shadow of water coming. It lifted me up. I dropped into the little squeezer and just tucked myself right in, crouching without ever standing. The dark water blocked the moon and made a curtain of ocean moving around me. For a second I felt safe, totally tubed. I shot out of the curl. It was unreal. I couldn't believe I was surfing, just like Gerry Lopez. Then there was another flash. It put an end to my flow, but I still rode the wave till I could walk off my board and onto the sand. Freedom and victory reigned.

It was the greatest moment of surfing I'd ever experienced.

"Hey! You!"

There was no time to celebrate. It was Glenn from *Tubed* snapping away. I recognized his English accent before I saw his face. My baseball cap fell off as I ran to the far side of State, and I didn't dare stop to pick it up.

"What's your name?" Glenn yelled.

I held my knotted hair tightly to one side so he couldn't see, and bent my head way down. Since I'd been jogging all summer, it was easy to outrun him, jam up the stairs, and hide in Mrs. Kinski's yard until the dogs stopped barking and the birds began to sing.

CHAPTER THIRTY-EIGHT

☾

Initiation I: The Rules

I had one day left to find Windy. Lisa and Jenni were not happy. No one was. Except Melanie Clearwater.

The morning after the big T. Rex concert, everyone was wearing their tour shirts, eating watermelon slices, and talking about how amazing Marc Bolan was. I wasn't sorry I didn't go because everyone was also gossiping about the blowout Rox and Jerry had.

The VPMs were goofing off, doing somersaults and cartwheels, and seeing who could do the longest handstand. Baby was picking her back tooth. She dug her hand almost all the way into her mouth, saying, "I forgot to floss. I don't want Lisa and Jenni to see any food in my teeth again."

I gave her a look. That kind of behavior would make it easy for Rox and Claire to give her a thumbs-down. Lisa glared at Baby and crossed her arms. "Do something," she told me. "You're the babysitter. You explain." Lisa made it clear that, as the leader, she couldn't be bothered. She and Jenni headed down to the water, where they strolled along the shoreline, watched Coco and Johnny surf, and flirted with every poor, unsuspecting guy in their wake.

And so, it was up to me to pass The Rules down to Baby. In the course of two summers, I had gone from the bottom to the top, like cream rising.

"Am I in trouble?" she asked.

This was an opportunity to give her *my* version of The Rules, not Annie's, and not Rox's and Claire's. By then I had really thought them through, and this would be the one time I'd say them out loud. The part I liked most was that it gave me a chance to help Baby be the best she could be.

I waited until Julie, Ms. ERA, and Mary Jo had joined Lisa and Jenni down by the water. I could tell from their looks they were *really* worried about the Topangas situation. The time was almost up.

I sat down beside Baby and looked right into her eyes. "This is mega important," I told her. "Here's how it goes. We live by a set of rules that are never written down or spoken about, and I'm going to tell you some of them now. Listen very carefully because you won't hear them again."

1. **We are not chatterboxes. We don't gossip or talk about other people unless it's one-on-one, and you're in an enclosed environment.**
2. **Whenever you talk, make your words count. We don't say every little thing we think.**
3. **Never talk in the stalls or go into a bathroom alone.**

Then, I added a rule just for Baby:

4. **Never pick your teeth again.**

Jean once told me something that remained so true I made it a rule:

5. **You can only make a first impression once, so make it count.**

Then I went back to my own rules:

6. **Stay in tune with the rhythms of the ocean, and you'll find your own.**
7. **We're organic, glowy, shimmery girls.**

"What does that mean?" Baby asked.

"Well, for example," I explained, "we all have beauty secrets. Mine is a little ritual that goes like this: Beauty Secret #1: Right after I shower I take some baby oil that has lavender in it, put it on a loofah, and give myself a brisk scrub to get rid of the old tan and make room for the new. Never use shea butter or that lemony citronella stuff. That's Rox's smell. Mine is Fireballs and primrose." I didn't tell her what was really amazing: that ever since I stopped smoking, people could actually notice what I called Eau de Nani. I continued:

8. **Carry extra money.**

Baby looked confused. "In case your date is a cheapo," I explained, "and so you can always make your own choices."

Then there were my die-hard rules:

9. Locals rule.
10. Keep your hair long; it has special power.

That brought me to Beauty Secret #2: "To brush long hair, use a wide comb and always start at the top, holding the center of your hair tight, to get rid of all tangles." Then I gave her the secret to super-shiny hair: "Rinse with vinegar and add a little fresh-squeezed lemon to enhance highlights."

Baby asked, "How come you don't have any pimples?"

"Pimples are a state of mind," I told her. "But when in doubt, there's Beauty Secret #3: Once a month I take an avocado and honey and make a beauty mask. Sometimes I get plain yogurt and mix it into the avocado and honey. If I want it to stick really firmly, I whip up some egg whites, add a dash of almond oil, put it all over my face, and lie still in the sun for forty-five minutes. It's messy. And to get my skin super clean, I add Vitamin E and fresh ginger juice, but not too much. It stings." I couldn't imagine Baby being more beautiful than she was today. She'd never need a facial. But I wasn't going to be the one to tell her. I didn't want her head to swell before initiation. I clapped my hands together to keep her attention, then continued.

11. Always have a bathing suit with you.

(That one was worth repeating.)

**12. No sex until a guy is one hundred percent
     your boyfriend. And you only get ONE
     throughout high school, so choose well.**

Baby asked, "Did you do it with Nigel?"

Finally, an opportunity to tell the truth. I was relieved to get to say, "No. Just because I had a boyfriend didn't mean I *had* to do it with him. I'm not rushing."

Baby laughed. "I thought you said I'm not Russian."

"Didn't you hear anything I said? Listen, if you're gonna be Little Miss Sassy, you'll get eaten alive at the initiation. Another thing: You have to wait for the higher-ups to talk to you. Think of it like crossing a dangerous street. You have to stop, look, and listen. Promise me you will?"

"Promise."

Baby swatted at a bee. I watched, mortified, as it landed upside down next to me. Then to make matters worse, she poured sand over it and threw a rock on top.

"Don't be a bee killer," I demanded. "Mana lives in everything! Who are you to take it away? Everything has a spirit."

I dug the poor little bee out and sent it on its way.

She looked like she was going to cry. Lessons like these aren't easy, but they're the kind you never forget. My dad had taught me about life's energy after I intentionally stepped on a spider, and I had felt as bad as Baby did right then.

She was such a clean slate, like a younger version of myself. I put my arm around her and comforted her. That's when I added some new rules:

13. Don't lie. Unless it's the little white kind that you tell so you won't hurt someone's feelings.

"What's the difference?" Baby asked.

"One is Watergate lying, and the other is when you tell a girl you really like her lip gloss but you really hate it. Okay," I continued, "here's the most important rules:"

14. **Think for yourself and dream big.**
15. **Never swear.**
16. **Start trends, don't follow them.**
17. **We don't toot our own horns.**
18. **We don't fight—and that way we never lose.**
19. **We support each other.**

Baby put her head on my shoulder. "I love you, Nani," she said. "And I hope you find Windy, so we can stay friends."

I tried not to think too much about what she had just said, and I smoothed her hair the way Annie used to smooth mine. "I saved the biggest rule for last." I explained what a Honey Girl is: magical, strong, and kind. I told her the rule that goes with that:

20. **We never call ourselves Honey Girls. It's an honor given to us by others.**

We sat there silently for a few minutes as Baby traced a heart in the sand. Then we heard drums banging in the distance. Everyone at State looked down toward the Jetty to see the Hare Krishnas jumping in a frenzy, singing as they splashed their way through the shallow water.

The Topangas danced to the shoreline, tossing sand on our towels. "Looks like we're going to win," Melanie said, sticking out her tongue. I was totally screwed, and it was Windy's fault.

Who cared about the Krishnas? Why did they all have bald heads, white dots painted between their eyebrows, and sing the same words over and over again?

Hare Krishna,
Hare Krishna,
Hare Krishna.

Bob pushed into the crowd with his life preserver, trying to get the Krishnas off State for good. Everyone cracked up when he tripped and landed in the water. From behind me, I heard someone say, "Lord Ricky's laughing so hard. It looks like he's gonna fall off his board."

I turned to see who was talking. It was Claire! I ran into her arms, then instantly apologized for getting beach oils all over her.

But what made me almost scream and tweak my neck was seeing Rox, standing next to her, smiling at me, a towel wrapped low around her waist. My knee-jerk reaction was to run, but Rox tightly locked her arm into mine and gave me a hard little kiss that singed my cheek.

I knew her air of friendliness was BS. Just beneath the thinnest layer of skin was a massive plane of hot, molten lava, ready to erupt.

CHAPTER THIRTY-NINE

Initiation II: The Royal Eight

Rox was here to judge the recruits. I had to hold my breath and count to ten, fighting off the desire to start the battle right where we'd left it. But instead, I just sort of looked at her and thought, *Oh, I see.* She would never expose the grisly falling-out we had had. As far as Rox was concerned, when it came to the lineup, everything had to look status quo.

Claire seemed more centered, not in a hurry. She was truly enjoying State, watching it as if it was a circus she went to as a kid that had just come back to town.

"I've missed this place," she said.

Out of the corner of my eye, I saw Jerry and Shawn intensely throwing a Frisbee back and forth. It gave me the feeling that neither of them was too happy about having their girlfriends back.

Jenni and Lisa ran out of the water, leapt into the air, and yelled, "Claire!" at the same time. They ran over to us and respectfully kissed Claire on her cheek. Rox, on the other hand, didn't touch anyone. She just sashayed around, acting all slick, and bumped her hip into Claire's when she wanted her to sit down. The rhythm was off between them, but no one else seemed to notice.

Claire showed Lisa and Jenni her hand-painted Monet slippers and how to kiss on both cheeks when you say hello. "That's how they do it in Paris," she told us. We do that in Hawaii, too, but I let Claire think it was a French thing.

When Mary Jo stood up to greet her and get *her* kiss, Claire gave her a dirty look. "What are *you* doing here?" she asked. I loved Claire's ruthless honesty.

"I'm back."

Rox put her hand into Mary Jo's. I almost gagged. She said, "Mary Jo is going to rule with Nani after Lisa and Jenni go."

"What?!" Claire and I exclaimed together.

I stood up so I could get right in Rox's face. "You said I would choose my Number Two."

"That was then, and this is now. Right, Claire?"

This kind of nasty standoff made the entire lineup slink back to their towels. No one took my side.

Claire was not about to react; it wasn't her style. "Whatever, Rox," she said.

She sat in her usual place: dead center in the lineup. Rox began drilling Lisa and Jenni about the newbies, as if Baby, Julie, and Ms. ERA weren't even there. Claire gave Ms. ERA a long, piercing stare. *Oh no,* I thought. *Here it comes.*

"Aren't you Ellie Katz?" she asked her.

Ellie nodded. "Yeah, a.k.a. Ms. ERA."

"You look a lot different in a bikini. Good."

Uncharacteristically, Claire rolled over onto her stomach and motioned for me to do the same. "Looks like Ellie is going to be your Rox replacement. Her body is actually better. Nice call."

She paused. "Speaking of Rox, I'm sorry. She's so out of control."

Claire whispered in my ear, "Is it true about you and Jerry?"

"No!" I told her.

"Oh, good. He's a prick."

She lit up a cigarette and offered me one. I wanted it so bad, I could almost taste it. I could just about feel the heat rushing down the back of my throat then out of my mouth into a long, wonderful stream of smoke. All I had to do was reach out and take it.

I had never said no to anything when it came to Claire. But there's a first time for everything. It wasn't easy, but when I had done it I was glad.

Claire talked about France nonstop for half an hour. It was so much fun to watch Rox have to sit there and pretend she cared. Claire told the lineup about Versailles, the way French women walk in high heels on cobblestones, and what it was like to sit in a café on the Champs-Élysées. She sounded proud when she told us, "I saw paintings by Matisse, Monet, and Manet."

Baby asked, "Do all French artists have M names?"

Lisa said, "Yeah, like that Mozart guy in Malibu."

Jenni laughed.

"Stop." I looked at Baby and said, "They're just pulling your leg." Then, before anyone could say anything about the bet, I changed the subject. "How was the Eiffel Tower?" I asked.

Claire reminded us that it was once the tallest building in the world.

Jenni said, "Isn't it a piece of art?"

Lisa answered, "No, it's a building. Because it has restaurants in it. Right?"

Claire nodded, stunned that the lineup was having a conversation about Paris without her help.

Ms. ERA mumbled to me, "Actually, it's a monument that was built for the 1889 World's Fair."

Then Claire started speaking French. Rox rolled her eyes. Of course, she was wearing her usual lemony citronella and shea butter, and really dark Jackie O glasses that dipped down her nose and left a mark when she finally lifted them up to say, "Must we hear about France all day?"

"*Oui, oui,*" I told her.

"*Parlez-vous français?*" Claire said to the group. Rox lit up and turned away.

I said, "*Quelle heure est-il?*"

Claire looked at her dainty watch and said, "Two o'clock." She didn't really know much French, and though her consonants were very good, she didn't pronounce her vowels sharply enough, which made it hard to understand what she was saying.

Claire looked over at Ms. ERA. She seemed to be studying her, and I could see that something had changed in her eyes.

"I went to Auschwitz," she said, which caught Ellie a bit off guard. Ellie shook her head and raised her eyebrows in total disbelief. Maybe that was the difference. Claire had witnessed that awful place where Jews were taken by Nazis to die. I guess it really affected her, and that's why she was trying not to be horrible to someone who was Jewish.

"Where's this Wendy Davenport?" Rox enjoyed my stunned look. "Missing?" she asked me.

"How do you know about Wendy?"

"Oh, I filled her in," Mary Jo slurred.

I ignored Rox and looked at Mary Jo. "She's still out of town," I lied.

Rox turned to me and said, "You better produce Wendy Davenport ASAP."

"Don't worry. She will. Won't you?" Claire said.

"Absolutely," I said to Claire, refusing to look Rox in the eyes.

"Besides, we have to have a royal eight," Claire reminded her.

It was obvious to me that Rox didn't want the new lineup to be as good as it was when she ruled, but, of course, that isn't what she said. "It *has* to be eight. That's right," she said. Then she looked at me again and sneered, "Why do you think we picked *you* up so quick last summer?" With that one sentence, I felt the hammer come down on what was left of my pride.

She had dismissed every other reason why she had anointed me into the SOS. They had needed me. That was it. Eight was a number linked to balance. Spiders have eight legs; octopuses have eight tentacles. Some people think the number eight is lucky. I wasn't so sure about that anymore.

When the no surf flag went up, Rox and Claire stood and fluffed their hair. It was time for the initiation swim.

"Are we going for a dip?" the innocent Baby asked.

"We don't dip," Rox said indignantly.

"We swim," Claire continued, leading the way. They were not amused. But I was. I loved that Baby. And I wanted her to survive, so I got her attention and sealed my lips with an imaginary zipper, telling her to stop talking.

Rox ceremoniously walked to the water and intercepted the Frisbee Jerry and Shawn were tossing. She made a point of flaunting her ownership of Jerry by touching his ass, kissing him full on the lips, and making him hold her hand for all of State—and me—to see. After another long kiss, Rox flicked the Frisbee back to Shawn. The lineup looked at me as they played.

"You guys better get going," I told them, refusing to dignify their nervous looks with more of a response. Anyway, Jerry would be on an airplane headed for my home, Oahu. I watched as the SOS hopefuls walked into the water. I wasn't worried about Baby or Julie. They were great swimmers, and would have no trouble getting to the fifty-foot buoy. But I'd never seen Ms. ERA go past the break.

And what about the riptide?

Rox went into the water and put her arms around Julie and Ms. ERA. Then she looked back as Jerry walked right by me. I could see by the way his feet dug into the sand that he was bummed out, but he didn't say a word.

I wanted to comfort him, but if I did, Rox would stir up all that ugliness again. I would not let her lure me into another fight. I saw her as a rattlesnake, and that meant she could not hurt me if I didn't try to touch her. Why reach out to a poisonous creature who didn't speak my language? Annie Iopa was right last summer when she told me, "That girl's got no *aloha*," and to watch out. What a drag that I didn't listen to her.

Mary Jo moved her towel close to mine, excited to discuss our future.

She checked her tan by spreading her toes wide and laughed, putting her head on my shoulder as she had seen Baby do.

I felt my whole body stiffen at her touch. "Let's not go there just yet," I said as I shrank back, never taking my eyes off the horizon and the almost-Sisters of Sand as they swam out. I was seething. Not only because Mary Jo was acting all cozy, but also because of Rox and the bet.

"Aren't you upset, seeing Rox and Jerry together?" Mary Jo asked, a cigarette hanging out of her mouth.

I scrunched my face up. "No."

Mary Jo continued, "Okay. But here's what I recommend: if anyone accuses you of having sex with your best friend's boyfriend again . . . just lie. I lied. And, look, we're best friends!"

"Are you telling me you slept with Nigel?"

Mary Jo laughed really hard. "No! I wish!" She laughed harder. "I just squirted in my bikini."

I glared at her. I was getting really good at freezing people.

"Oh, Nani. I'm sorry I put the acid in your drink last summer."

I gave her another long, hard look and counted to ten before I exhaled. How was I going to rule with this nut job?

She continued, "But I promise I'll never do it again. Now, just find that Wendy Davenport." I wanted to punch her in the face. But that wouldn't set a very good example for Baby, when I just told her we don't fight. I had to follow my own rules. I couldn't believe when she went on. "Speaking confidentially, I told Lisa and Jenni I didn't dose you so we could all get past it and be friends again. And now we are. So just lie."

"I don't have to lie," I told her. "Nothing happened."

"Okay," she said, drawing the word out like she didn't believe me. "I'm going up to the liquor store. Do you want a Fresca?"

I looked at her like, *You have got to be kidding.*

She laughed again and waved me off. "Don't worry. I won't pop the top." She was cracking herself up as she walked away.

CHAPTER FORTY

Initiation III: The Ins and Outs

Rox and Claire would have kept the initiates swimming for hours if Bob hadn't hoisted the surf flag. The swell was picking up, and the VPMs, Shawn, and creepy Lord Ricky were going out for Jerry's last afternoon. More photographers were at State than ever, but Glenn held the primo spot with his tripod. Although he was done with the *Tubed* article, he was sticking around.

The SOS ran out of the water and back to where I was sitting. They readjusted their towels in the direction of the sun, trying not to drip water all over me.

When the strained, pointless small talk began, I got nervous. Nobody knew what to say. Everybody was joking around about shaving their legs, eating potato chips, their favorite TV shows, and talking on the phone at night, while Rox slammed a new box of Marlboro Reds loudly into the palm of her hand.

Claire shifted and whispered, "Here she goes." I prepared myself for the worst.

First, Rox pointed at Baby, whose little face went bright pink. In a harsh tone she said, "You are too young to be in the lineup . . . but you don't look it. IN."

Then she took aim at Julie Saratoga, who lit a Sherman, trying to be chill. Rox stood over her. "I like the way you suck in your stomach muscles. And it's chill how you sit in a lotus position—even though I don't think you know you are. You've got that Rio de Janeiro 'Girl from Ipanema' tan. It's sexy. So . . . IN."

I didn't like the way Rox's eyes lingered on Julie's suit. I had a bad feeling she was thinking Fiji.

Rox pointed at Ms. ERA. Then, just to be mean, she went over to Bob's tower to ask him what time it was—even though Claire was still wearing her expensive waterproof watch. Rox liked making people suffer as they waited. When she came back, she acted like she had forgotten what was supposed to happen next. "You . . . were going to be a floater. But after you stripped off your top at the buoy and went belly up with those beauties like some *Playboy* foldout, you are definitely IN."

Ms. ERA said, "I think women should be able to go topless, just like men. Equality doesn't just happen in the office." She was trying to make a point, but it went right over Rox's head. "Gloria Steinem was a Playboy Bunny," Ms. ERA said to me, on the down-low.

"Really?" I asked softly, keeping my eyes on Rox.

"Yeah," she whispered. "She was a journalist, you know, and she went undercover and exposed the Playboy Club in New York for what it *really* was—a male chauvinist pig land."

Rox cleared her throat loudly to shut us up. "Do you mind?" She pointed at me, shook her head, and said, "Where's Wendy Davenport?"

The rest of the lineup turned their heads, but nobody dared say a word. They knew by now that Scorpios, like Rox, are brilliant at inflicting pain. Naturally, she looked like she was enjoying herself. Rox stood up, freezing me. She held up her pinky stiffly, bent it a couple times, and said, "Bye-bye. You don't belong here anymore. Unless you're sitting next to Wendy. Whoever the eff she is. Go get her."

That was Initiation Day in the old regime. It wouldn't be like this if I ever got in charge. Because, even though I was far from perfect, I would never let myself sink as low as Rox did. She was deliberately hurtful and humiliating. I packed up my stuff abruptly and looked to Lisa and Jenni for support. There was none. Julie, Baby, and Ms. ERA didn't know what to do.

Claire was the only one who didn't ignore me. But, nonetheless, I was surprised when she gave me a big hug goodbye. "Will you come visit me in Santa Barbara?" she asked. "UCSB is supposed to be a party."

"Of course," I said. Then she walked to the water to be with Shawn.

Even though I was getting thrown off the beach, not saying goodbye to a leader was a huge break in protocol. Of course, Rox made a big issue out of it. I had challenged her power in front of the group.

"Oh, don't be a boo-hoo, Nani," Rox said.

There was no time to grapple with my feelings. Enough was enough. I went right up to her and said, "Up yours."

Rox backed up. Before she could say anything, I told her, "You don't rule me anymore."

As I said it, a bee landed on the top of her head. Not where she could feel it or hear it. It was just sitting there. Rox let loose with yet another torrent of swear words, but I couldn't pay attention to the awful things she was saying because I was fixated on that bee gingerly trailing down her hair, closer and closer to her face. Rox was terrified of bees. I mean, when it came to bees, she was almost mental.

"There's a bee in your hair," I finally said.

"Oh," Rox laughed, "you think I'm going to fall for that?"

"Stand still," I commanded.

Rox looked at the lineup again and said, so the whole beach could hear, "First she lied about Jerry. Now she's lying about a bee in my hair. Because she knows that if I even heard a b—" She stopped mid-word. I could tell by the look on her face that the high-pitched buzzing sound was now close enough to her ear that she could hear it. She went hysterical, flailing her arms, which pissed the bee off and made it buzz louder and twist deeper into her hair.

When she frantically tried to swat at it, Baby grabbed her hand and said, "Don't be a bee killer. Mana lives in everything!"

Amazing! She had repeated exactly what I'd told her!

Between Rox trying to get the bee out of her hair and Baby trying to stop her from hurting the bee, I didn't know if I should laugh or cry, until Rox screamed at Baby, "Get away from me, you idiot."

Everyone on State stopped. Even Lōlō was startled by the disruption. I flicked the bee out of her hair and said, "Really?" Rox was standing there, furious, her hands by her sides, clenching her fists. She stepped back onto Lisa's towel, splattering sand everywhere. Poor Baby turned to me, unglued. "Don't listen to Rox," I told her. "She's a bitch. You did fine."

"I am a bitch?" Rox yelled. She was furious and completely off center. This never would have happened in the old days.

I stood protectively between her and Baby, but I wasn't done with Rox just yet. I wasn't going to let her ever obliterate anyone in the lineup again.

"She was only trying to help you. Say you're sorry," I commanded. The lineup watched me and Rox like a tennis match, concentrating on our every move until Rox shooed Lisa away and took over her towel, ignoring all of us.

I crossed my arms and turned to Lisa. "Why do you let her do that?" I insisted.

Lisa shrugged me off. "What? It's nothing. It doesn't matter."

"Yes, it does."

Jenni stepped in and took Baby by the hand, leading her away. "Don't make a big deal, Nani. Just go find Wendy."

I looked straight ahead and caught Baby's eyes. She buried her face in Jenni's shoulder and looked away. No matter how much I wanted to sink my teeth into Rox and tear her apart with my words, I couldn't. Not just for poor Baby's sake, but for mine. I was better than that. I dropped the tiny bee at Rox's feet and said, "She's dead, just like us." I flipped my hair in disgust and gave a swift kick to the sand as I walked past the gloating Topangas.

I was halfway up the beach when Mary Jo caught up to me. She took the cigarette out of her mouth, exhaling the smoke off to one side, and dropped it into the sand. "Do you want help looking for Wendy?"

You could have blown me over with one of Melanie Clearwater's feathers. I was shocked.

She continued, with the flash of white teeth, "I can't rule without you." Maybe it was because she wasn't stoned or drunk, but I believed her. Out of the whole lineup, wouldn't you know—it was Mary Jo who came to my rescue. "It's kind of my fault that this all happened," she said apologetically.

I consoled her with a quick hug. "Don't blame yourself. Rox has been pissed off at me all summer. Maybe State isn't my beach after all."

And that's when the idea got planted. I looked back at the shore. Rox was sitting alone. Jerry Richmond was surfing. Claire and Shawn were strolling by the water in their own little world, oblivious to everything going on. The lineup was already wading into the water. I could see the Sisters of Sand were taking care of each other. So what if I never returned? It wouldn't make a difference to them.

Finally, I really understood that nothing was going to change unless I changed first. I paused and stared at State one last time. Then I looked at Mary Jo and said, "Aloha." This time it meant goodbye. It felt right as I turned away and headed through the tunnel.

CHAPTER FORTY-ONE

The Weirdest Day Ever

When I got home, I put on my ratty Outrigger sweatshirt and baggy shorts, braided my hair into long pigtails, and locked myself in my room. I would have given anything for a turntable right then. Living with no music was hell.

I decided to rearrange everything to make it look less like a Fiji-girl den. I didn't want anything around me that reminded me of Rox. Now my room would be more like an apartment, the studio type where everything you need is in a single space. I pushed my bed against the farthest wall. As soon as I had enough money, I'd paint over this crystal-blue color with Swiss coffee white. It was more practical and grown-up.

Jean never got a bolt for her door, but I got one for mine. I used some of Joyce's twenty to keep myself safe and make sure my room was officially Mom-proof. There was no way she could get through my window. My closet was now going to be a pantry. It was dark enough to keep apples and bread fresh, and a good place to store peanut butter and jam after they were opened.

It was time to throw away my childhood. It was over, and I knew it. I put everything into a bag for charity—Liddle Kiddles, surf trolls with rainbow hair, and all my Hot Wheels. I kept my peace beads, my collection of Dr. Seuss books, and *Charlotte's Web*. And, of course, I kept Mrs. Beasley, the doll from my favorite TV show, *Family Affair*. Mrs. Beasley was never leaving my side. As for the trinkets I collected with Rox—the starfish we found together on our long morning walks before dawn patrol and the tower of blue-green sea glass—I would return them to the sea. I put my lava lamp in my Barbie suitcase and stuck it in the giveaway bag. I also emptied the basket of driftwood. Each stick told a story that no longer mattered to me.

While I was at it, I went through two big boxes of stuff: old muumuus, toys, and some spin art I made when I was six. I threw them all into the charity bag, along with some old training bras, flower stickers I had never used, and my clackers—hard-as-a-rock toys that were like poi balls but made of solid Lucite. I tore my Lucky Locket dolls off their necklaces and tucked them into the knitted slippers Jean had made for my eighth birthday.

Someone else could make use of this trash. I didn't need it anymore.

After fixing my room, I decided to say goodbye to the lineup the proper way and make a lei for Baby's birthday. I picked all the double camellias off one of Jean's shrubs. The trick was to do it after the sunset, so the flowers would be moist in the morning.

I pierced a long needle through the base of each one. Instead of using thread, I used dental floss, like I was taught to do in Hawaii. I strung it through their thick cores, pulling gently out of the petals, just like sewing. I checked for bugs as I went along, twisting each flower around in the palm of my hand until they all faced the same direction. I liked these mainland flowers; they looked like carnations with big, round heads. I alternated bright pink, soft pink, bright pink. The finished lei wasn't as fancy as the white ginger blossom ones that have winding patterns, but it would definitely do.

I wrapped it in newspaper to keep it fresh, sprinkling a little water on the inside, then tucking it way back in the refrigerator before Jean got home from work. She was doing night shifts again. We barely saw each other, which was fine with me.

Since my bookshelves were just about empty, before I put *Rubyfruit Jungle* in my new library, I sat down to read it. It was the last of the three books the vanished Windy had left me in the sand.

Reading it was like opening a jar of candies. It had lesbian sex a-go-go. It blew my mind, and I could hardly believe what the author bio said about Rita Mae Brown. It said, in print, that she was gay! What happens to people who say they're gay? Don't they get in trouble? I guess not if you're Rita Mae Brown. She was my new secret hero for life. I couldn't stop thinking about her and her main character, Molly Bolt. It made me nervous to even write their names down, but I did, over and over, until the back page of the book turned black. I must have read the whole book in less than two hours and, ironically, I placed it next to Nigel's highlighted Bible, which was another favorite keepsake.

I wondered if there was a hidden reason Windy gave me *that* book. Maybe she was trying to tell me something. Was she sending me a message? What if the book spoke for her in some way she couldn't? The thought almost curled my hair. I didn't realize I was pacing back and forth. I had to find her. It was not just about being in the lineup. This had gotten personal.

I rode my bike around the Palisades. I went to the Bay Pharmacy, the taco buffet restaurant where everybody hung out, and finally to Pali. I stayed until the gym closed at nine, but there was no sign of her. I had to suck it up and go home.

When I got back to 33 Sage, there was Jerry—half in, half out of my window, his butt crack peeking out of his shorts as his lower half dangled below the sill. I was tempted to tease him and tickle his feet or something, but instead I just said, really loudly, "Jerry!" He banged his head as he dropped out of the window.

"Hey, Nani. I was just, uh . . . my top hat fell off in there." He grinned kind of sheepishly, and held up a pink envelope that looked like it contained a Hallmark card—the kind you give for Mother's Day, with lots of flowers and sparkles. "I wrote you a note."

I had to ask. "First Nigel, and now you. What is it with you guys and notes?"

He went red in the face. He didn't have an answer. But I did: guys wrote notes because they're a lot worse at communicating than girls. So I helped him out. "Would you like to talk about what's in that note, Jer?" His mouth hung open. I asked, "Are you becoming a priest?"

He laughed. He was so cute with his baby-blue corduroy pants and unbuttoned *Aloha* shirt. He looked one hundred percent native. He was ready for Hawaii.

"Let's go to Fong Wong," I said, "and get some takeout."

"Excellent," he said.

Once we had gotten our little boxes of food, we went to Temescal, the jock beach. We'd never run into anyone we knew there. We sat in the van talking about tomorrow. The sky looked like a black box full of stars.

"What time are you leaving?" I asked.

"Solomon, Annie, and little Jimmy are picking me up at six a.m."

"I bet you'll be on the cover of *Tubed*."

"Aw, you think?"

"Definitely."

"Yeah, I'm kind of bummed I won't be here when it comes out, but . . ." He didn't finish the thought. Instead, he pretended his chopstick was a sword, and we went into a duel. Noodles and bean curd sauce went everywhere, and chili oil splashed on the dashboard.

When we were done with our little food fight, I opened the envelope to read what Jerry had written.

Dear Nani,
     I wish I'd gone for you when Nigel went all priest. I should have dumped Rox and made you my girlfriend. I will be bummed out the rest of my life about it. I don't know why I even got back with Rox, but when we broke up forever today, she told me about that other guy.

I've been a dork. I will always love you, Nani, and I love surfing with Dodger. He's totally extreme. Be careful.

Peace Love Dove
Jerry

"I want to give you something," he said, and he cleared a path into the back of the van. There was sand and junk everywhere. When I saw what a pigsty it was, I started thinking about how I'd give it a good cleaning tomorrow after he left, when it would officially be mine. Maybe I'd even move into it.

"Earth to Nani," Jerry said. We sat on Nigel's thin mattress and ducked under our boards. He pushed a large box toward me. It was covered in newspaper and had tape everywhere, with a floppy, gold bow falling off to the side.

"I'm not a good wrapper," he said.

To say I was stunned would have been an understatement. I was blown away, blown over, blown back. No guy had ever given me a big box of anything before.

"Open it," Jerry coaxed. I didn't know where to start, so I just pulled every which way, like a little kid.

It was a brand-new stereo with speakers, radio, and a turntable!

"Are you crazy? This must have cost beaucoup bucks."

"I guess, uh . . . I don't need another surfboard," Jerry said sheepishly.

That was off the hook. Unreal. What a sweetie. I kissed his cheek. Now I had something to plug in to again. Music and

Bowie singing. I could dream of him all day long: Bowie dressed in his red Kansai Yamamoto jumpsuit, with a pirate patch over his eye and the coolest stiletto boots, singing just to me for hours. And then I'd listen to T. Rex to honor Jerry Richmond.

"Thank you so much." I went to kiss him on the cheek again, but he turned his mouth into mine.

I pulled away as he said, "No, remember? Rox and I broke up! Over that Scotty guy. He can't even surf. What a poser."

"Are you bummed?" I asked.

He kissed me again. "Not really."

Then he tenderly unbraided my hair, put his fingers through it like a comb, and pulled it down to my side. "I'm in love with your hair," he said. He buried his face in it and slid me around to give me a bona fide make-out kiss. I wanted to tell him I was a virgin, but instead I said I was a Virgo, which basically means the same thing. I also told him my lucky day of the week is Wednesday, my favorite color is blue, and I love sapphires. He told me he already knew all that. Our lips parted wider and wider as our kisses became deeper and harder.

He lifted my arms up, and I let him pull my sweatshirt over my head. He looked down at my shorts. We gazed at each other for a long moment.

"Listen," I said, "you have to use a rubber. And I can't ever be your girlfriend."

He nodded vigorously and curved himself around me like a vine growing too fast. His pelvis pushed into mine, moving my whole body forward while the weight of the world lifted.

He tickled my earlobe and nipped the top of my shoulders before he kissed his way down to my chest. I had read *The Happy Hooker,* and she said that when you're with a guy, if both of your hands weren't holding something, doing something, or moving something, it wouldn't feel good for him. But the fact that this was going to feel good for me was a total surprise. Maybe it was working out because I was thinking about girls while feeling Jerry.

He slipped his hands around the back of my legs and positioned me like some weird yogi. I let him tilt me back, and just like that, we fit perfectly. I thought it would be more hazardous or painful, but it wasn't. Every nerve ending in my body connected with Jerry. He was like a chunk of marble, rock solid—everywhere. I think just looking at him naked would have been enough to keep me busy, but as I gave myself over to him we went way, way, WAY past that.

Sex with a guy was just like being caught in a riptide. You had to go with the flow.

When it was over, and I was lying in Jerry's arms, listening to his heart pound, my mind started churning. I couldn't help but imagine the future. I closed my eyes and wondered what it would be like to live forever with Jerry Richmond on Oahu, just past the Gold Coast under Diamond Head, having kids, getting old, and surfing side by side at Tonggs. The only problem with this picture was . . . Jerry Richmond.

Jerry was great, but I was ready to take him home, since the van was now mine. This was nothing like going to Fiji. I was definitely still in Santa Monica.

Finally, I could stop lying to myself. I *had* to be with girls. Even if they broke my heart. When he got his boards out, I said goodbye to Jerry for good. I told him, "Don't forget, *aloha* isn't a shirt. It's who you are. Now, go surf some big waves for me."

He had such a strange look on his face. I hoped he wouldn't say it, but he did. "I love you, Nani."

I didn't say it back.

CHAPTER FORTY-TWO

(

A.M. Horror

I dreaded opening my eyes. Today the Topangas were going to take our spot, and the SOS would have to look at the back of their heads and endure the stink of patchouli for the rest of their lives. I pulled myself from my sheets and threw Mrs. Beasley against the wall. Jean was home from her night shift. I could smell the pot drifting from her bedroom and hear the TV blasting. I knew she didn't care whether I was coming or going anymore, which was fine by me.

I put on my final-day-at-State outfit: my smallest bikini, my feel-good poncho, my three-inch shorts worn down low, and my Levi pocket purse, which I slung over one shoulder. My bangs were grown out. I could finally tuck them behind my ear. Hallelujah. I dabbed primrose behind my ears and twisted the boa around my neck.

Jerry's top hat was right where he'd dropped it last night. I put it on to max out my glam surf. If I was saying goodbye for good, I'd make sure State never forgot me.

I tossed my Don Ho wraparound shades into my pocket, along with some Fireballs, so my breath would be fresh when

I said goodbye to the lineup. Since Jean was home, I snuck out the window and went around to the kitchen to get Baby's lei. When I opened the fridge, I realized how starving I was. I drank some milk from the carton and sucked down stale Cheerios until my stomach felt full.

There wasn't one clean dish, piece of silverware, or glass in the whole place, and something sticky covered the floor. I wished I had put on my flip-flops before coming into Jean's side of the house. Nixon was still on the front page of every newspaper lying around, and the stories were the same old shit. Why wasn't he getting thrown out?

But I sure wasn't going to let a messed-up government—or mom for that matter—ruin my day. Screw them. I wouldn't be a sucker anymore and believe that these guys were going to make it *pono*. In fact, I'd believe in the government again when Nixon surfed.

I giggled to myself, which gave me an inner blast of hope. Oddly enough, after Jerry, I felt more intact. No, it was beyond that: I felt more like myself. Knowing I wasn't going to do it with him—or with any other guy—again had told me for sure who I was, and I felt like I was solid for the first time all summer. Maybe even for the first time ever. I grabbed Baby's lei, and before I slammed the fridge, I heard footsteps behind me.

I turned to find a furry, little man in boxer shorts. I screamed. My dad always said if a guy's a freak I should kick him in his *kahunas* and run, so I slammed my foot between his legs. Why hadn't I done this when Lord Ricky and his hunters grabbed me? Then I hauled to Jean's room to warn her.

"Call the police!" I yelled. Jean was as drunk as a skunk, and she looked more stoned than I had ever seen her before, holding on to the wall outside her room, wearing a faded kimono.

She yelled at me, "It's Willieeeee!" I grabbed her arm and tried to pull her back into the bedroom, but instead I fell against the door with all her weight on me. Jean was so drunk, I couldn't move her. To make things worse, she started laughing. But her glass of vodka never spilled.

"Don't you remember Willie?" she asked, pulling a feather out of her mouth. "You met him at St. John's when Rox was . . . you know . . ." she joked, making air quotes, "'. . . sick.'" Her eyelids drooped. Then she totally closed them.

"Snap out of it!" I said, pushing her away. "What are you talking about?" I kind of remembered Willie as the orderly from St. John's—the guy with the broom and bedpans.

He peeked around the corner, clearly still in pain. "We were celebrating your mom's review," he squeaked in a strained voice, still holding his *kahunas*.

Jean reached out, placed her hands on my head, then put all of her enormous weight on me as she stood. She offered to help me up, but I pushed her hand aside.

"I got a Satisfactory," she said, swaying her hips back and forth like some tourist doing a bad hula, as she danced over to Willie.

"Barely," Willie chuckled. They acted like a Satisfactory was some great achievement. Was Jean screwing up at work? Or worse—getting drunk there? Were things going to get even worse?

"Why is he in his underwear?" I asked.

That made her laugh harder. "Why?" she said coyly to Willie. They laughed until they were almost peeing.

That's when I figured out the answer. "No!" I said. Jean had told me she would never have a boyfriend. Dad was her always and forever—the only one. She and Willie looked at each other all lovey-dovey. It laid me to waste.

"Mom, get up," I ordered.

"Blah, blah, blah. Nag, nag, nag," she said, slurring her words. "What's wrong with you? And why are you dressed like that?"

Willie looked at my outfit and laughed. "It's Halloween!"

I turned in disgust. Out of the corner of my eye, I saw Jean fall into Willie's lap. "Hey, I could use another 'lei,'" Willie said, looking at Jean and wiggling his eyebrows.

I stormed out of the house, slamming the door behind me. Small birds fluttered from the roof to the overgrown bougainvillea shrubs. I peered up at the sky and cursed the morning sun.

I threw Baby's lei, which was miraculously still in one piece, into the bike basket and rode up and down the winding curves of Amalfi Drive, not stopping until sweat dripped down my back and I was standing in front of my father's *puuhonua*, his sanctuary, and the place I lost his ashes. I hadn't planned to end up here. It's just where his bike took me. I pushed the top hat further down onto my head, so the hot wind wouldn't blow it off. The Santa Anas were back.

My eyes wandered over the canal. Water was flowing out to State. Not a trickle, but more like a current in the Anahulu River. It was making the most beautiful sound. I loved it. Hearing it allowed me to settle back into myself, as if my feet had sprouted roots to hold me down and make me strong.

The Santa Anas came every year. How could the wind be so predictable, and my life be so out of control?

I whispered, "Hi, Dad. Mom has a boyfriend."

I cleared my throat and looked around. Even though I was alone, I spoke in a whisper, "You know, Dad, I like girls. One hundred percent. Like I said, I'm a *Funny Kine.*" I think deep down I was hoping my dad would see me as special, like his ancestors, who thought *Funny Kines* and *Māhūs* were spirit people with a purpose.

For a while, I just stood there watching the ducks and hummingbirds in the shimmering water. It was painful being here, but not the same as it was before.

"Grief changes," Joyce had said.

I made myself laugh when I thought about Jerry and Rox last summer, standing exactly where I was standing, kissing, and tearing me apart. The way I had felt that day had given way to a completely different reality. A year ago I would have never believed I'd lose my virginity to Jerry Richmond and like *him* better than I liked Rox.

As I sang my dad's favorite song, a melody about Hawaii, I heard a small, soft voice joining mine. I peered over the bridge. Lōlō was lying on a piece of cardboard, hair knotted in his face. That weird dog of his was still wearing my rabbit's foot around its neck. It dangled like a crucifix. I looked at Lōlō; he seemed like a lost child. I kept singing until he rolled onto his side, closed his eyes, and clutched his empty bottle of wine. My secrets were safe with him.

CHAPTER FORTY-THREE

（

Legend

I was back in flow, riding my bike to State. I stopped for a moment to watch a rainbow kite flying, untethered, through the sky. I pledged my allegiance to it. In Hawaii, rainbows are a symbol of new beginnings, forgiveness, and enlightenment. They are blessings. It was a blessing that I knew who I was. I also knew who Jean was. Who Rox was. Jerry. Nigel. All of us were finally wearing our true colors.

And I could have all the secrets in the world as long as I knew my own truth. I was beyond Rox's grip. The black feathers of my boa blew behind my arms like wings of a great warrior.

At the corner of PCH and Chautauqua, I glanced across the street. My heart stopped. There was Windy, hitching up the coast.

I yelled her name, but she couldn't hear me with so many cars speeding by. I rode as fast as I could, putting all my weight on one pedal as I zoomed closer. I was so happy to see her, I just jumped off and let the bike drop.

"Are you nuts? Hitching alone?" I said.

"I'm having a bad day, Nani," Windy lashed out.

I acknowledged what she'd said with a nod and cautiously approached her. Windy stood her ground.

I pulled her thumb down. "What's wrong? Where's Pete?"

"Gone. And my Nurse Ratched of a mother is making me see a shrink."

"Why?" I asked.

"How do I know you can keep a secret?" Windy said.

"Besides the fact that I'm loyal beyond reason?" I was so nervous I was twirling the tips of my hair. I steadied myself. I had to convince her. "I want to be your friend, and I think you want to be mine."

Windy turned away, as if dust had blown into her eyes. I knew secrets were not easy to say aloud, so I stood still as I waited for her to say something.

"I know you've probably heard the rumors about me," she said.

"Don't worry," I reassured her. "Nobody believes them."

"Well, you should. Because they're true. Now my mom says she'll send me to a mental institution in Camarillo if I don't see a shrink. Up there they give people like me lobotomies and hysterectomies." There was a tinge of fear in her face. "It runs in my family. Adam has it, too."

"What do you mean?" I asked.

"I mean that Pete is *his* boyfriend. Not mine."

"Oh," I said, trying not to sound too happy. This was the best news I'd heard in my entire life. "I totally get it. Really, Windy, everything will be okay."

Why didn't I tell her I was that way, too? What was I waiting for? Now was the time. I was trying to work up the courage, but instead I just looked at her.

Windy glared at me. "That's easy for you to say." She turned away, then looked back and said, "And I'm not going to say another word to you unless you really mean it."

"I do. Absolutely." I took my shades off and looked her right in the eyes. "I think *Rubyfruit Jungle* is the most amazing book I've ever read. If I could be anybody, I'd be Rita Mae Brown. I *love* Rita Mae Brown."

Windy understood. Right then and there, we established a code—without even trying. A look of relief spread across her face gradually and to such an extent that it made me want to hug her. But I didn't.

"I had a feeling you'd like that book. I've been so worried about what you'd think."

"Is that why you've been avoiding me?"

Windy looked down.

"You don't have to worry about anything with me. I'm—like—you," I told her. We both just stared at each other. I wanted to tell her everything, but there was no time to waste.

"Tell me another secret," she said. She was stoked.

"Only if you come with me to State."

"I don't have a towel."

"That's okay. You can share mine."

Her whole face lit up. We walked along without saying a word. With Windy, the sky was bluer and the air felt cooler, even though it was almost noon. I didn't want to look like I was panicking, but time was of the essence. I knew that, any minute, the Topangas would take over. But before we went through the tunnel, I stopped Windy and said, "I have to tell you something." I was afraid I'd lose her again, but I wasn't going to deceive Windy. Telling the truth was a risk I was willing to take.

I told her about Mary Jo's bet and how she was in it. She listened intently. Turns out, Windy Davenport's most favorite thing in the world was winning. It was her religion. And this was just another competition she could ace. She instantly liked the idea of being in the number one spot and blowing away the Topangas.

"Just explain to me what makes this spot so special, so I'll know."

"Well, State has three main areas: the volleyball courts, the gay side—" I paused when I saw a hopeful expression come over her face. "It's just men," I said. "I have no idea where the women go . . . and there's the locals' area, which we dominate. Our spot is like the top of a pyramid. It's where everyone wants to be. It has mana—you know, energy. It is the sweet spot, the vortex, and no one sits in front of us. We're the only ones the surfers can see from the takeoff zone."

As we went through the tunnel, I told her my greatest secret. "I surf."

She looked stunned. Even in the half-light of the cement underpass, I could see she was impressed. "No way," she said.

"Really. I dress up as a boy and go out at night."

"That's one of the best secrets I've ever heard. But if I'm going to sit in that spot, you're going to have to prove it."

Just when I locked my bike up and got Baby's lei from the basket, Windy took her first steps onto State. It was like seeing a bird learn to fly. She just intuitively knew what to do. She strolled a bit slower and let her arms dangle gracefully at her sides, then she flicked her blond hair away from her face. Her sleek, oversized tank top made her a real stand out.

I hadn't realized we were the exact same height and that we both had long, narrow legs with strong calves and thin ankles. It's why we walked at the exact same gait—together but separate. We were a sight. Everyone was looking at us like they used to look at Rox and Claire.

"I think everybody likes your top hat and boa," Windy said. She had no clue how good-looking she was.

Thankfully Lord Ricky was out cold at his post, lying like a lump in what looked like a new backrest, so Windy got a free pass that first day. Oh, yeah, Lord Ricky was definitely dipping into his own stash of drugs. His bathrobe was strewn over his chest, and his red-tinted glasses sat cockeyed on his sunburned face. His jaw dropped low, and he snored so loudly, I felt confident placing a small shell on the tip of his nose. I encouraged Windy to put a shell on top of mine and told her, "When he's awake, stay away."

Then, so everyone walking by would see, I wrote in the sand around him: SCUM OF THE EARTH.

The VPMs had the waves all to themselves. I was so jealous. It looked really good out there: five-footers. But I couldn't think about surfing now. I had to take care of Windy. "This is scary," she said as she took my hand. I did not let go. "But," her voice lifted a bit, "I like the fact that so many people here read."

I hadn't noticed, but everyone—I mean *everyone*—sprinkled around State was staring at *Tubed* magazine. I had almost forgotten.

As we reached the volleyball courts, a page blew out of this old regular's hands. He stood up quickly. On the back of his legs were crisscross marks from his folding chair, creased deeply into his skin. "Hey! Grab that!" he yelled.

I slammed my foot down on the page, and Windy picked it up. There I was in a dazzling photograph. I mean, there was Dodger, totally in control, tubed under the moon. I stopped in my tracks, paused, and looked at her with a big smile on my face.

"I *told* you I surf," I said.

"What?! Is that you?"

I nodded, and we broke into a major case of the giggles.

"Shhh!" I said. I slammed my finger to my lips so fast, I stuck the tip of it up my nose. Windy and I cracked up even more. It felt so good to laugh with her, and so amazing to see myself in *Tubed*. So much for the No Girls rule!

The old fart put his Pall Mall back in his mouth. Windy creased her nose and pretended it itched to cover her face from the smoke as she handed the page back. "Thanks, ladies," he said. The rest of his copy of *Tubed* magazine was tucked under his arm.

"Can I borrow that?" I asked, trying not to grimace as he slid it through his armpit. I took it with my fingertips.

As we walked away, Windy waved her hand in front of her nose. "I hate the smell of smoke," she whispered.

"Me, too," I commiserated. I was so glad I didn't smoke anymore, or else I would have stunk. In the distance, I saw the lineup—and the Topangas starting to gather their stuff.

On the cover of *Tubed*, there I was again. Excitement jolted through me. It read "The Mystery Surfer of State Beach."

Windy said. "You're a legend!"

I flipped to the article about Dodger. These photographs were A-M-A-Z-I-N-G. But my favorite was the one of me with the Oscars. My baseball cap was pulled tight over my head, not revealing a single feature of my face.

I was safe.

"You're famous. No, infamous," Windy said, with a gleam in her blue eyes that made my knees buckle and sent goose bumps flashing up my tanned arms. And just like that—ZAP—girl love took hold of me again. Like it had happened with Rox, only better.

"Come on. We've got to go." I beckoned to Windy. The Topangas were moving their towels down. It was a matter of seconds before they'd be sitting side by side with the SOS.

Just as we took off, a volleyball came out of nowhere. I looked up and saw Rox standing in the courts. Windy gracefully dropped to one knee, picked the ball up, and gently spiked it back to her. A fake smile stretched across Rox's face.

I shook off her scalding glare and gave a little pinky wave, just like she gave me yesterday. She raised one eyebrow and clenched her teeth. She was never going to get her kicks off me again. Not with Windy Davenport standing next to me.

Windy and I wove our way through scattered towels. State looked different without Claire. She was probably halfway to UCSB by now, packed and gone for good. But still, we admired pretty surfers all around us. They were all mouthing the words as they read *Tubed*. As I passed them, I saw a tiny picture of Jerry under the spread about Dodger. I felt bad and good at the same time.

Melanie Clearwater was the first of the Topangas to see us. She did not look happy. I tried not to act smug as I said, "Melanie, say hi to Wendy."

"Hey, girl." Melanie said, disappointedly.

I plucked a feather from my boa and offered it to her. "No hard feelings?"

She stuck it into her braid with all the other feathers, put down her towel in her old spot, and settled back in. The rift between us didn't dissolve with my peace offering. I had just helped her save face, which she appreciated.

"That was about as friendly as a pre-game handshake," Windy observed as we sashayed forward, in full sight of the SOS.

For Baby's fourteenth birthday celebration, there were paper pinwheels blowing in the sand and orange balloons tied to the lineup's bikinis. Everyone had a fan or a parasol in cherry-blossom pink, the pretty-colored paper kind from Chinatown.

Windy gave a modest little wave and whispered, "What if they don't like me?"

I had to fight the impulse to hug her. Instead I gave her a quick hip bump to keep her moving. Baby pranced over to us in her new, pale tangerine bikini. I said hello to Lisa and Jenni without looking at them and pulled back, so they could barely air-kiss me hello.

"We knew you'd do it." Lisa beamed. They appreciated me, but their congratulations had nothing to do with an apology. Windy and I stood in front of the lineup. No one but me would ever call her Windy. She was one of those special Honey Girls who could look super sexy without a single accessory. And when she nonchalantly lifted her tank top over her head, she revealed a magnificent, hard body and showed why she was the high priestess of volleyball. A surge of excitement rippled through the lineup as they greeted her. Lisa and Jenni melted like candles over Windy's handmade coral-and-gray-marbled bikini, which stuck to her like a second skin.

While Lisa and Jenni welcomed Windy, Baby, Ms. ERA, and Julie flocked to my side. "We were turds yesterday," Julie admitted.

"Can you forgive us?" Ms. ERA asked. They embraced me, and I felt the love in their super deluxe group hug. I knew I mattered.

When I looked around, I got the warmest, safest feeling. State was home—the only one I really had anymore. Even if it wouldn't matter to anyone else if I left, I realized it would matter a lot to me. And now, with the notoriety of being the Phantom Surfer, I'd be the most famous girl who ever walked this sand.

Baby bashfully dipped her head. I placed the lei and arranged it on her shoulders. She didn't complain about its weight. Usually a lei weighs nothing, but this one was heavy. Most *haoles*—no, I will call them visitors—take a lei off as soon as you put it on. They don't know that's an insult. I kissed Baby and said, "*Hau'oli lā hānau.* Happy birthday."

Of course, the lineup showed me the pictures of Dodger, who they were convinced was the most unshakable and magical surfer ever. They were in awe.

"If this guy ever comes to State during the day, I'm going to jump him," Ms. ERA said. "Really, I'd go on birth control for that."

I wanted to tell them I *was* Dodger. I was practically dying to divulge my secret. But after that comment I thought I'd better wait a while to do it. Maybe I'd let them calm down a little, then get my board and just hammer the waves for everyone to see. I didn't have to be afraid of Lord Ricky or any of his guys. Even without Jerry to protect me, I'd be safe, now that I had Windy and my other friends to watch my back.

I studied the lineup left to right, watching them all get cozy with Windy. It was really special. But something was missing. "We need a floater," I announced. It was important that we always kept an extra SOS member in the lineup. We would never slip below eight again. Not on my watch.

Lisa and Jenni nodded. I wasn't surprised that they hadn't thought of this themselves. All they wanted to do was be with their boyfriends.

"Who should we get?" Lisa asked.

"Nancy Norris," I said, without a second thought. There was a long silence, but nobody argued.

And I knew exactly who we should send to get her. Mary Jo was passed out and had missed most of the festivities. I woke her up, and she took a deep gulp of whatever she was drink-ing—it smelled like ouzo. I told her my plan, and she nodded. It was as if she was bowing, conceding to my strength as she looked up and saw Wendy sitting next to me. She gave me a look, that knowing glance that made me want to be her friend last year. Then, obediently, she dragged herself up and into a jog toward the Jonathan Club to find Nancy. I felt a twinge of hope as I watched her go.

Bob signaled me to come to his tower, and I motioned for Windy to join. He zipped down the weathered planks, keep-ing one eye on the riptide and the kid heading right into it. He had his red buoy over his shoulder.

"I need to talk to you, Nani," he said. He looked at Windy.

I told him, "She's my best friend. You can talk in front of her," and Windy stood up taller. I wondered what Bob could possibly be so serious about.

"Sometimes I sleep in the tower here," he said, pointing to the lifeguard station.

That's weird, I thought.

"Driving home to Encino is a little too far to go some nights," he explained.

"You live in Encino? That's the Valley!"

"You don't get it, do you, Nani?" he said. He handed over the Dodger cap.

That's when I understood. The night Glenn was taking my picture, Bob had seen the whole thing.

"When this hat flew off," he said, "and I saw that hair, I knew it was you. You can rip, Nani, but you're playing with fire. If Ricky or his goons found out, I won't be able to protect you. That means no more State. I can't be responsible for a girl surfing by herself."

"What does being a girl have to do with it?"

"Everything," he said.

Nobody at State listened to Bob, and I wasn't going to be the first. I knew I'd keep surfing, but he didn't need to know that. I nodded toward the water, and he looked up, then darted off to make his first rescue of the day.

When he dove under a wave, Windy tapped me. Rox stepped out from under the tower, holding a volleyball as if she had chased it all the way down the beach.

"Look what I dropped," she said.

"You never drop anything," I told her.

"Aren't you going to introduce me to your *friend*?" she said sarcastically.

I knew she knew who Windy was. But just to humor her, I said, "Wendy Davenport . . . Roxanne West."

"You can call me Rox." She looked Windy up and down in that chilling way she had inspected me the first time we met, and then bit her lower lip. She asked seductively, "Ever been to Fiji, Wendy?"

"Yeah," Windy said matter-of-factly, "have you?"

I knew Windy's family traveled a lot. But what Windy didn't know, of course, was what Rox was actually referring to. I fought a smile as I got nervous. That vicious look appeared on Rox's face as she snapped at me, "Don't act all innocent."

I didn't know if I was going to succumb to her nastiness or start laughing harder. Most importantly, I didn't want Windy to get caught up in this, so I moved her off to one side and told her to go back to the towels. She looked at me uncertainly. I told her, "It's okay"—even though it wasn't.

Rox gave Windy the stink eye. It looked like she would never run out of hate. She offered me a cigarette, then sniffed. With a condescending smile she said, "Oh, that's right. You quit."

She lit up and then exhaled right into my face. Could I really despise someone I used to love so much? My palms started to sweat as I asked her, "How long have you been hiding under the tower?"

"I don't hide." She crossed her arms and pushed her boobs up, grinning. "Long enough, though, Dodger."

Obliterators love it when they've got the upper hand. "Why are you this way?" I asked.

"Why are *you*? You must *really* be a dyke if you dress up like a guy and surf," she said flatly, exhaling her smoke into my face. But this time I inhaled it and blew the stinky air right back at her. Rox didn't say a word. She tried to freeze me. When I didn't look phased, she said, "I'm going to tell everyone you're a dyke. Right now."

"No, you won't," I countered. "Because you're one, too. Even if you won't admit it." I thought of my goddess, Pele. She would help me stand tall. *'Onipa'a,* I told myself.

But Rox sneered. "I have a boyfriend. You don't. No one will believe anything you say. I'll make sure of that."

And she would. I could see it in her eyes.

"No one would take you seriously," she went on, "if you said that about me. But I'll send rumors about you to every break from here to Hawaii. I'll make sure it gets across the ocean, even if I have to scribble the words 'Nani Nuuhiwa is a dyke' and toss them into bottles to get them there."

She was obsessed, and I could see that she wouldn't stop. I stared at her. I had to pretend I didn't care.

Rox was surprised. "You think you're so tough, but I know you're not. So give in right now, or you'll regret it. Say girls don't surf. Come on, say it so I can hear it."

"No. That's stupid."

"Say it, or your new pals Wendy and Baby, Julie, and Ms. ERA—which is a stupid nickname—and even Jenni and Lisa—all of you will be labeled dykes by the time I'm done. All of State Beach will hate you. They'll tar and feather you." She slapped at my boa. "Well, it looks like you've already been feathered."

I pushed her hand away and looked over at sweet Baby, wearing my top hat as she twirled her pink parasol. Then there was Ms. ERA with her balance of beauty and brains, and Julie Saratoga, starting a new life at Pali, so delicate on the inside and tough on the out. There was Lisa, in her prime, ruler extraordinaire, and Jenni, finally out of her cocoon, soaring like a great enchantress into Coco's arms. Above all, there was Windy, seated in the middle of the lineup on her first day. I had just promised I would keep her secret. And now I had to prove I would.

No way was I going to let anything happen to them. I saw Mary Jo walking down the beach beside the perky Nancy

Norris. Watching how nice she was being, I could actually for-give Mary Jo. She would do anything to be in the lineup. It was more important than her pride or common sense. She was just messed up and burned out, and I wasn't going to let Rox hurt her, either. I couldn't be that selfish.

"Okay, I'll say it." I looked at Rox. "Girls don't surf." I said it really fast, so it wouldn't hurt as much.

"Now go tell them." Rox pointed at the lineup. When I hesitated, she said, "Are you going to say it, or should I?"

"This is so stupid."

"You better choose fast. My boyfriend is waiting for me." She licked her lips and glanced up at the courts. Scotty was sitting down, drinking a beer. He wasn't even looking at her. He didn't care.

Even so, I got it. That's how Rox did it: she always had a boyfriend to make her look un-gay. No one would think she liked girls when she had a guy on her arm.

All of a sudden, I felt sorry for her. She would be like a room without furniture—empty and alone—for the rest of her life. I gently touched her scar with my fingertip and said, "You might not call yourself a lesbian, Rox. But you are."

That sent her into another raging fury, and she stormed over to the lineup. I was hot on her trail. Neither one of us wanted to run, because it would look dorky, but we both wanted to be the first one there, so we did a weird fast walk until our toes touched the first towel.

She started to say something, but I stopped her. I said, "I'll tell them."

The lineup turned around attentively. I yanked the Dodger cap out of the back of my bikini and stuck it on my head. Rox reacted as if I had just done a magic trick. Lisa looked at the photo of Dodger on the cover of *Tubed* and then at me. "Isn't that . . . the Dodger's cap?"

I put it on. "Yep." And before anyone could say another word, I said, "I'm Dodger. And I surf."

Rox froze. Windy covered her mouth so no one could see her smiling. Then I lifted my boa and tossed it into the wind. There was no need to say a word. Rox choked on her smoke and spun around to get a closer look. The lineup went wild, and Rox went quiet.

"You've been sneaking around *with* Dodger?" Jenni asked.

"No," I said. "I *am* Dodger." It was the one time I think it was okay for the lineup to squeal, which they did loudly. They started flipping through *Tubed*, pointing to the pictures of me sailing though the waves under a bright moon.

Rox staggered back in disbelief. "You guys!" she said. "It's going to make all of us look bad if one of us surfs. Girls who surf are gross. Next thing you know, she'll be growing hair under her pits and telling you to stop shaving your legs. Do you know what I'm saying?"

Julie Saratoga spoke right over her. "Where did you learn to surf like that, Nani?"

Baby jumped up and hugged me. It was as if Rox weren't even there. "You're so amazing, Nani! Someday I'm gonna be like you. Will you teach me?"

"Me, too," Ms. ERA and Julie said at the same time.

Even Nancy Norris joined in, waddling into my arms and hugging me, too, though she had no idea what was going on.

But it was Lisa who asked Rox, not so politely, "Don't you have somewhere else to be?"

Rox couldn't say a word with all of us standing there together, united, staring her down. She pointed her finger at me, stabbing it repeatedly in the air, as she walked away without a word. And that was the absolute, final end to her rule.

I sat down beside Windy and whispered, "Are you still going to run away?"

"Definitely not. You're way too interesting." Our hands touched accidently, but neither one of us moved.

"Girls, a photo?" Glenn Martin asked in his sexy accent. I could tell everyone was stoked, but nobody showed it. The SOS moved slowly and methodically, getting their towels into place in the new order: starting with Ms. ERA, then Julie, Baby, Windy, me, Lisa, Jenni, Mary Jo, and Nancy Norris on the far end. I took off the baseball cap and shook out my hair.

"I thought girls weren't allowed in *Tubed*?" I said.

"You never know. Things could change." He winked. That cracked everybody up. "Come together."

We put our arms around each other, playfully entangled our legs, and laughed as he clicked away.

I cherished this lineup. These beauties really cared about each other. I knew that, together, we would discover what life meant beyond the sand and State Beach. The world was waiting for us.

Here's something else I knew: girls *did* surf. And soon we would be free to surf everywhere guys did. Surfing would be open to any girl strong enough to go for it. But they'd have to have courage. I didn't want to stand alone, but sometimes that's the only way to get things started. I swore to myself, to Nāmaka, and to all the goddesses above and beyond, that someday I'd surf State Beach in broad daylight, for all to see.